Tamara Faith Berger
Little Cat

Coach House Books, Toronto

first edition

 Canada Council   Conseil des Arts   ONTARIO ARTS COUNCIL
for the Arts   du Canada   CONSEIL DES ARTS DE L'ONTARIO

Published with the generous assistance of the Canada Council for the Arts
and the Ontario Arts Council.

LIBRARY AND ARCHIVES CANADA
CATALOGUING IN PUBLICATION

Berger, Tamara Faith
    Little cat / Tamara Faith Berger. -- Rev. 2nd ed.

Reissue of revised novels, Lie with me and The way of the whore,
    in one book.
Issued also in electronic format.
ISBN 978-1-55245-271-4

    I. Berger, Tamara Faith Lie with me. II. Berger, Tamara
Faith The way of the whore. III. Title.

PS8553.E6743L58 2013   c813'.6   C2013-900220-0

Little Cat is available as an ebook: ISBN 978 1 77056 271 4.

Purchase of the print version of this book entitles you to a free digital copy.
To claim your ebook of this title, please email sales@chbooks.com with
proof of purchase or visit chbooks.com/digital. (Coach House Books
reserves the right to terminate the free digital download offer at any time.)

LIE WITH ME

ONE

One time, Jupiter, happy to be idle,
Swept the cosmic mystery aside
And draining another goblet of ambrosia
Teased Juno, who drowsed in bliss beside him:
'This love of male and female's a strange business.
Fifty-fifty investment in the madness,
Yet she ends up with nine-tenths of the pleasure.'

Juno's answer was: 'A man might think so.
It needs more than a mushroom in your cup
To wake a wisdom that can fathom which
Enjoys the deeper pleasure, man or woman.
It needs the solid knowledge of a soul
Who having lived and loved in woman's body
Has also lived and loved in the body of man.'

– Ovid, *The Metamorphoses*

B ut if I told you everything you'd probably think I was a slut and I can't deal with that so I'm not going to tell you absolutely everything. I mean, I can't fully deal with myself if I call myself a slut. It's just that I know there's all these problems with a girl like me having sex so much. I think if a guy loves sex it comes from the pleasure he feels in his cock – which is why he's never called a slut. But because it's easier for a girl to get disconnected from all the feelings she has down there, she can get lost trying to *know* herself. Do you see what I'm saying? Being a slut kind of implies getting lost, going astray.

I think the trouble, too, is that a slut understands that there is not as much pleasure having sex as she wants there to be. Pleasure roams around her body like a runaway. I am speaking from experience on this. I used to hop from guy to guy, always looking to feel more down there, and I got so disappointed. I felt like I was missing something, as if my body were lacking the basest enjoyment that was supposed to be there. I'd seen how pleasure touched a cock and made a guy look like he was never coming back. Pleasure hurled right through him! But *my* pleasure never felt done – even when I came, there were parts stuck inside. Pleasure clung to my stomach, it swelled up my throat.

See, I used to be the kind of girl who'd walk down the street and practically call out *fuck me fuck me fuck me* to strangers. I'd get dressed really sexy and go out to clubs to pick up. In the secret pit of myself, I felt like a lunatic loose on the street, legs in the air, eyes popping wide. I wanted men to grab me and fuck me right there.

There was this time when I went out by myself and I wasn't wearing any underwear. I straddled the bar stool, toes swinging over the ground. My pussy lips were pressing on the leather. My whole body was balanced like this, legs wide, back arched, clit stampeding like a bull. Then this man got near to me and started checking me out sideways. I saw his hands grip the bar. I knew right away that this was the person who was going to fuck me.

'Can I buy you a drink?' the guy asked.

'Okay,' I said. 'Anything.'

A grin started widening all over my face. It was like it was mocking my part down below. I thought I was going to start laughing out loud. I couldn't put words to what was going on, but my stomach felt like it was going to erupt under my skirt, my body kept getting these warm continuous blows. I thought every person in that bar could see that coming off me. I mean, how much I wanted. How I could've fucked all of them from the way I felt. It's always the same, I thought, getting sex like this is always the same. It starts from this feeling of flagrancy, which expands until it flattens, until I forget where I live and I forget what I like, until I don't even recognize my face in the morning.

The man at the bar started laughing with me, as if he knew that I was holding myself back. Then he stole my hand and pressed it on his dick. We both straightened our backs, like we were bracing ourselves. All my flesh pulled toward his flesh. I gulped my drink and banged for more.

'More!' I shouted. *More! More! More!*

I started rubbing that guy with my fist up and down under the bar. His cock was a hose, all coiled up and bulging. I wanted to hold it forever. But my cunt was breathing like a small animal, begging me to do something.

'Let's go!' I pleaded.

The man looked at my eyes, as if he were confused by my need, then he opened his mouth to say something. I looked above his head. I didn't want to see how he was going to say yes. I didn't want to see if his mouth was trembling. The guy took my hand from his dick and held it tight. I slid off the bar stool. My cunt was so wet. Both my shoes hit the ground.

I followed him out the back door of the club to the parking lot. I felt air rising under my skirt. The darkness was drying all the stuff on my thighs. The man led me to the end of the lot by a fence. He leaned up against it and pulled down his zipper. I wanted to cling to his body like wind. But when I saw the glare of his long hanging thing I went down on my knees. His cock started swelling in front of my face. I opened my mouth. I took the head of his dick between my lips. My whole neck arched up and circled round. I was sucking and sucking and I heard a car starting behind me. I couldn't stop, my heart was speeding. The car was coming closer behind my back. I couldn't stop. I felt the lights burning onto my ass, pumping as I sucked. I closed my eyes, I jacked my jaw. I kept sucking in a pulse going on and going off. I thought I heard two men laughing behind me. Then it got dark around us and I couldn't breathe right.

'Hey,' the guy moaned, lifting my head by the hair. 'Hey, come up now – easy, baby.'

My breathing got rapid, ragged, the second the head of him popped from my lips. I'd wanted it faster and harder. I didn't care who was watching.

'Don't. I want more!'

My tongue was hanging out, my palms were on his legs, I was breathing so fast.

'I wanna fuck you,' the guy said. 'Come back up.'

I saw the guy's stretched-out neck. I wanted him to fuck me too. I pressed my breasts into his legs. The sky looked so large and so black that I felt like I could fly underneath it.

The man raised my dress as I climbed him. My naked ass was exposed and I felt it clench in his hands. Then he slipped his palm through my thighs and put two of his fingers inside me. I was so wet down there, dripping. I tried to squeeze his fingers up me but I didn't have time. He was poking my cunt like a madman.

'Let me do it, just like this, let me feel you, lemme fuck you, just for a second, just for a second.'

My thighs were splitting and I started to shiver. I was rocking back and forth, my whole pelvis in his hand. My pussy was sticking to his fingers like a leech. I wanted to fuck, to feel his cock just like this, his skin on my skin. I wanted to plug up my hole, feel his whole naked part up my whole naked centre. I wanted to jolt myself, fuck myself, make myself cum. My hands went to the guy's chest. I wanted my fists to pound until I hurt him.

It was like I was stuck. I knew where I was and I knew what I was going to do.

'Get a condom. Come on!'

The man reached down. I couldn't look at what he was doing. My face was turned up toward the sky. We were pressing back into the fence. I was swallowing hard. I couldn't stop now. I felt the man's bone pressing up in my thighs, he was bending his knees. I was trying to stop myself from moaning too loud. My lower body felt like it was going to flare open. Then he pushed up so hard that it shocked me. My legs went all locked. My mouth filled up with air. He was lifting me up, right from the ground. It was like my cunt lips were sliding out of my body, growing, and I thought I heard men laughing again. I squeezed my legs, clipped so tight, we were fucking and rocking back into the fence. I tried to shift myself more and more in his hands, move with his thrusting – god, he was in me …

It was all going too fast, I couldn't keep up. The man was gripping my hips, his head to the sky. Still stabbing, he opened, lips unfurled, eyes jacked wide, his temples were beating all over his face. I held his shoulders, our lips almost came together, and I clamped my hands on his head: *you're beautiful you're beautiful you're beautiful*. Then he made this noise like a tied-up dog. Still pounding and thumping, his knuckles dug into the sides of my ass. I knew it was over. My breathing sounded almost like crying.

I started to stretch my legs toward the ground and his cock slipped out of me. His shoulders came down. The guy was prying me off his body too fast and I fell in front of the fence. I wasn't steady. My arms reached back to find something to hold on to. I just wanted to lie down – it was over, all over, I wanted to go home.

I saw the condom crumpled up on the gravel beside me, there was cream shimmering on the top. My skirt was still hitched at my hips. I was just sitting there, panting. I wanted to go home. I heard the man zipping up his pants. People were coming out of the bar and starting their cars. I straightened my skirt and got up. The man looked around. I knew that he was ready to go. I could barely move my legs to walk. All I could think was over and over: *Am I safe? Am I safe? Am I safe?*

I bet you think I'd have deserved it if I got a disease that night. You'd say I was just being a dumb slut walking around all tarted up and having sex with a stranger in a parking lot. You'd say that, or you'd think it at least. But you don't really know why I do it. I'm not hooked on danger or anything like that. And of course I don't want to get a disease. It's just that there are times where I don't see what's safe before losing my footing. It's that feeling of falling, I mean, falling into someone's strangeness – there is no way around it for me. It's like I walk into someone in sex and I know: I am losing parts of my body in this, my body dissolving, my body for his … Following, falling, fucking like that, until every split second of being open wraps around me. My flesh looms so close and so large in this light. When I can have sex with a stranger my body is filled to its ends with these kinds of murmurs:

I need your cock to touch my cunt.

I need us naked for only one second.

I need us forever to be here forever.

I have always had to feel myself like I've never felt myself before. The very first time it ever happened, I was young, maybe seven years old. It was late at night when I was put into bed with a boy. It was just the two of us, under the covers, completely awake. We stared for so long at each other, until his eyes felt like my eyes in buzzing grey light, until our breathing turned fast. The places between our legs became opening and shining.

I remember how we went toward each other, really slow, like we were moving through water. We got so close to each other's faces. Then we moved at the same time down each other, until his face was at my thighs and my face was at his. He lifted my nightgown, I pulled down his underwear. We stared at each other down there. His mouth pressed the line that was beating between my legs. My lips touched so light on his animal skin. His penis looked like a bloom I'd never seen open. I thought I was staring at the softest, warmest thing in the world. He was putting his lips on my vagina. We stayed together like that all night.

When I remembered much later what I'd done with that boy, it felt like the worst kind of secret. I had this cold wind racing from my head to my stomach every time I saw in my head how I'd touched and kissed him, over and over, and how I'd been touched and kissed down there over and over … I didn't want that boy to remember what we'd done. I wanted to think that it never even happened. See, I didn't understand how I could've already been touched down there. I had never even touched myself down there. I couldn't stop feeling my face stuck in that black and warm place between his thighs. The whole thing between us kept playing in my head in slow motion. I couldn't get it out. What happened between me and the boy was tying me up so tightly that I couldn't fall asleep without thinking about it.

When I was around twelve, there was a guy who started liking me. He was a few years older than me and he invited me over to his house. He took me down to his basement. We sat on the couch and we were just watching a movie when he started touching my breasts. He turned my whole body away from the TV. I didn't know why he was doing that. It felt like his hands were pawing these lumps that were attached to my front. Then the guy moved his hands up to my face and cupped my cheeks. It made my lips part open the way he pulled a little. I watched his face coming in toward mine. His eyes were closed and he pressed his lips down onto mine and all of a sudden from that cupping on my cheeks, he opened my mouth and his tongue pushed inside. He started licking around. It felt like his tongue was made of something plastic. I watched him like that, inside my face, and I knew that my tongue was licking his too. The guy's face was swelling, his eyes were flat shut. It looked like he was having a really good dream. I slit my eyes and shifted them away. I didn't want to see how he was liking this and I was not.

When I was finally alone back in my own bed that night, I kept thinking about the way that his face looked so close to mine, his hands on my tits, his tongue moving inside me. I knew that I never wanted that to happen again! I felt like a monster. I never wanted something like that to happen again. Because I thought: *There is nothing on my body to touch.*

I mean, who was I to let that guy touch me? I never said a thing when his hands squeezed my breasts. I didn't say a word when his tongue left my throat. It felt like words gurgled up to my lips but those words disappeared when I swallowed. What would I have said? Would I have said *please*? Would I have said *stop*? Would I have said *lick, suck, cat, dog* or *dream*?

I remember how, afterward, I couldn't even tell my friends that I'd kissed or made out, that a guy had touched my breasts. It was just me with myself, every night in my bed, saying *you will never let that happen again*. After a while, I guess, I felt fine keeping it inside me. But maybe when you never say a thing, your thoughts spread like mould.

See, I kept feeling ugly. And I let it happen again even though I said it never would.

I heard someone say that once a girl opens her legs she can never close them again. In my case that's true.

I was dancing at a party in someone's basement when I was in high school. We were all drinking when it happened. I remember how my body felt thickened with juice. Only my breasts felt alive then, thrust out from my chest. They felt so good that I was jumping! I was gulping drink after drink, and all I wanted to do was move like that, feel my flesh shaking loose on my bones, my arms in the air. I started to push my tits into all those dancing people. I laugh at myself when I think of that night. See, I ended up going to the bathroom with this guy. I don't exactly remember how we got there but I think he pulled me out of the crowd. I remember he said: *I was watching you dance.*

It was dark in the bathroom and it smelled like a wet plant. The door was locked. I really had to go pee but this guy was pressing me down by the shoulders until I was on my knees. The bones in my back pressed against the slick side of the toilet. That guy was pulling down his pants and he was holding my head with one hand so I wouldn't move. He was calling my name but he was so far above me. I felt all this hair at my mouth. I didn't think *that* was what it would feel like. He held himself and his body got bigger in my face. His hips started rocking. His thing that had no hair pushed into my lips. It was there on my tongue like a water balloon. My mouth had to really open. I wanted him to stop moving, just let me feel it for a second, just let me feel what it was like. But he slid it in my mouth until it felt too deep. I had to open my jaw and it hurt. I was ready for it to stop. But he was too tight with his hand on the back of my head. He kept horsing the thing and his hips in my face.

'Please, please, please,' he moaned. He sounded like a girl.

I started moaning too. I heard myself gag.

Then this strange sour cream flew into my throat, the guy's grip went slack on the back of my head. I quickly yanked away and looked up. There was this flash where I saw his head reeling. But I knew he was happy, he kept saying my name, saying *yes* saying *yes* …

I sprang off my knees and I ran out of the bathroom. I ran up the stairs and ran out of the house. I was running and wiping that cream off my face. Racing home so fast that what I'd just done made itself known everywhere in my body. My heart felt like a twisted muscle.

I think I kept running after that night, I mean running to and from men. I only wanted to do things with them once. See, this is what I was trying to say to you right at the beginning, I mean why you'd probably call me a slut: because I started having sex all the time, just one time. I wanted to know what would happen with another guy and another guy when I was down on my knees, with a pulsing water balloon in my mouth. I started getting good at what I was doing too. I mean, hearing guys above me groaning, just like they were dying. I sucked everything coming through them; I sucked them to feel sex right in my mouth. Sucking their cocks for this feeling, too, but all the stuff that they were doing to me didn't ever really feel like it was happening in my body. It's what I was saying before – something was getting stuck inside me. Like the pleasure I was feeling was sticking up my throat, buzzing through my ribs. And when I swallowed, it was like there was this big pile of people at the bottom of me, all their limbs shooting out. I think I kept sucking dicks like crazy because I wanted so badly to plow through.

Something did burst for me eventually. I mean, I'd been fucking so much, always trying to feel myself more, and I think I fell in love. It's hard for me to say that. Are you surprised to hear me say it too? You probably think that sluts don't love. It's true in a way, you know, sluts don't love. But they can love flesh, so I guess they fall in love from having sex. Well, some girls can, I guess. I think I got more fucked up falling so hard for some guy through sex because I didn't know how to suck a cock that I thought I was in love with. Trying to love this one felt like I had to jump in the centre of that twisted mound of people.

If I back up for a second, I'll tell you more, because I want you to understand. See, through all my sucking and fucking, I thought that men's hearts were in their cocks. I mean, that their cocks were the way that they loved. And so I was feeling their hearts by sucking them. This is the real beginning of what I wanted to tell you about.

When I met that one guy who I fell in love with, I sucked his cock better than I'd ever sucked anyone's before. I lay my head on his stomach and I put him into me endlessly. It was simple at first, because I finally felt like what I was doing with my body was right: I had all this longing for sucking the life out of men, and now here was a life that I finally wanted.

But you know what happened? This guy didn't notice. I mean, I was sucking his heart the best that I could and he didn't even care! It wasn't like I expected him to fall in love with me because of my sucking. I know you probably think that I think that and so you think right away I'm a fool – but all I'm really asking right now is: how do you have sex with someone you're in love with?

I couldn't look this man in the eyes. When we fucked I looked down at his cock coming in. I looked there so hard my sight blurred. His cock poked and pressed into the place where I wanted to feel myself most, but all I felt like doing was crying after sex because somehow I knew I was letting slip what I couldn't even see. I mean that the feeling I wanted was slipping away without my even feeling it. I was fucking and fucking him and nothing was staying. I always came back to this guy's body for more, to grab what I felt that I already missed.

I bet if you could've cut me in half right then, you would've been able to see what was making me cry. Do you believe me? Has this ever happened to you? The feeling that you're sprouting something so disgusting and it only comes out around the person you are in love with? I wish I could explain this even more to you but I'd have to squeeze you up and throw you back into my body when I was feeling this way. I swear you'd never have come out of me alive! It was like there were these tight, pimpled lumps in my stomach. I had flushed cheeks on the outside, but I was rotting on the inside. I was trying to love this person who didn't love me back. That man had some kind of lust for me, sure, but I knew it wasn't serious. I was just a puppet sucking his dick – one who would've split open her tongue to serve him better!

Maybe you can already see it so perfectly, how everything I thought was so wrong – how this was not love, how I was perverting the word by even calling what I was doing *that*. But I just had no experience with this kind of thing. Go ahead if you want, be disgusted with me. I know it must look bad. Having sex with this guy turned into a nightmare, it became the very worst that it had ever been for me. I couldn't stop sucking, I couldn't relax. My body was rigid. My lips didn't kiss. Sex with this guy was like digging a hole. I was watching us do it, watching us dig. And I wanted more of it and more of it until I thought I could see our dark holes matching up. It was leg striking leg, it was cock into cunt. I was so deep in the mud with this guy that I knew: we are the same. But I thought the man didn't see that! He didn't understand. And so I couldn't do a thing. I couldn't talk, I couldn't fuck and I couldn't run away.

I guess this is why I'm telling you this story. I want you to understand. Please, stay with me right now. I will tell you everything that happened. My mouth works like a deep, deep ditch – there's always more, one inch deeper. Please trust me, please. I'll tell it all. Just stay with me here for a little while longer.

It all started with me and that guy at a club. I remember seeing him across the room. His eyebrows were thick, all in one line. He was watching me dance and it made my stomach stir. This guy looked as strong as a bull. I started moving over to him. The music was so loud that my whole body vibrated. As I got closer and closer to this guy's chest I thought I wanted to marry him. I swear I'd never felt it before like that, that I wanted to be near to a man, barely moving, forever. My head reached his chin. Our bodies were almost rubbing. I felt like a lioness under her king. I wanted to look up and lick him, clean him and stroke him. I am saying that the very first time I met this man, his body made me feel like I was near it for a reason, that I was living how I was born to be living.

Of course me and the guy got together that first night. I thought that there was a branch that was burning between his legs and it filled my mouth, every inch of me, with fury. There was practically nothing left when he was inside me. I sucked and I squeezed my throat muscles, I kissed and rubbed his flesh with my red-hot insides. I wanted his white-hot expulsion to drip down my throat. When he was inside me the very first time, I had the feeling that a real person was finally inside me.

But I didn't know how to get what I usually got from a man. I wanted to be having sex with this guy even more, all the time.

And I didn't know how to make it happen. I thought about him in my bed, on the street, it didn't matter. I stopped thinking about everybody else. I was paralyzed. What was playing so clear in my head – my face at his stomach, my mouth on his cock, sucking and staying so near to his skin – this kind of vision was swelling me up and then when I saw him I clenched like a fist.

All he wanted was sex from my mouth. Then sometimes we did it me up on top of him moving too fast, and sometimes we did it him pushing behind me, me arching my back, my face in the bed. My whole body ached like this thing that could crack. My heart was a bargain-priced dim plate of glass.

I knew for sure that things were really going to hurt me the first time we did it, sex in my ass. The guy had told me that he'd wanted to do that with me ever since he first saw me. My ass is kind of plump and it moves in circles when I fuck. I was always scared of having sex there because men usually hurt me when they put their fingers in there. I swear, I thought that if I let this guy do it to me in the ass I'd be this open-assed dog howling forever! I mean, I knew I was in for some kind of trouble that night because I'd been dancing up close to other guys at the club.

'You're a slut,' the guy said when we got back to his place.

'I'm sorry. Come on. It was nothing. Look, I'm sorry.'

'You saying sorry means nothing to me.'

I don't remember what I tried to say next. His voice was so mean. I remember him unbuckling his belt. It slithered between his palms. The guy got so livid, his eye whites turned red.

'Take off your dress and your underwear,' he said.

'Come on, don't.'

'Do it.'

'I can't.'

'Do it.'

He'd backed me up against the door. There was a lump in my throat that was going to burst. My teeth were clenched. I didn't want the guy to see me cry. So I started slowly taking off my clothes. He was so close to me. He was looking all over. I was cradling my body with my arms trying to hide myself.

'Please,' I was begging. 'Don't.'

'I've had it from you.'

For some reason we both knew what kind of thing was going on between us. He was seething and I was making these pressed-together cries. His hands took my wrists and he dragged me into the living room. Then he reached under my arms, gripped me like a child and pretty much forced me down on a chair on top of him. I was hanging like a dishrag over his thighs. I made my whole body go as limp as it could on his legs. I was shivering, afraid I was going to piss. My stomach was pressing into his knees. He tore down my underwear. My ass felt huge and cold. It was right there for him. The belt was whipping above me like a flame.

'Don't hurt me! Please!' I was choking and trying to kick back or shimmy my legs. My underwear was not all the way down. My underwear made me hog-tied.

The man let the belt crack down on my ass. It was like a magician cutting through a lady's neck. I froze. I really froze. And I heard myself cry. But it didn't feel like I was making real noise. I wanted to tell the man to stop it. I wanted to tell him to put his tongue on my ass, to put it right where it hurt. He kept whipping my big white behind with that belt. I humped on his knee trying to get away.

'Stop!'

I was stuck.

'Please!'

I squeezed my eyes. My fingers, my toes were spasming like fish.

The man pushed me off him and onto the floor. I was wobbling there, a runt, on my hands and my knees. My ass cheeks were naked, all tilted up. I tried to look back at him through teary fuzzy eyes. We were in the middle of the living room. His house. His TV. His books. His rules. The guy was looming over me. My hand went down between my thighs. I was trying so hard to hold myself in. I didn't know why I was wet.

Suddenly the guy reached down for my hair. He grabbed it and pulled me like the runt that I was down the hallway. We stopped at the mirror beside his bedroom. When I saw myself I started breathing so fast. My cheeks were bright red. My eyes were running black.

'God. God. God. Everything hurts … '

I think the guy must've felt sorry for me right then. He sank down to his knees behind me. For one second I saw his face and he was looking at what he did to my ass. Then he moved his mouth down there. He put his lips right where he'd hit. It was making more heat burn all over my skin. The side of my face was pressed up against the mirror.

Then, without letting go of my ass, he lay on his back underneath my thighs. He brought his face up toward my pussy and he pulled me by the hips down to him. It was the first time that he'd ever done that. It felt too good, his lips kissing near my clit, his tongue coming out, his whole head moving, he was doing it so fast. I'd never felt myself move like that. I was moving so fast in time to him. I couldn't control myself. I was buzzing all over, it was leaving from my throat. Then still too fast, the guy slid out from under me. I couldn't feel his lips anymore. I wanted more. He was up there behind me. We were still in the hallway. I could smell the kitchen and his bed. The guy's hard body pushed up against my ass. He was rubbing the head of his cock on my asshole and gripping my hips. I was rocking into him and he thought that I wanted it, but I just couldn't stop it, my hot ass moving in circles and circles. Inside my throat the buzzing was just getting louder. I thought I was screaming: *No! No! No!*

'It's okay,' the guy said. 'Shhhh!'

My elbows weakened. My mouth touched the floor. My ass moved up in the air like a dog's. It felt like the buzzing mass in my throat was going to fall, smear the ground with something thick. The guy was spreading my cheeks. He wasn't going to stop. I felt the air blow over my asshole. My cunt was getting so big underneath.

'That's it, shake your ass.'

A weird grunt raced out of my throat. I knew he could see me.

'Just wait! Wait! Please!'

'Shhhhhh! Let me do it.'

I was shaking my head side to side. I felt the belt slaps on my ass spark like wires.

'Wait!'

My ass was starting to let in his cock. It was unbearable, stinging so deep.

'Careful, careful, careful, please!'

'Shhhhhh!'

He leaned his face toward me, he breathed through my ears. His cock was burning the walls of my ass. I was stuffed like that to the end of all ends. My teeth on the floor. Him scraping my hole, slow in and out, my muscles were ripping, he kept pumping and pumping. I tried to move out. I was suspended like that. A rabbit stuck in a wolf's mouth. I was hanging and I kept wanting him to fuck me, but I knew he had to stop. I thought he was going to kill me like that. I don't know, maybe if he had said something then, like: *I know how you like it, I know that you like this* ... But the way that he fucked me, just that, in and out, all I could think of was how was I going to take pleasure?

Well, it went on like that between me and this man. All the time I kept doing it, all the time asking *how*. I was scraped out, teetering on one tiny line, loving him, sucking him. I just kept on. Having sex where I felt like I was drowning and he was floating over me with a life jacket laughing. It was like I heard him thinking every time we fucked:

I will never love you or your sex.

I will never love you or your sex.

I will never love you or your sex.

I'm embarrassed to tell you what happened next. I know I must really look like a fool now. It's not easy for me to tell you what I'm going to tell you, but I can't skip this part. Please wait, understand: I was trying to see if I could love a man! Just wait. Please. I want you to stay with me until it's all over.

I'd been out dancing at a club with some friends this one night and I decided to go over to the guy's place afterward. I'd never done that before. I mean, I always waited for him to call me. I guess it wasn't the best idea, because I'd been drinking a bit, and there I was, ringing his buzzer over and over. When he let me in, I remember I was hopping around in the elevator because I was so excited to see him. I felt a line of sweat around my hairline. My hips were still shaking and my throat was all hot.

The guy's door was open for me when I got up to his place. I went rushing down the hallway toward the bedroom because I heard some banging there. He was looking in one of his drawers. His back was toward me and I started dancing for him. I was just happy, you know, still reeling. I must've been dancing for at least a minute when I stopped. I stopped because I saw how his eyes were. He wasn't moving. He had the worst look on his face. I didn't know what to say. I was going to say it, I wanted to say it: *I love you I love you I love only you!* But I couldn't say a thing. The guy was pursing his lips like he was going to spit in my face. I heard saliva collecting in his mouth and all I could do was stand there. He was coming toward me like that, bull's-eye. I felt my lips opening up. I thought for a second it would turn into sex. I knew that I would've done anything for him right then. But the guy crooked his arm round the back of my neck. He widened my lips with his fingers and stuck his thumb down. I started gagging. He pushed in another finger and hooked it hard at the roof of my mouth. I tried to bite down but my teeth had lost their ridges.

'Is this what you want?' the guy finally said.

My neck got all knotted. My stomach started bubbling. I had no idea what he meant. I wanted to love him! I didn't want this. Then his knee hit my groin. I fell to the floor. The bones of my legs thudded like wood. I slumped over my breasts and coughed up his fingers.

Then the man's palms started flashing in front of my eyes. I heard myself scream but all I was doing was choking. He pushed me down more. He smacked both my cheeks. My back bones were rubbing against the floor. He pinned my wrists and he spread me. I felt his knuckles at my thighs.

I tried to lift my head up but the guy was slapping my cunt. I could barely see, I was squinting and I was trying so hard to squeeze my thighs shut. I wanted to make myself go toward the smacking because I thought it wouldn't hurt as much if I could go closer and closer. I felt my lips move. It was wet underneath me. The man didn't stop coming over me, coming closer. I didn't know if he was hitting me or fucking me or what.

But the next thing I knew the man's face was hovering over my head. He had his palms on both sides of my skull. It felt like he was scraping my forehead with a rock, digging hot pits in the bones of my face. I felt my body falling through the floor …

'Open your eyes!' he yelled.

I tried and I tried but my sockets were filled. 'I can't, I can't … '

Are you still there? Can you see me? Look! Please look. My legs, were they spreading? I didn't know how to move. I thought that the man was still on top of me pounding. I didn't know, I couldn't look but I thought he was still there above me, still coming … I kept fixing on to that hook that he gave me: his finger down my throat, the hook that we were fucking, I kept fixing on it, fixing on it. I wanted to get out so bad …

'Come on, girl! Come on, open your eyes!'

I heard my own voice in my head. It was speaking too loud: *You wouldn't be here if you hadn't wanted more. You're lying flat like a corpse on the ground. Your throat's running open from sucking the cocks of all men. Your body is ripped into so many pieces. All you can do is scavenge yourself like a crow.*

Listen to yourself, still talking! You haven't stopped saying bad words and thinking bad things ever since your first time. If you can ever suck someone without looking for his love, you'll stop running like a slut all lost for your cunt. Look at you. Look. Your temples are burning! Stuff is pouring out of you. Look, it's coming …

Rolling around in the darkness, my face was scraping something flat. My cheekbones were poking like knives into the floor. I was calling for my lover. I was calling, I was calling, but my flesh had no sound.

'I can't do this, I don't want to do this.' I heard the guy talking from way up above me.

'Why?' I was crying now.

'I just can't. I don't want this. I don't want to do this to you.'

What don't you want? What can't you do? I was screaming in my head. But my fucking mouth was glued shut. I was never coming up for air. I dragged myself away from him on my stomach. My face pressed against the floor. Water poured from my eyes.

'Stop.' He was still over me. 'Stop. Stop crying. I just can't do this.'

'Why, why, why?'

'I can't. I don't know. Stop crying, please stop crying.'

'You don't love me. You don't … '

I broke open. I was gasping from the back of my throat. I couldn't stop. I heard him walking down the hallway. He was leaving me like that! He slammed a door. *Fuck you! Don't leave me!* I was crying, I kept pulling down the hall and toward the couch. *Fuck it. Fuck it.* I finally pushed my weight up. I rolled onto my back on the couch and sunk in. Pain kept coming and going in waves through my chest. Pain throbbed down the backs of my thighs, it burned my knees, it prickled all through my ribs. *I'll never be with you again.* That was pain. My body was tight and packed into a tube. Over and over in my head it was playing: *I don't want this. You don't love me.* God I wanted it to stop. I wanted to fuck. I wanted to get rid of myself, alone like a fool at his chest.

TWO

Jupiter laughed aloud: 'We have the answer.
There is a fellow called Tiresias.
Strolling to watch the birds and hear the bees
He came across two serpents copulating.
He took the opportunity to kill
Both with a single blow, but merely hurt them –
And found himself transformed into a woman.

'After the seventh year of womanhood,
Strolling to ponder on what women ponder
She saw in that same place the same two serpents
Knotted as before in copulation.
'If your pain can still change your attacker
Just as you once changed me, then change me back.'
She hit the couple with a handy stick,

'And there he stood as male as any man.'
'He'll explain,' cried Juno, 'why you are
Slave to your irresistible addiction
While the poor nymphs you force to share it with you
Do all they can to shun it.'

– Ovid, *The Metamorphoses*

MAN NO. 1

It was just turning light in the room. I saw her lying there, dead to the world. Her head was hanging off the dirty beige couch. I walked up. I stood over her. I touched her breast, it was heaving up and down. My finger sunk in and I gripped my cock.

Her cheeks looked puffy. Her eyelids were dark. I pulled up her skirt. I was breathing so hard that I thought I might wake her. I started peeling down her underwear. My finger got stuck around the elastic. She was shifting around. I knew I had to go faster. I pulled her underwear down to her knees. I felt like I was running without moving. I thought she was going to wake up. I held the head of my cock, put it right where she was splitting. I spread her lips with two fingers.

Then I climbed onto the couch and grabbed her thighs with my knees. I pushed my cock up her. Fuck, I couldn't help it. She started making these grunts. My heart was pounding.

I dropped so my palms ended flat on the couch beside her tits. There was a coffee stain beside her neck that looked like a smeared star. I felt her warm jiggling against my wrists. I was sliding my dick in and out of her now, it was going all the way in, my cock hard inside her. I couldn't stop doing it, grunting with her. She felt like she was coming through the back of me. Every time I pumped toward her head it made her boobs shake more. I saw the slits of the whites of her eyes. I didn't know if she knew it was me. I couldn't stop fucking her body. And her insides were getting hotter, her hips pushed up to meet me. She was breathing faster than me now. Her lips were limp, I saw her tongue.

Moving in and out, I wanted to finish, I wanted to come, my cock was going in and out and she was whipping her head side to side. On one stroke, we stuck together with my dick pushing up in her before bursting, and I toppled to pull out, my come shooting on her stomach.

I lay there breathing heavily, flat on her flesh. I wanted to say something to her, my lips were near her neck. I could smell food behind her in the cracks of the pillows.

These little whines were curling out of her mouth. I wanted to say something to make her stop. I didn't know what to say. *I'm sorry*, I wanted to say something like that, *I'm sorry*. But I felt a stem in my throat and I started coughing. The next thing I knew I was pushing off her completely. Standing over her. She was still lying there dead to the world. The smell of something humid, that dirty beige couch, the smell of her was all over me.

'I can't open my eyes!' she whispered.

I felt sick to my stomach. She was scaring me now. The whites of her eyes were flickering under her lids. It was like she was watching me from the window of a train. I'd pushed off her too roughly. I walked out of the room, fast, down the hall. I shut myself in her bathroom. The bath mat was burgundy, shaggy and wet. I heard her yelling after me, 'You fucked me in my sleep! You fucked me in my sleep!' I knew that if I stayed in there long enough, she would fall back asleep so I could leave on my own.

MAN NO. 2

My friend knew that I hadn't been with anyone in a while. He told me about this girl at the bar where he worked who'd been coming in for about a year. He said she always came alone, and she almost always left with someone different. He said she was really good-looking. My friend told me he thought that she'd just broken up with someone, because she'd hadn't come in for a couple months and now she was back, a few nights a week, sitting alone. She hadn't let anyone take her home yet, my friend said, but I bet if you came you'd get her.

The night I decided to go, I was feeling pretty good. I remember the second I walked into the club I saw my friend and her talking already. He saw me right away too. He pointed to me and she turned around and smiled. She was really good-looking. Her hair was long and dark and kind of wild at the bottom. Her breasts were large. She was wearing a short skirt, bare legs. Her legs were uncrossed. We didn't talk so much right away. I felt like I couldn't really speak to her. We just sat beside each other and drank. I saw her hands were gripping her wineglass and rubbing up and down the stem. I moved in a bit closer to her so that our arms were touching. She didn't pull away.

Then my friend started giving us a bunch of drinks on the house. We began talking, I don't even remember about what, and I let my hand go under the bar. My fingers started touching the top of her thigh. She was letting me, I mean she relaxed into it, and I could feel that feeling of knowing in us both. I wasn't used to that kind of knowing in a girl. And she was smiling, pretending like it wasn't even happening, which was turning me on more. I began rubbing her thigh, feeling up the crack of her legs pressing together.

When I got up to her panties she turned to me and her eyes were glassy.

'I'm going home now. You want to come with?'

We were drunk. I grabbed her hand and we left the bar fast together. I'd forgotten to say goodbye to my friend. While we were sitting in the cab on the way to her place, I started feeling up in the exact same place on her thighs. This time she spread her legs open a bit for me. I slid my hand under the bottom of her skirt. My fingers dug into her thighs. Her relaxation was tightness now, it was amazing, it was like she knew how to play with that line. I felt this heat coming from her pussy. Her panties were wet. She was squirming for me.

When we got to her building, she led me up two flights of stairs. I watched the parts of her ass move together and apart under her skirt. She knew that I was looking at her ass, so she pushed it out more and started laughing.

She didn't turn on the lights in her apartment. She just let me in and shut the door behind us. We passed through a living room area with a couch and a TV and I followed close behind down a hallway to her bedroom. I kept looking at her ass, so round in her skirt. I was happy for the street light outside that came through her bedroom window at the end of the hallway. The light outlined her ass, it made her so fucking sexy.

She walked over to the window and pressed her hands up against it. I got behind her and pushed myself against her ass. She was still kind of laughing. I reached around and squeezed her big breasts through her shirt. She started pushing back and circling her ass into me. I put my chin on her shoulder, my lips to her neck. She smelled like wine. I kept opening my mouth on her skin. I looked down at my hands on her tits. I was pinching her big nipples through her shirt, which was blousy and flowered and thin.

Then she squirmed out of my grip and turned her body around toward me. Her tits were thrusting into my hands. I started to feel up under her shirt and her bra but she held down my arms.

'Wait,' she said.

She stood a few inches away from me and leaned her head back into the window. The glare from the street light was stronger here and it made a halo of greenish light all around her. She lifted up her arms slowly and took off her blouse. Her breasts looked so huge. I'd actually never seen breasts so big on such a short girl. Her nipples were hard under her white bra. It looked like a sports bra, which wasn't too sexy, but the shape of her nipples, rectangular, made me not care. Then she unzipped her skirt and walked out of it. She was standing there so close to me in her sports bra and panties. I really wanted to fuck her. She unbuttoned my shirt and took it off. She unhooked her bra. There was pounding in my ears. I couldn't stop thinking: *I'm seeing her naked tits right in front of me and she wants me to.*

Then she walked behind me and rubbed her breasts into my back. I let out tight breaths. She lay her hands on my shoulders, slid them down and around my chest. She started pinching my nipples. She kept doing it, pinching harder, until my breath got faster. She was putting her mouth and her tongue all over my back. Her lower body was grinding against me.

My whole body went hot for a second, like I was going to come right then. I turned around quick, I needed to fuck her, her chest rising, her nipples purple and hard. I looked toward her bed. It was a double bed low to the ground, heaped with sheets and plaid blankets. She crossed her arms over her tits like she was amused. She watched me take off my pants and my underwear. She was staring at my hard cock.

I opened my arms to her and tried to kiss her but she jerked away. So I grabbed her. She started squealing. I bent her body in two and I gripped her hard by the waist. Her head was near the floor and she was bracing her hands on the edge of the bed. Her hair was splayed out like a broom. The cheeks of her ass were opening up.

We were moving in and out with each other in the rhythm of fucking. Then for one second the girl stopped. I don't know from where but she handed me this condom.

'Put it on,' she said.

My cock was pointing right at her asshole, not her pussy. My hands felt like they weren't working right, my fingers were filled with jelly. The girl's panties were still on, they were stuck in her ass crack because she was so wet. I started putting on the condom and she was moaning, I thought I heard her say *do it do it*. She was wiggling her ass and pumping her knees. I wanted to fuck her ass. She reached up to pull her panties off.

The girl was grinding her naked ass toward the head of my cock. I steadied her. I pushed my cock near the entrance of her hole and she pumped her ass up so I slid into the bottom of her pussy. Fuck, it was hot. She started grunting really deep. Her back looked like a slide. I reached around her waist and started feeling for her clit. It sounded like she was praying; saying *yes*, saying *please*, saying *god*. I just kept gripping her hips, going in and out fast. Sweat was running down my face.

Then she let go of her hold on the bed with one hand. She stuck her fingers in her mouth and started sucking. I thought she was trying to stop herself from screaming. She was pumping her whole body back and forth under the street light. I slammed her into my hips, I saw her ass shake. I was watching my prick going in and out of her but I couldn't, I couldn't, if I looked I was going to come. I just kept thrusting into that place, my balls were buzzing, fuck I was gonna come, I wanted to tell her how much I liked her right then, this dirty hot girl, I was fucking so hard, I was going to come way too fast, her ass was squeezing, still moving. I bit my lip. I was bolting my weight through the cave of her, coming …

We both fell forward onto her bed. I thought she was cursing. I didn't know if she came or not. When I pushed up off her, I was breathing hard. She was writhing, still pumping, moaning *fuck fuck fuck*.

I was kneeling on the floor beside her bed. It smelled like food, like scrambled eggs or something. I thought it was the sheets. She pushed up off her stomach and turned around. Then she climbed on me and started showering my neck with these soft kitten kisses. I felt like an animal. My stomach churned.

'Look,' she whispered, holding my shoulders. 'I want to talk for a while. Stay. Will you stay?'

'Okay.' I stared up at the ceiling. There was a long silence where I knew that she knew that I didn't really want to.

The girl motioned me back up beside her. She pulled up the huge heap of covers at the foot of the bed. I got in and we lay down on our backs as she covered us with a bunch of the smelly sheets and also a plaid woollen blanket. She grabbed my hand tightly and laid it on her stomach. We were lying close enough together that her breast was touching my side.

'Look … Look, I just … '

She started to speak a few times like that, but nothing would come out. I lay there and stared at the ceiling. I noticed a hook for a painting coming out of the wall. She was trying and trying to speak but she kept swallowing her words.

'Just tell me,' I finally said. 'It's okay.'

'Okay. Okay. I had this friend, he did it to me once … '

'What, like I just did?'

'No, no. Not like that.'

'Like what?'

'I wanted to feel like that again … '

'Like what? Tell me.'

'Do you really want to know?'

'Yeah. I'm right here.'

I was stroking the back of her hand and playing with her fingers. Then I turned on my side and put my thigh over hers. She had gotten so worked up about something that she was shivering, even under all the covers.

'I like being tied up,' she said quickly. 'He tied me up.'

'How?'

'How did the guy tie me up?'

'Sure.'

'I was looking at some pictures of girls like that. I found this magazine, it was pictures of these girls hanging from the wall by hooks, from the ceiling by hooks, with their ankles up and their wrists knotted together. Girls with ropes between their legs, I mean, rope tied in knots all over their naked bodies and then the biggest knot was between their legs. Their knees were bent underneath them. Their elbows were stuck together. Those girls' eyes were open, they couldn't move, they were being watched! Someone was taking these pictures!'

'Yeah, I've seen those kinds of things.'

'So I bought myself some rope, because, I guess, I wanted to see, you know … '

'By yourself?'

'Yes.'

'Why by yourself? I thought it was with a guy.'

'Wait. I just wanted to try it first and see how it was. Listen: it didn't stay that way, being alone.'

'Okay.'

'I was lying on the floor in front of the mirror in my bedroom, actually just right over there, and I tied one of my wrists to my ankles and I put the rope – this miniature brown hairy ball of twine that people probably bought for their little cats – I put it underneath me. I mean, I put it under my ass. And I had to touch myself, it was the feeling, that fraying twine on my skin, how I couldn't move normally. I was locked like that with that texture all over me … '

'Yeah?'

'I wrapped my whole chest. I did it so my tits pushed nearly back to my chin. I pulled up the twine up between my legs … My back was arching, these sounds were coming out of my lips and I held the ends of the rope down on either side of me and I started thrusting my chest in the air, feeling the rope go up into my pussy and my breasts fucking jiggling and I couldn't move my legs, all right?'

'Yeah?'

'And he walked in on me!'

'Who?'

'The guy I was seeing.'

'Who was it?'

'I'm not going to tell you his name … '

'That's not what I meant.'

'I was in love in with him.'

'Oh.'

'And he started yelling at me: *What the fuck are you doing? What the fuck are you doing?* I saw his face. He looked like he was going to hit me.'

'He did?'

'My eyes squeezed shut.'

'He hit you?'

'He was so mad at me.'

'I could never hit a woman. Never. Absolutely fucking never. I don't care what she was doing.'

'I felt his breath over me, these rapid huffs. And I thought for sure he was gonna hit me and I just stayed there, god, I couldn't move away. I was trying to stop from even breathing … But when I opened my eyes, I just opened them in a blurry slit, I saw that he was in my underwear drawer looking for something. Then he came back to me, down at my legs, he was crouching right at me, where the biggest knot was. He had my camera, my clit was pulsing so fast … '

'So he didn't hit you. Thank god.'

'He took pictures of me. He took all these pictures while freaking out and sweating and unwinding the rope and throwing it twisted all over my body!'

She was shaking. Her arms were strangled so tight around her chest that her tits came up near her chin. She ripped the plaid blanket off herself.

'I hated him right then. I told him: *Fucking tie me tie me tie me back up!* I tried to relax my eyes, look him straight in his face, but I couldn't, I couldn't.'

'He sounds like a violent asshole! I'm not surprised. Why were you in love with him?'

'No, you don't understand. I crunched my teeth together until tears came down my cheeks … I wanted that feeling, I wanted that strangling … And it was like he finally heard me, like he was finally paying attention to me the way that I wanted. It was amazing, I swear, he started doing it. He was taking the rope from my stomach and winding at my ankles. He lifted my legs up and wrapped my thighs tight. He coiled my stomach with the rope and it burned. Then he yanked up my wrists and slapped my face.'

'Holy fuck. Who raised this guy?'

'He was the kind of guy who never said what he meant.'

'But he'd hit you before, hadn't he?'

'No … No, he only did that once, the last time. Fuck, I don't want to tell you any more.'

'Why?'

'Because you hate him. It's clear. And I get it. But, I mean, you don't know how I felt … '

'Why do girls like you always go for the guys who treat you like shit?'

'I couldn't help it.'

'Because you were "in love" with him, right?'

'Please. Stop.'

'Why are you shaking?'

'I didn't tell you what he did with the pictures.'

'Let me guess. He blackmailed you.'

'Blindfolded.'

'Brilliant!'

'I started to hallucinate. It was like the space under my eyes got white. It was like being outside, like a river was rushing close by and I felt something squirming up against my back, as if I was lying in the gunk of the earth. The ropes were still burning my gut but I felt something cold and curling, like it was trying to get up under me. Like it wanted food. Like a million tiny snakes were moving toward my thighs. It got sharp there, underneath me, like their mouths were open, like all their tiny teeth were starting to bite me and it was all focused at my cunt. They wanted the skin and juice of me. I was arching my back, trying to shake the pain off my skin, but I was squeezing my thighs, squeezing inside, trying to not let them go in, but I kept getting wetter and wetter, they were slipping inside me, the million tiny snakes ... I was going to come. I was on the verge of the biggest come of my life.'

'And what happened?'

'I heard stomping downstairs. It broke me. I mean, I couldn't see. And there were people downstairs banging at my door! A bunch of them pounding up the flight of stairs, my front door was fucking open and I heard them running down my hallway and there I was, I was blindfolded, tied up, flat on the floor, squeezing my thighs – god, I couldn't help it, I couldn't help it!'

'Hey, you're okay now. You've already said the worst.'

'No no no! I haven't! He was laughing, they were all laughing at me like that. There were at least four guys in my room. I heard him coming over to me. He was whispering to the other ones, watching me there. I was cold everywhere, I wanted it to stop.'

'Why didn't you just say that?'

'Because I was too in it. Can't you see that I was in it?'

'In what? I don't fucking understand.'

'The guy stroked my hair. I thought it was his fingers. I couldn't see. He pressed into my cheeks, my lips, my whole face, and he said, *I brought them back for you*. Here she is.'

'That's creepy. Didn't you think that was creepy?'

'The men were breathing around me. I couldn't help it. My body was leaking open through the spaces in the rope. I knew they were all looking at me. My pussy was growing between my crushed legs ... Men's breathing rushed at me, it was stuffy and sweaty, filling up the room. They were crouching around me, I could feel them coming in for me, and they started touching me, their heads and hands leaning in. They first started pinching my tits. They said, *Look, she's moving her hips!* I knew that they were all going to do it to me. They kept pinching me and laughing, *Look, she wants it.* And I felt a cock press between my thighs. I knew it wasn't his. And he told the rest of them, *Hold her legs up in the air!* I got stretched from underneath. It was like I had wings coming out from my pussy or something. My whole stomach started throbbing through the rope. I knew those men saw everything about me right then … '

'Wait. Wait. You really liked it?'

'I felt like the one I loved, I mean, he was there too, *he* was directing it with all those others. I was opened for *him*. I didn't know if he was turned on or turned off. I didn't know if he liked me like that or hated me: tied, wet and eyeless, in front of those guys … I wanted to know how far it would go in front of him.'

'Man … '

'They were holding my legs up in the air. Cocks poked underneath me, guys grunted, *Look, she loves it, look at her go, her hips are so wild, look at her now!* I was getting fucked and this cock dropped into my mouth and I sucked and they kept on, they kept on, pressing my ass and pressing my cunt and one of their bodies slid underneath me and one went on top and they both drove up me and I felt them inside me. I didn't know which part was in and which part was out. I was the centre for all of them fucking. Over and over each time it felt better, each time it got worse. I knew this was it. Getting fucked by so many, being seen, being known … '

'You really liked it. That's incredible.'

'Yeah. And then, I mean, I was ready for it to stop. I remember how I opened more to try to stop it, and it felt like my heart was rushing too hard. My stomach started bubbling. I thought I was going to shit or piss. Something started filling the backs of my eyes, my ass was my cunt and my cunt was my ass. It was like I was tied to a stick in the ground. I was tied to a stick as they punched holes in this earth!'

'God, I'm sorry, I'm sorry. It's okay. Look, I'm sorry. Let's get up.'

'No. You don't get it. It just makes me see that sex is always like this!'

'But you said you loved that guy!'

'I did!'

'Come on, don't cry. Please.'

'I'm sorry.'

'Why did you stay there? Why didn't you leave?'

'Have you ever loved someone who didn't love you back?'

'No. I don't know, maybe I have … '

'Talking about him makes me … '

'Look, let's stop talking about it. Let's get up. I should go now.'

'It doesn't matter who fucks me! You or him or all of them! I know that guys think they fuck me, but guys who think they fuck me think they know what they're doing when they don't, they really don't! The morning beside them always stinks. It's that stink of men in their sleep and all I want to do is get out of their bed.'

'But … '

'I don't want to see myself in the morning. Looking down between my legs. I know there's stuff dripping out from me, even in the morning, my cunt is still wet. I don't know why my cunt is still wet! I mean, I know what's happened in the middle of the night, I know what happened with all those men. But my body awake, in the morning, it's like it's bloated from the feelings. I am heavy and wet and my body wants to fuck again. It's never enough! It's like my cunt has taken in all the thoughts I didn't speak. It's like it has drowned all my need in itself! Don't you see what I am saying?'

'No. No. I have to go … '

'The only thing I feel after sex is: this is how I have to fuck.'

'I've got to go. I've really got to go now.'

'No! No, you can't go. Don't go now! One more time. Please. Come on.'

'I don't know, after that story, I mean, I can't.'

'Please.' *Why do girls always say* please?

The girl was licking her thumb. Both of us were sweating, a cold kind of sweat. She started rubbing her lips in circular motions on my cheek. Her saliva was burning. She was making my face wet like hers.

Then she wrapped her thighs around me. She took both my hands and put them on her breasts. *Please*, she moaned again, really sexy this time, like there was something in her throat. She was making me feel like I was being let out of a cage. My fingers were twisting her nipples, my mouth was on her neck. I felt how her hips were churning like a motor, it was making me hard. She was using her wet fingers to rub between her thighs.

Fuck me, she mouthed.

And then she pushed herself up onto her hands and knees. Her ass was toward my face. She looked like an animal. I saw her ass and pussy spreading. This blaze went ripping through my groin.

'C'mon, fuck, fuck, please!'

Her voice was matching the jerks of her rear. I could see all those guys doing it to her. I didn't want to be like them. I could see how she still wanted that shit that she loved. I wanted to fuck it out of her. That man was an abuser. An abusive fucking beast! I got up behind her. I was kneading her ass cheeks. She was moaning like something inside her was going to crack, she was moaning like she knew what I was thinking.

MAN NO. 3

'd been watching her dance. Loved her ass shaking. The way she looked down at her feet, shook her hips and got into herself. She made me get up and want to dance too.

So I made my way close and when she sensed me right near her, I was surprised for a second – she stared straight at me. Her eyes looked like they were going to cut through my face. But then she smiled. It softened her eyes.

She looked down again and danced closer with me. She started pressing herself into me, reaching out her arms. She was wearing a tight little skirt. She let me feel around her waist and then down, until I was holding her ass. I loved this girl's ass. She let me feel how it could move.

Then she snaked her arms up to my shoulders, I thought it was to hug me, but she just pulled my face down close to her and whispered, 'I want you to come to my place tonight.' It was exactly like that, so easy, no problem.

When we got to her place, though, there were a few moments where we just stood in her living room not talking or touching. She lit a candle and bent down really provocatively, on purpose, to pick books and takeout containers off the couch that looked all stained with coffee marks or something.

In this strange kind of childish voice she said, 'So … what do you want to do?'

I knew she knew what I wanted to do! It had all been so clear back at the bar. She was playing around with me. I just wanted to have everything go smoothly.

'I like the way you were dancing back there,' I said, trying to make her feel good.

'At the bar? Oh, thanks.'

'How about I see you dance some more?'

'Here? I don't know, come on ... '

I couldn't believe she was acting so innocent all of a sudden. Like she didn't have it in her. She'd been so hot with me at the bar, it couldn't have been more than twenty minutes ago!

'Come on, baby, let me watch you move some more.' I sat down on the dirty couch and pushed the small coffee table over to one side. 'Dance for me.'

The girl looked down toward the floor. She was wearing these high-heeled shoes that made her feet look naked. Her hair was swinging in front of her eyes. She started moving her hips side to side, then laughing.

'I can't,' she said.

'Come on, you can, baby, that looks really good.'

I think I gave her some confidence for it. Because then she lifted her leg up and put one heel down on the table. Her legs looked strong in that position, both calves bulging out, her foot arched so high. She started rubbing her hand along her open inner thigh almost up to her pussy, stretching the edge of her skirt with two fingers so I couldn't see her panties. She put her other hand on the back of her ass and started rocking back and forth between her palms, one near her pussy, one on her ass.

'I can't dance without music!' she complained.

'Yeah you can, baby. You're doing fine.'

I was getting hard. I loved the silence and watching her grind. She didn't know how sexy she looked.

Then she raised her leg off the table and stretched it out straight, trying to point her toe. All the muscles in her leg hardened. When she put her heel back down on the floor, she started dancing toward me. She turned around and showed me her ass. It looked so high in her skirt. She put both her hands on her ass cheeks and started splitting them open, pressing them closed, making the fabric of her skirt stretch to the limit. Then she bent herself in half, putting her fingertips on the floor. Her ass raised open even higher. Those heels made her legs look so firm and stretched. She started inching her skirt up over one side of her ass.

'More?' she asked, looking under her open legs at me.

'Yeah, baby, it's sexy, come closer … '

She teetered her way back a bit, shaking her ass in tiny movements. Now she was laughing. The blood rushed to her face. I reached my hands up and forced her skirt over her ass in one yank. She wasn't wearing underwear. Jesus Christ. Her naked ass was right there. I saw her inner thighs shining.

'I don't like wearing underwear,' she said quickly.

My cock was huge, pressing at my pants. I reached down and unzipped myself. Then I helped the girl move even closer to me, until both her calves were steadied against the edge of the couch. She reached her arms through her legs and grabbed for my hard cock. Her hands clasped around my shaft, stroking up and down, while I was trying to bring her closer to my face. I kept trying to split her ass cheeks open wider so I could make out her dark little butt hole, flickering in the candlelight. I could tell she was a bit uncomfortable, all of a sudden, being that stretched open overtop of me. She knew how closely I was looking at her pussy and ass. She started squirming in my hands. She was moaning now, trying to get away. But I knew it was turning her on that I wouldn't let her move from that position. She wasn't making sense, mumbling, 'I … I … want to try … God, yes, that feels, I want to try I want to … '

She started pumping her knees up and down in excitement and her ass kept almost touching my face. On one of her down motions I let my finger move into her crack. She liked that, gasping, and she started moving down more slowly so that I could rub right on her asshole. It twitched when I got it.

Nasty girl, she likes it up her ass! With an ass like this, I'm sure she takes it.

'God, that feels good, god, god, it's good … '

Her whole body was getting hotter each time I got it and poked her hole. She started to let my finger inside her ass. Little by little, I was trying to pull her down to me, my finger getting hugged by her asshole. I wanted her to sit right down like that on my cock.

'Come here, baby.'

The girl let go of my cock to try to rip off my pants and she got them down to my knees and that was enough, God, I wanted to fuck her wiggling ass! I'd only done it once before and that girl didn't like it, but this one wanted it, I could tell, I knew she did, the way she was moving herself. I wanted to feel how big her clit got when I was up her ...

'Come on down, baby, sit down,' I said, straining.

She wasn't letting me pull her down, she kept opening and closing her ass cheeks, moaning and struggling with me. I didn't know if she was doing that on purpose, delaying or what, so I gripped her flesh harder. 'Come on come closer come closer ... '

'I've only done it once before,' she said, breathing hard. 'You've got to stop if I say so, okay?'

'Of course, baby, of course I will. I don't want to hurt you.'

She handed me a condom from somewhere. I have no idea where. I put it on as fast as I could, I was serious, this was fucking amazing. I got it on just in time, it was all happening so fast, her ass going down on the head of my prick, I watched her cheeks split, her hole start to open, second by second, the head of my dick going in her, so tight, down on my dick, her asshole alive.

'It's good, it's okay, it's good, it's okay,' she was saying.

The juice from her pussy was coating my balls as she sat her weight down, and she started bouncing up and down, up and down on my lap, rocking back and forth. Her voice got gruffer than I'd ever heard a girl's: 'Fuck I'm gonna come, I'm gonna fucking come.'

Holding down the sides of her ass hard on my prick, pumping up – it felt so good. I banged my head on the top of the couch. My prick was throbbing and everything got tighter in her ass. It was a trigger, her coming. My dick shot up into her ass spasm. We both screamed. Yes, fuck, yes! Fucking hell yes, I came in a girl's ass!

When I eased her up off me she yelled like she was hurt.

'What? What is it? Are you okay?'

I thought she was in pain but she started laughing. She couldn't stop. Her voice got high and then low. 'I feel like I'm flying. I feel like I'm flying!'

I watched her crumple down on the floor in front of my feet. Her back was shaking. I couldn't tell if she was still laughing or if she was crying.

'Are you okay?' I asked. I wanted the lights to go on.

'Yeah, yeah, I'm okay, I'm okay. I needed that. Thank you.'

She was talking into her hands. Thanking me! Man. But she didn't move from the floor. I had to wipe off my dick. I wanted to get up, get it clean and go home. I would think about her all night. I'd think about this for a long time. Maybe I'd get to do it with this girl again.

MAN NO. 4

'd been watching that girl at the bar thinking: no way, no way was I going to get that lucky. She was wearing a tight black top with short sleeves that made her tits look too big for her body. Her ass was round through her skirt. Her legs were pretty muscular. She wasn't tall but she wore shoes with big heels.

She had hiked up her skirt and was shifting her body around on the bar stool. She was drinking red wine. She'd started a conversation with another woman by asking for a cigarette. There were only the two of them sitting at the bar, even though the rest of the place was busy. I was standing at the edge of the dance floor. I couldn't stop watching the girl's lips move. The other woman was older, kind of good-looking and laughing with her. The girl was taking big gulps from her drink. I could tell she was getting drunk because she was sliding her lips together and liking the feel of it. The girl was leaning into the woman to get another cigarette when she caught me looking at her. It was like she knew I was looking at her mouth. Her tongue slid along her upper lip. I think for a second she thought she was shocking me, licking herself like that. But she wasn't shocking me. I was amused watching her flirt with that woman, sure. And I was thinking about how her lips would feel on me.

I was staring for too long, though, and I looked away for a moment. When I looked back up, the girl motioned me over by patting her hand on the seat beside her. I hadn't really thought she was going to do that. I smiled at her and her cheeks turned bright red.

I felt my heart beating up near my throat when I walked up to her and the woman. I squeezed in beside her stool and the wall. She didn't even say hi to me. She just started giggling with the woman who I could tell wasn't happy that I was now there too. The woman had a few wiry grey hairs near her ears. She blew her smoke in my direction. I leaned my back against the wall. *I got the hint, lady.* I looked past the two of them at all the people dancing. Everyone was dancing alone. I like watching people together, really grinding. I was so close to the girl's body and I felt heat coming off her. I felt like she was doing that to me on purpose. The woman whispered something into the girl's ear. I kept looking at the dance floor.

I ordered another drink. I noticed that the girl's back really curved in at the bottom before it turned into her ass. I wanted to hold on to her there. I wanted to see her on her hands and knees, her big tits swaying, her ass humping. I wanted to see what she moved like naked.

But the girl kept on ignoring me. It was bullshit. I didn't want to be there anymore. I gulped down the drink I'd just ordered and touched her lightly on her shoulder.

'I'm going,' I said.

'No, wait up.'

It was the first time she looked at me. Her eyes were glazed. She assumed she was going with me? I didn't even think I heard her right. I turned and started making my way out through the crowd. I wanted her to follow me but I wasn't sure if she was coming. When I turned my head to look, I saw her kissing the woman. I stopped and stared at them even though I didn't really want to. I felt a bit embarrassed. I just wanted to get out of there. I saw the woman's hands squeezing the girl's ass. Their tongues were going in and out of each other's open lips. It was pretty incredible, their age difference and everything. That woman was really taking pleasure with the girl's body. I felt it in my throat.

Then I saw the bartender moving toward them. He was smiling and talking – he must've made some kind of joke because the girl peeled herself away and they all started laughing. The girl jumped down off the bar stool. The bartender and the woman looked at each other. The bartender rolled his eyes. I saw the girl look around for me. She looked kind of worried. I was near the front door. When she spotted me, her mouth broke into a smile. She started walking quickly toward me, making her way through the tables and the people. Everyone was looking at her. She started running. She ran past me, yanking my hand and pulling me outside with her.

It was raining. There were barely any cars on the street.

'Come on!' she yelled, still running. 'Let's go to my place!'

I was almost out of breath running after her. 'Slow down!' I yelled. But I liked watching her ass move as she ran. She kept whipping her head around looking for a cab, waving frantically.

When I caught up to her, she was standing by the cab, chest heaving up and down. I climbed in after her. She rolled down her window. Then she leaned her wet body over my legs to roll down the window on my side too. She arched her neck up toward me. She opened her lips. I reached under her head and brought her face up to mine. Her tongue poked into my mouth. It tasted like wine. I let her do all the movement. I liked taking her rhythm like that and she was pressing her breasts into me frantically. I wondered if this was how she was kissing the woman in the bar. The girl's hands were running all over my neck. I was getting hard. I held her shoulders and pushed her back a second.

'Why were you kissing that woman?'

'Because I wanted to,' she answered, sitting straight back up beside me. 'Why'd you think I was doing it?'

I rolled up my window. The girl started laughing, with hiccups. I wondered how much she'd had to drink. I didn't say anything. I really wanted to get her home with me. I wanted to see her naked. I wanted her to suck my cock. I knew she wanted to too. We started kissing again. She was rubbing her hand up and down on my cock. I felt like she would've done it right there if I pushed her down.

When we got up to her place, though, she wanted to just sit down on the couch and talk. It was weird: she walked up to her bookshelf and tilted her head. All I wanted to do was fuck her. She was right there in front of me. She didn't turn on the lights. I grabbed her hand and led her to the bedroom, which was down at the end of the hall. I tickled around her ribs, I got her laughing again. She was looking up at me, trying to get out of my grip and talking dirty, saying things like: *Come on, guy, take off your clothes! I want to fuck you, take off your clothes, I want to suck your dick, baby, come on!*

We were both taking off our clothes and throwing them on her floor. The outlines of her body were so sexy. I didn't even care about her sucking my dick right then. I grabbed her by the waist, pushed her down the bed, which looked dirty with piles of sheets. She acted like she was trying to put up a fight.

'Come on, you can fuck me, can't you?'

Her breasts were jiggling at the top of her chest. Her skin was so hot. I wrestled with her a bit. She wouldn't lie still. She was still laughing. I used all the strength I had to turn her on her stomach. She was half on the bed and half off, her legs stretched wide in an upside-down V toward the floor. I stood over her, I felt so much bigger than her. Now I wanted to turn on the lights. She was thrusting her pelvis up in the air and reaching under herself. She was spreading the front of her pussy with her hand. I wanted to see that better. She was mashing into the sheets furiously, never stopping for a second, going, 'Fuck me fuck me fuck me!'

I never knew anyone could say it so much. I wanted to tell her to shut up. But I was totally possessed. I grabbed hold of her ass cheeks and I spread them so wide. I could see her asshole and her slit underneath. The two were so close. I watched my fingers knead hard into her ass cheeks. I was thinking: I know I can make this girl come easily.

So I let go of her for a second and she turned around to watch me. I got a condom from my jeans on the floor and put it on. She was humping her pelvis up, watching me on her elbows. I knew she was drunk.

'Turn back around,' I whispered.

On her hands and knees, she got up like a little bunny. I loved her like that. It was fucking amazing. I put my cock at the edge of her pussy. She was moaning in these short little gasps. The head of my cock was getting fucking grabbed by her pussy. I couldn't do it slowly. She was moving her ass so fast she was sucking me inside her. I started pushing in these shortened hard thrusts. I couldn't stop how I was doing it so hard, I thought of her tonguing that woman at the bar, I felt like punishing her ... I knew I was going to let it go too fast because she kept moaning that she liked it. I saw her face for a second turned my way from behind. Her eyes were closed, her lids were black, her lips rubbing together, moaning: *More, more, more.*

I noticed this picture hook up above her head sticking out of the wall. There was a piece of rope hanging down like a noose.

Her ass was rolling all over my hands, her whole body was bucking, her breasts swung underneath – it was like I'd been there right from the beginning of time or something. Me and her, just me and her. I was going to come ... I pulled myself out of her, caught my breath.

'Come outside!'

'What the fuck?'

The girl had bolted up fast. She started running naked down the hallway in front of me like a ghost. She opened a door off her living room to a balcony. It was still raining a bit. With the air on my skin it felt like her panting. I grabbed her from behind and pushed her up against the railing. My hand reached down and felt in between her legs. She was swollen and soaking. My fingers spread her lips and found her clit. She started squealing and pumping her ass back into me. I put my hand over her mouth. I felt her lips vibrating. She was trying to be quiet for me, but when I got my cock back inside her she started moaning through my hand. I was looking down over her shoulder at the city at night. And her tits were so big, her nipples were hard. My hand slid off her mouth and squeezed her tits together.

'You … ' she said, breathing, turning her head, eyes rolling back.

All of a sudden it was like she wasn't really with me. All she was doing was splaying herself for me, her pussy inflating its mouth on my cock, her ass pulsing into my groin. I couldn't help what I was doing. She was coating me with her wetness, fuck, sucking me, taking me. Sirens at night.

'Put it in my ass. I want it in my ass … '

She was like an animal. I didn't care anymore, her body got hotter every time I thrust deeper. I took myself out of her pussy and shoved up her ass.

'Yeah, that feels good yeah that feels good … '

Then in one shriek her asshole contracted and I thought she was coming. My cock got pushed out. The globes of her ass in the night, my come had streamed and stuck white. I was thrown backward, weak in my knees. I wanted to stretch out underneath her, down where it was wet and concrete. I heard her heart beating somewhere above me, my heart was pounding, taking in the rain.

'Come on!' She was hissing and yanking me by the hand. 'Get up!'

I was so exhausted. I could barely breathe enough to get up. I started coughing, trying to catch my breath. She was pulling me down the hallway back to her bedroom. All I could do was stumble behind her. I heard her muttering *fuck, god, fuck*.

When I finally felt the bed underneath me I crashed. I wanted sleep. I felt like I was lying at the bottom of the river. My eyes were closed but I could feel her hovering …

'Why do you have to fucking fall asleep the second it's over?'

'I'm tired. I'm just tired.'

'Why do you all always finish too slow or too fast?'

'No … it felt good, that's all. Can I sleep here? I'll leave in the morning, baby, I'm just tired.'

'After you come and it stops I want to kill you.'

I looked up the wall to that hook. The noose was still there.

'I feel like smothering you with my pillow when you sleep. Your breathing gets heavy and I'm still up. You're sleeping and my cunt is still beating. How can you sleep? I can't sleep. You don't know how to have sex. I want to stick my fingers down your throat or up your ass. I feel like sticking your head in the ground.'

'Man, maybe I should go … '

'It's like you're dead there in front of me.'

'I just need to go to sleep for a second.'

'If you don't wake up then I want another. I want you down between my legs. If you won't do it then I want another. I want ten of you between my legs! I want you lined up to have me. It doesn't matter who you are. I'll just get your wiggling tongues. I'll watch you go down on me, eat from me, drink from me. I just want your heads, your rough little cat tongues … '

I didn't know what she was doing. She was grabbing for my head. She was sticking her fingers in my ears! I wished at that moment I'd never come to her place. She was pushing my head, but it didn't feel like my head. I wanted to tell her to stop it. But everything was stuck. Her fingers in my ears like two twigs. I wanted to go to sleep. But she got stronger with me, shaking my whole head. Yelling, 'Wake up! Wake up!' She pushed me toward her thighs. It felt like she was rolling my head up a hill.

'Just put your tongue in me. Put your tongue in me!'

Her fingers were hooked inside my head. She forced me to her cunt and locked her thighs at my ears. Then she started bucking her hips. My mouth was slipping on top of her cunt. She was so wet that it felt like I could've drowned in her. I wanted to come back up for air. But she moved her pussy harder on my face. She was forcing her clit on my tongue. It felt like a bulb. Her thighs were shaking against me. She was breathing loud, I heard it coming from her cunt. I kept moving my tongue over her clit. She got bigger and bigger. I squeezed my eyes shut until everything turned black. I kept licking and licking. I think she was coming, it tasted like sugar was pouring down my chin. She was screaming so loud, it felt like she was going to pound through my face! I finally found my arms and I grabbed her ass and split it open. She came when I did that, it was like I heard it – this unlocking, this total release. I'd never felt that before, I mean a girl coming right on my face.

When she climbed off me she was quiet. I rubbed my face with her sheets. They smelled weird, like eggs.

'Listen,' she whispered. 'Listen … '

I nodded that I was listening to her. I felt sort of sick, dizzy. I couldn't stop licking my lips. That taste of her was keeping me awake. My lips still felt like her pussy. Then she reached her arm for my neck and drew me close to her. I put my head on her chest, but I felt nervous, I don't know. That noose was right above us and I didn't want to ask what it was for.

'I had this friend once,' the girl said, stroking my cheek. 'She did what you just did. You listening to me?'

'Yeah, I am. I am.' I was glad she wasn't mad at me anymore. And her kissing that woman at the bar now made sense. She liked girls. She was bisexual.

'Listen: to get inside someone you really have to be there. Every second, right there. It's at the back of your throat, inside your lips, all over your tongue. Can you hear me?'

'Yeah, of course I can hear you. I'm right here.' She was at the back of my throat, inside my lips, all over my tongue.

'It's like you're looking down a highway at a turn in the road. There's this car coming toward you, and you know that the car is going at the exact same speed as you are toward it, but you both can't slow down, so it's like your car's racing into her car, coming closer and closer … '

Her voice was making my head all thick and sleepy.

'So that's what happened with me and this girl. We were really close friends. I used to go over to her place for dinner and we'd talk and drink, I mean we did it every week. Then one night, we had a fight. It had to do with why people get hurt. I remember she said that rejection was the worst of all kinds of pain. And I was disagreeing with her because I was saying that rejection didn't make you bleed, so it couldn't be the strongest kind because there was no physical pain attached. Now I get how that is totally simplistic, but at the time it seemed like I was supposed to be opposing her. And I was talking a lot. I said that the worst kind of pain would be rejection where blood really starting pouring out of your heart! She rolled her eyes at me and said that the kind of pain she was talking about was *real*. I started laughing saying that her kind of rejection couldn't have that much reality in it because it only applied to the person who was feeling it. And then she got so mad, all of a sudden, I mean, I wasn't surprised, I was being an asshole for some reason, I just didn't know why. But I think she knew why. I think she already had these kinds of feelings for me. And she jumped up off the couch, her voice got deep and she said, "You don't understand anything I say, do you? You don't understand anything about me."

'She was on the verge of tears, my friend, and I tried to pacify her. I said I was sorry, I mean, I really didn't want to hurt her. But that just made it worse. She couldn't speak. She ran to her room. I wasn't sure if I should follow her or if she would come back out or if I should leave. I found myself walking down the hallway toward her bedroom. The door was slightly open. I knocked and asked if I could come in. She said okay. She was kneeling on her bed. It was the first time I'd ever been in there. She had a special area walled off for the bed. The walls were painted yellow and there were red lights everywhere. She was wearing a red fuzzy sweater that was clinging to her chest. Her breasts were pressing out high. The light was so strange. It made the place look like it was swelling. And she almost looked like a child, on her knees, begging me to play. "It's okay, just come here," she said. Her voice got lodged in my throat.

'I climbed up on her bed. I didn't feel sure, but I did it. I lay down on my back. She did the same. It was too warm. She whispered something, I didn't hear what, we were lying side to side, not touching.

'I was stuck there on my back. But I knew where I was and what we were going to do … '

'Tell me what you did.' I got that out. The girl hadn't stopped stroking my face and I was totally turned on again listening to her story.

'Uh, well, she whispered again and it travelled over my neck. It sounded so much like she was saying my name. I turned my eyes toward her. My skin was throbbing. Her sweater was itching against my arms. We were too close. It felt like she was reading my mind. Her gaze was so steady on my face. I couldn't hold it. I looked at her neck. I wanted to touch it. I heard her hand move along the sheets. I was too hot, it felt like the kind of heat from a fire in the middle of winter, if you move just one inch you'll be cold … She was coming closer and closer to me and she said I should take off my clothes. I couldn't, though, I still couldn't move, her hand touched my waist. It felt like the skin there was splitting in two. Her fingers worked up under my shirt. The tips were freezing. She traced along my ribs. She was moving up toward my breasts. She got there, she squeezed me. We both moaned when she did it. She used her other hand to lift up my shirt. I was breathing so fast. She pulled my bra over my breasts and she moved her head in, she jutted out her lips. She was wetting me. She was sucking on my nipples. It felt so good, I was beating all over. I put my hands on the back of her head. I wanted her to suck more, my whole breasts, the flesh and the nipples, I wanted every part of me in her mouth. I pulled her hair in my fists. I wanted to come. I felt like a man touching a girl, a girl who was writhing all over him. Do you hear? Are you listening to me?'

'God, yeah.'

'Girls are like this. What they want, it's never over. I wanted to fuck her. My hands went all over her body – I wanted to fuck her, flat on her back, her body on fire, her lips were opening. I rolled over her and I started to move, see, that's when I felt it, that I wanted to fuck, my breasts were above her, that I could fuck, that she could take me in more, and I took off her sweater, her underwear, her bra, and I pulled off my own so that when I pressed down we were naked to naked. Our bodies rubbed like steam comes off the ground. Breast to breast, thigh to thigh, our cunts moving, I couldn't help it, my ass was up and down, my ass was in her hands, I wanted to fuck her and fuck her so bad. My knees spread open her thighs. Wetness shot down. We moaned, we were together right there, cunt to cunt, water boiling. I was licking her neck, my teeth bit her skin, her fingers dug down between both our bodies. She was splitting me wide, doing the same to herself. It was one flashing second, my clit to her clit, the walls went on fire, my clit to her clit, it all buzzed in my blood and the dark opened up on our brightest red skins. Oh god, wake up! I want you to know how this feels. Fuck. Just wake up! I want you to touch me, really touch me. I can't stand this. I really can't. Fuck. God. Fuck.'

I was falling asleep to the sound of her cursing, afraid of the noose being tied round my neck.

MAN NO. 5

I drank too much. I don't remember exactly how I got there. I remember being at the bar, not leaving it. The two of them were sitting beside me at first, their bare legs swinging over the bar stools. They looked exactly alike from the back. Laughing and smoking. The same long dark hair. When I glanced down I saw one girl's hand playing up under the other one's skirt. It startled me. I wanted to see that. And they knew I was watching. They looked over at me a little. I didn't look back at their faces but at their hands on each other's bare thighs. There was just no way they thought I couldn't see them. Fuck, I was sitting right beside them.

'Let's take him home with us.'

'No, I don't want to.'

'Come on. Why not? It'll be fun.'

'He's not going to be enough for us.'

'Oh, come on! Let's do it, it'll be fun. I'll get to see you fuck.'

They were talking in these jokey voices. Now I knew they knew I could hear them.

'Look at his feet.'

'Whatever, look at his nose!'

'I like big strapping dicks.'

'So do I.'

'It's not worth it to fuck a small dick.'

'Stop it!'

The two of them were laughing hysterically now.

'Come on. He looks nice.'

'But I like it when they're not so nice.'

'I know you do, you little slut! Come on, let's take him to your place. I feel like fucking him.'

'Only if I get to see your face when you're coming … '

'You know you can see anything you want … '

The two girls were ordering another round. Then the one closest to me, the one the other one called 'little slut,' turned to me and smiled. 'Can I get you something?'

I didn't know what to say to her. She was offering to buy me a drink? What the fuck did that mean?

'Come on, Loverboy, drink with me and my friend … '

The girl put her arm around the other girl and drew their faces close together.

'Yeah! What do you want to drink?'

They really looked alike. Their lips were so glossy.

'Come on, Loverboy, drink with us!'

'Okay,' I said. 'Anything.'

So they bought me a beer and we all started talking. I bought the next round, and the next, and the next. I guess we just kept drinking. Then I think we got in a cab. I remember I was walking in the middle of them, arm in arm, up some stairs. They let me go when we got inside the apartment. I saw a couch covered with takeout containers. The two of them ran ahead of me, laughing, down a hallway. I followed them, stumbling, my hands along the walls. It was dark and too hot in that place and I was drunk. The bedroom at the end of the hallway seemed as small as a closet. The bed was near the floor.

I was taking off my clothes in there because I was sweating. I listened to the sound of them kissing. There were lumps of sheets all over the bed. It looked like an obstacle course. I was feeling around for the wall to lean on. My dick had gotten hard because they were below me, sighing out moans between their kisses. I was starting to make out their legs in the darkness, twisting together like they were glued. I saw two tongues flicking around. They were drawing each other's lips in circles. That's what I thought I saw.

With my palms sliding along the wall, I ran into a hook for hanging a painting. It was fucking sharp and it cut me. Then I banged my shin on the edge of the bed and cursed. The girls stopped their kissing for a second and started laughing: 'It's Loverboy!'

It was like they'd forgotten I was even there.

I held my cock. I was cut and bruised and I needed some air. But I was down in near to them now, kneeling at the edge of the bed. The bed was too close to the floor. It smelled like old eggs. I reached in for one of their thighs. I dug deep into it with my hand, I felt like I was shovelling that thigh into the mattress. I heard moaning.

'Oh god, he's got me, he's got me!'

'Make him wait, you little slut, I'm gonna come, I'm gonna come from you first.'

I kept on squeezing the top thigh, the little slut's thigh with one hand as I stroked my cock with the other. Their breaths heated up, as if they were hyperventilating. I heard their cunts clicking. It sounded like a nightmare.

I let go of my dick. I didn't want to come yet. I lay down on my stomach, my knees hit the floor. They were kissing again, mumbling. Their four legs rose up. I smelled their pussies in a hot stuffy gust.

'Put your fingers in us now, Loverboy.'

Both my hands reached inward to feel for their cunts, along their thighs, I was following the heat and I found one, I found the other – they were hot and smashed together and I went in each one. It was like I was sticking my fingers into soup. Both their cunts were so thick. I spread my hand so I could do both at the same time with one hand. I had one with my ring finger, one with my thumb. The little slut on top clutched my finger on and off with her pussy. I wanted to see what I was doing. It was making them breathe fast again, I was pushing in fast and rhythmically, it was making me breathe faster too. I started to shove my second hand, reversed, into each of them, spreading, hearing them kiss, god, stretching them wide, two fingers in two pussies, god they felt big, hugging me, wetter, I couldn't go slow.

'More. Do it more!'

I inched in even closer, they were sucking me deeper, keeping me there.

'Suck us now. Suck us. Come on!'

They were on top of each other. They spread their legs wide behind them in a V. They got so excited rubbing and sliding, trying to touch their two clits. The whole bed was wet. I got my face right up there, breathing into the two of them stacked on top of each other. I didn't know if I could do it.

'Do it, do it, do it, do it!'

In between their tongues and saying *do it*, they were breathing fast again. I got my lips wet. I stuck my tongue out. I licked from top to bottom. Pussy lips vibrated and smashed against my tongue. I knew which one was her, the little slut, the one whose place we were in – she was tight and tasted like cider. She was growing behind herself into my mouth.

'More, more!' she screamed. 'Fuck, yeah, you know how to do this, Loverboy! Thank god! God I love him, he's fucking skilled like a magician!'

Yeah, a magician! I concentrated on her with my mouth because she loved it and she needed it. I poked the other girl with my thumbs. It was hard to please two girls. I had to keep licking. I couldn't stop. Saliva was pouring down my chin. I felt like my mouth was moving inside the mouth of a beast. Lips purple. Throat wide.

'I want to fuck you,' I could hear myself gulping. 'I want to fuck you.'

Again I heard them laughing. They were licking each other's tongues. They untangled themselves, moving quickly, and they dragged me up by the arms so that my whole body was finally on the bed. They rolled me over on my back.

'I told you it wouldn't be big!'

'It's amazing. My magician has a big fat dick,' said the slut.

They were passing my dick back and forth between their hands but I knew that my girl was squeezing it harder. Then they got close and started kissing each other around me. Their mouths formed a suction at the head of my dick, their hot spit poured down. It felt so good I heard my moans fill the room. I was going to shoot in their faces and that made them do it faster, they were making me moan like that, *she* was doing that, I couldn't help it, they kept licking each other so fast around my cock, hot sucking, dark kissing. I was about to come but they stopped and started laughing.

'No, Loverboy, not yet! Oh fuck, you tell him. He likes you better than me.'

The little slut who smelled like cider crawled over me and she whispered in my ear. 'We're all gonna come, Magic Man. I got a present for you first.'

And then she climbed up to my neck and pinned her knees at my ears. The other one stayed down at my cock. I could feel she was straddled on top of me, too, her knees pressing hard into my sides.

'The condoms are under my bed.'

The one down at my cock reached away, leaving her hand on my balls. The slut at my neck started inching closer. My nostrils were so close to her. I could feel everything charge.

'I know you love pussy juice,' my slut said, way up above me. 'I know you love it so much and you make all the girls you fuck so happy 'cause you suck them off for hours and hours, don't you?'

She was making me embarrassed. Also proud.

I watched as she stuffed two fingers into her pussy. Then she painted them on my lips and dipped them into my mouth. I sucked her hard as she scissored her strong little fingers and tried to pick up my tongue.

'You want even more of me?' she asked.

I nodded.

'You make me happy,' she said. 'Because you know what's good for you.'

Then she took my tongue and pulled it up and shoved it inside her. She sank down. It was humid up inside her, my nose pressed up against her hair. I could barely feel the condom rolling over my prick. I was nailed down now by her tight cidery snatch, just my tongue, my tongue, my tongue swimming up. Colours were flashing in front of my lids. *Keep licking, keep licking, keep licking her there.* I didn't know what I was doing, with who, who she was.

'Good, he feels so good in me,' the one down at my cock said. 'His tongue is slowing down.'

Then I felt it, I mean, what was going on down there. It was amazing, it was like the girl was swivelling on me. My hips started fucking her right off the bed. The girl was humping me back and I forgot about the one I liked because that cunt down there was picking up my dick like a fist. Then I felt the slut's hand grab roughly under my chin.

'Keep it moving! Come on!'

My cock was about to explode from the mechanical squeezing when I opened my eyes to the one there above me. She was angry now. I looked way up at her dark, street-lit face surrounded by hair falling in a circle: her eye whites crackled like the eyes of an owl. I wanted to stop licking her cunt but she still had me locked by the knees.

'I wish you were my boyfriend,' she said. 'You're really, really good at this.'

I was confused. The confusion made me mad. I just wanted to come, and I could feel myself getting soft. The one down below pushed off my cock. My dick bobbed in the air, the condom was sagging, fuck … What the fuck did they want from me now?

Quickening breaths got loud through my nose. I was going to kill them using that hook in the wall.

'Did he come?' the girl down there said.

'I don't know, I don't think so,' the mind-game slut said.

'I want to see you suck his cock.'

'Okay.'

My slut slid down me as if I hadn't just been tonguing her, as if she hadn't just told me she wanted me to be her boyfriend.

She pulled the condom off with her teeth. She put me all right inside her mouth. But I was half done, I was pissed off, I didn't know if I could come. I really didn't know anymore if I could ever come. Her hair was warm and long, covering my balls; her mouth breathed and tongue-sucked me hot and so tight, the head of my cock got hugged in her throat, I heard myself grunting, as helpless as her. Then, in her lips, down her throat, in one last flash I went off. She swallowed my jerking but she pulled off too fast. She left a drum beating too hard in my crotch.

'He came in me. He came in my mouth!'

'I want to taste it on your lips, baby!'

Now there was more hair on top of me, two bodies, four eyes and the slurping of tongues. They were passing my come like plasma between them. I was running out of air. Both of their bodies smashed me down, leg over leg and ass over chest, sucked into this dirty egg bed. Bloated, sweating, I wanted to bury my face.

When they finally toppled off me, the slut turned on a light by her bed. She laughed with wide eyes when she looked at my face.

'You're all wet, Loverboy!'

I looked up at that hook coming out of the wall. I looked at my hand. It was bleeding on the side.

The girl looked at me with sympathy or something. She handed me part of the sheet and wiped my chin dry.

'You can sleep out there on the couch out if you want,' she said. 'Just dump all the shit on the floor.'

I heard the other girl grunting with exhaustion, trying to get comfortable in the bed at the wall. I looked around on the floor for my stuff. By the time I found everything and got my pants on I heard breathing going steady with sleep. My mind-fucking girlfriend was wrapped around her friend's back. I turned off the light and left that place quickly. I never wanted to see her again.

MAN NO. 6

The first thing she said when we got back to her place was: 'I was watching you, you know. I was watching everything you did back there.'

I couldn't say anything to this girl. We were standing just inside the doorway of her place. She wouldn't let me come in. 'You think everyone didn't see you?' She started laughing.

She was making me feel bad. I wasn't sure I should've come here with her. Then she suddenly snapped her boot foot and kind of jump-kicked me in a ninja spank move. She started laughing at herself. It didn't hurt but I was in.

Then she locked the door behind me and turned on the switch beside my head. The hallway lit up. Her place was a total fucking mess. There were pizza boxes on the floor with half-eaten slices still in there. Empty wine bottles and Chinese food boxes all over the couch. It was nasty.

'Are you thinking about how dirty you were?'

I knew she was talking about what she'd seen me doing at the bar. I'd been sitting there watching her on the dance floor. I felt like she was dancing just for me: she kept licking her lips, shaking her hips. Her breasts were jiggling up and down under her T-shirt. She turned around and showed me how she moved her ass. I had to put one hand on my cock under the bar. It felt like it was going to go off in my pants like a trigger.

After a few songs like that, she came up right beside me where I was standing. She squeezed herself in between me and some other guy at the bar. She was smiling this huge smile, there was sweat around her forehead. I wanted to say something to her but I didn't know what to say. I felt the heat coming off her. She got a drink of water and then she started moving her upper body in time to the music. Her breasts kept touching my arm. Suddenly she turned to me and said, 'I'm going home now, I want you to come.' I'd never had that experience before – I mean, of a woman coming on to me like that.

'How'd you think that everyone couldn't see you? Don't you think there's a problem with exposing your cock like that in public?'

Her voice sounded so mean now. She was making fun of me. I looked down at the lines in the floor. Then I heard her boots stomping down the hallway. I followed her. I felt like a child. My hands were clasped behind my back.

When we were in her bedroom, she stood by the dark window and looked out. I tried to approach her but she pushed me away. It was like she was mad at me. I didn't even know this girl and already she was mad! She motioned for me to come over in front of her. She arranged it so that my body pressed right up against the window. Then she went behind me.

She put her hands on the sides of my ass. Her breasts were pressing into my back. That felt good. But then she moved her palms down to my tailbone and she started tapping. It made me shift on my feet. Then a rush of heat blew up in my face, so hot that I thought it was the radiator or something. She was scooping her hands under my balls. She started squeezing my sac. I let out deep groans, I couldn't help it. No girl had ever touched me there like that. It felt really fucking good.

She heard how I was enjoying it, though, and she stopped. She put her hands back on my tailbone for a second and then she reached around and unzipped my pants. She took off my shirt and pulled off my pants and underwear. She stayed completely clothed. She turned me by the hips to face her. I didn't really know what she wanted. She put her hands on my shoulders. Her arms were so strong. She pushed me down until I was on my knees.

I had the urge to yell, to say something, but my breath was coming out in these short sucking gasps. I'd wanted her so bad at the bar. Now it felt like long lines of heat were shooting from my ears to my knees. I was getting all soft in the gut, hard in my cock. The girl was cradling my chin in her palms. She slid my head toward her like that, by the jaw. My face ended up at her crotch. She pulled up her skirt and put my head under. My nose got crushed in her warm underwear. She opened her thighs a little. She was clutching me so hard by the back of my head.

I put my tongue on her underwear. I was trying to lick through. I heard the girl moaning. She was swivelling her hips, bending her knees around my shoulders. I opened my mouth wider so that I could take down her panties with my teeth. I got them down like that to her thighs. She wiggled the rest of the way to step out of them. Now she really spread open her thighs. Her naked pussy was over my face. It was wet and swollen. It got so hot under her skirt. My whole face was melting. Her cunt above me was a balloon about to break open. I started pushing my mouth up to her thick lips, moving my whole head side to side. She started rocking her hips in time with me, her pelvis humping back and forth. I could feel her thighs quivering on my cheeks. I heard her murmuring and I rubbed my tongue all over the place where she was hardest, soaking. I wanted to hear her keep moaning. It was fucking hot.

But then she started pinching the skin on the back of my neck while I was sucking. And she cranked her hips at my face, side to side, so it felt like she was punching my cheeks. I was going to get bruises. I wanted to stick my tongue like a beak all the way up her pussy to hurt her too. I kept letting her lead, though, touching her clit with my lips while she banged me. The girl's nails were clawing at my neck. I knew she was trying to come. She was someone who had to try hard to come. It was crazy and it hurt but I loved feeling her tries. I whipped my head to help her along, I wanted to go deeper inside her, bite her, make her fucking freak out and scream. She kept grunting. It got faster and faster but I didn't know if she was coming. It felt like her cunt was opening all over my face.

Then, I don't know why, she started sliding away from me, wiggling backward. I couldn't stop moving my head. My face was all slick with her. Her skirt flew up over my head like a parachute. I was kneeling there, on her bedroom floor in the dark, holding my hard dick with one rubbing hand. My tongue was numb. I knew she was watching me. She looked like a gold-plated statue of God. She looked like the shining evil angel of some dusty store window. I was pumping myself, doing it so fast, I couldn't help myself, and I felt a spurting, one white second all over my fist! I did it right in front of her. She started laughing at me.

'Fool!'

She glared down at me from her leather-booted perch. 'Look at you. Look what you just did.' She took a pillowcase off a pillow from her bed. She threw the thing at me. 'Clean yourself up! Come on. Do it.'

I used the pillowcase to wipe around my cock. My chin felt like a rock on my chest.

'You can do that faster, can't you?'

The pillowcase smelled. I wasn't sure if she was serious, I mean, her reprimanding tone. I was trying to go faster, but my fingers wouldn't move. The pillowcase was sticking to my cock. Then she slapped the side of my head and yelled, 'Come on, do it faster!'

I felt like I was going to burst out laughing. But I also felt like I was going to bawl. I couldn't belive what she was trying with me.

The next thing I knew she had a handful of my hair and she started yanking me down the hallway. I had to scurry like a big dog behind her. She stopped when we got to the bathroom. I felt my knees hard on the shining white floor. It was bright, almost blue. I wanted my knees on the shaggy bath mat. My head was still hung.

'I want it again,' the girl commanded. 'And I want you to do it better this time.'

Her knees lined up in front of my eyes. I was into her game because I wanted to beat her. She was sitting on the toilet, lifting up her skirt. Her boots looked fucking ominous. I tried to stop smiling. She opened her thighs and pulled my face in toward her cunt. I had never seen a pussy so close in bright light. It was red and smashed and shorn under there, her dark purple cunt lips coming apart. I saw something inside, too, that was beating in pulses. She was spreading herself even wider with her fingers. There were short hairs all around her lips and her thighs in the pattern of water. She got wider and wider, it was like a circle was breaking deep up her centre. It looked like a wheel, with spokes facing in. Her pussy skin shone. I wanted to suck it and kiss it. I never knew it was so bright like that, I never knew.

'You are my slave. You are my knight-in-shining slave.'

I laughed. Yeah! I could be her fucking slave. She held the back of my head and forced me into her. It was exactly what I wanted her to do. I used my tongue like a big fish going up. I wanted to push it even harder this time. I didn't want to mistake this girl's orgasm again. I slid my tongue in and out and in and out and then I rubbed her cunt with my lips from her ass to her clit, using my hands to hold her ass cheeks apart. I slid her forward on the toilet. She was shocked by my grip. I was breathing in time with her thrusting, in time with her cunt, us both going fast, and when I poked my tongue in her asshole she screamed and she tightened. I could hear her pussy like a heart pumping blood. I went back to her there because I knew she wanted that more and I put a finger in her ass and I fucked her completely. I rose up, attached, with her screaming and coming, not letting her go. Her pussy convulsed all over my face. I was right there inside, I was right there for this.

MAN NO. 7

She was walking toward me on the sidewalk. It was a weird time to see her because I thought she worked during the days. I hadn't seen her in a long time. Or it felt like a long time. Her face had gotten bigger. Maybe just her lips were set tighter. It was strange. Her eyes weren't as wide or as glassy as I'd remembered. She looked almost menacing. I was thinking: *She still looks good, the way that she walks, the way she walks and shakes her hips.*

When she saw me, though, it was like she froze for a second. I caught that even though we were still pretty far apart. That was when she got this 'fuck you' look in her eyes. She kept walking the same way, looking over the top of my head. I could feel my tongue going dry. I stood where I was and waited for her to get to me. My thighs felt stiff. I didn't know why I was swallowing so hard.

I knew that I wouldn't be able to tell her what I was thinking. How I wanted to say that I was sorry how it ended with us. I'd felt like shit for four months. Fuck, her face *was* menacing. I thought that maybe she was going to get mad at me for what happened. I didn't want to hear it. I couldn't think about that last night that I was with her: the line of sweat on the top of her forehead, her hair pulled back, how that anger like a blackness took all of me. She'd taken me over, but not as this person in front of me now. I mean, she'd been a weak girl before, a needy girl, a girl not taking care of herself. I hated what she'd done with her body that night, how she looked dancing with her lips pushing out like she wanted to kiss me.

'Hey. How's it going? I haven't seen you in a long time.'

She was smiling at me. She wasn't mad. I realized up close that her lips weren't tighter, they were actually more relaxed. And her skin almost looked like it was golden, shining. I didn't understand the pull of this girl. I wanted to hug her or reach for her, but I couldn't. I was still uncomfortable. I knew I had to say something to her.

'Yeah, it's been a while. I'm okay. How are you?'

Fuck. I wanted to be as casual as she was. I knew she didn't forget that night. How could she? I'd never hit a girl before. It was a nightmare. It took me over. I'd never hit a girl before! Thinking about her with all those other men, the sweat on her forehead, her licking her lips. I didn't want to see how she was in the world. When I saw her like that I got rabid. I got sick.

But with her in front of me now, I remember how she was with me: she made me feel so good, too, she made me feel like she loved me. I wanted to believe her smiling at me. I didn't want to think she was lying. I felt anxious for a second, what to believe, her standing, her smiling, right there in front of me. All I wanted to do was set the whole thing right.

'So ... do you want to come by?' she asked.

The expression on her face was open, but I still didn't know if she had really forgiven me.

We started walking toward her place. We weren't talking, but I realized that just walking with her was relaxing me. I'd been with a few other girls since I'd last seen her and things were okay with them, but it wasn't the same. I didn't know what it was about *this* girl. She never asked for anything from me and she wasn't asking now either. For a second I thought: *She's just like me.*

When we got up to her place, though, something changed. The air in there was heavy. It smelled like an animal's pen. It was cramped. I couldn't believe how much takeout garbage was on her couch. Empty wine bottles with candles lined the walls. Who the fuck lives like this? This girl lives like this? Right away I thought I shouldn't have come. I started sweating. I didn't know if I felt like having sex with her. I didn't think I could.

I followed her down the hallway into her bedroom. It was filled with the sun. She seemed like she was in such a good mood.

Her bed was close to the floor. It was piled with sheets. I

couldn't look away from that bed. There was a bloodstain, a coffee stain, the smell of fucking sex.

'Look up,' she said, smiling.

There was a hook screwed into her ceiling with a piece of rope hanging down. There was another hook linked to the rope that stuck out of the wall, a pulley system.

'What's all that for?'

The second I spoke, though, I wished that I hadn't even engaged. My whole face got cold. I knew I shouldn't have trusted her, trusted that she forgave me.

'I can't believe you left me like that.'

Her voice had turned furious. My eyes went down to the floor. I knew it. I was sorry. I thought for a second that I was going to scream that out. My fucking *sorry*, my humble, my need for her again. But I pressed my lips together. I didn't know what I felt in my life anymore.

'You never cared a thing for me, did you?'

'That's not me. I did.'

I said that too fast.

'What. Fuck, what exactly did you feel for me?'

My teeth started chattering. She'd never talked to me like this.

'You didn't feel a thing for me and you know it.'

I couldn't speak now. She was doing something bad to me. My eyes were stuck on the squares in the floor.

'I can't be with you,' she said. 'I can't be with someone who doesn't feel anything for me, someone who never says anything good, like you. If you're going to hurt me, see, you'd better love me. I can only be with someone who hurts me if they love me. You can't do it. I can't be with you.'

I was trying to understand her. I didn't understand everything she was saying. The sun was making me drip with fresh sweat. I felt it on my forehead. It was like she was talking for me, and what she was saying wasn't what I would say.

'You felt nothing for me!' She was yelling now. 'I don't even care if you did feel something. I don't care what you felt for me!'

God, it wasn't true what she was saying! I knew that if I spoke now, though, I was going to cry. I swallowed hard. My chest caved in.

'I know what I'm saying is true, okay?'

Her voice softened up a bit when she said that, but I knew now that she was disgusted. She was disgusted with me. All the things I never did for her. I wanted to leave her place right then. I felt like I had nothing. My teeth chattered more. It was hot in her bedroom. She walked up close to me. I felt like I was in a dream where I was trying to yell but I couldn't, where I was so angry but I couldn't say a word, where all these people were forcing me out of a room, groups of people, hating me. I felt my mouth cranking open in slow motion but there was nothing coming out, nothing.

She was pulling a chair up behind my back. She stood up on it so that her body was near my head. She gripped under both my arms and lifted them up. She started fixing my hands together with hanging rope. She wound the rope around my fingers first, then tight around both my wrists. I remembered what she'd said when she'd made me do the same thing to her: *tie me tie me tie me back up!* I heard her breathing hard. Then she went over to the wall and stood on her bed to yank the end of the cord from the hook that was there. My two arms were being lifted over my head. I couldn't stop it because I couldn't tell her what I wanted to say.

When she came back around in front of me, holding the rope like a leash, she looked like she was proud of herself. I was swallowing, swallowing, still trying to say something.

'Look,' she said impatiently, 'it's okay. Nothing matters now.'

Then she unzipped my pants. My cock got hard right away. My armpits were open. I felt the sun burn my back.

She pulled off my pants and stared at my penis. She was looking at it without love. My weight sunk in my gut. I thought I was going to be sick. My arms felt like they were invisible.

'The last man I had was a lot like you, you know,' she said.

She was pulling her shirt over her head. I'd never heard her talk about anyone else she'd been with. My eyelids got heavy. She stripped to her bra and underwear. It was a sports bra, panties.

'I think that guy might be wounded for life!' she laughed. 'I mean, how can you go back to regular sex after you've been held down and fucked by a hot bitch like me?'

She was speaking so clearly. I didn't want to hear it and I wanted to hear it. There was nothing I could do. I watched her mouth move.

'That last guy really begged me to treat him the worst that I could imagine. It was a bit strange at first, but then I got into it. When I yelled at him things like: *Get on the ground, fool*, and *Don't you fucking hear me?* it was like I always knew how to curse at the men I'd allowed to go inside of me.

'That guy's head would wobble on his neck like a chicken. He didn't know how to look up at me directly. I felt like I could pinch his balls. I could kick him, choke him, put things in his ass. I wanted to see that guy cry. I wanted to see blood come out of his nose. I wanted to straddle him naked, fuck on his face.

'I liked how his fear filled up my bedroom. Every time I sucked in, I got a mouthful of it.

'This one time I put the spike of my heel right on the rim of his asshole, his asshole that I made go up in the air. I couldn't stop laughing when I did that. He was howling and I was laughing. I pushed my heel in, gently, but I did it, right in the hole. These horrible sounds came from his gut. I kept doing it, pushing in like a dart, like I had a bull's eye. I knew it was too much for him because just one extra, tiny little thrust and he bolted away from me, his whole body jerking spastically. *Fool! You fool!* I was screaming. *You're going to get it!*

'I hated him so much right then that he couldn't take it. I caught him and I stuck my heels into the back of his wrists. I walked up and down his arms in my heels. I wanted this guy in agony. And even though he was howling, I knew he wanted it. I walked on his ass. I poked holes in his flesh. Nothing I was doing felt like enough. I bent down and started slapping and scratching the backs of his thighs. I couldn't stop until I broke through his skin. Until the welts I'd made were shining with blood, until he was barely moving.

'*Roll over now,* I yelled at him. *Now! Do it now!* He wasn't responding. I had to force his torso over by yanking his right arm over the left. The guy winced and screamed as I did it. His open skin burned. I didn't care. I really didn't care. And I pretended like I didn't care either.

'I was standing above him. He was breathing too fast. I opened my thighs. I was spreading my pussy and I hovered above him. He pursed his lips and made kissy noises, like some helpless baby who wanted his mummy's breast. I wanted to stuff something down his throat. *Shut up!* I told him. His eyeballs popped open, so white and so wide.

'I was smiling. I distinctly remember that I was smiling. I spread my cunt lips and I sank there, right there, I felt how it touched me, the ball of his eye. My body felt like it was made to be flying. It felt too good, so good, eye on my cunt. Actually, I didn't know if I knew how to feel that good. How to make us both feel that good at the same time. I suspended myself for a second, caught my breath, heard his moans, and I did it again. Back down on his face, his eye on my skin, this time I couldn't stop, I was sliding all over his nose and his cheeks, his throat and his lips. Both of his eyeballs were silk, they were rolling with me. My palms flattened down on the floor at his cheeks, I felt his whole head being held by my thighs, his eye on my clit, slipping and moving, both of us screaming and slippery, connected alive.

'That's how it was between me and that guy. God, it was good. Can you see how I thought he was something like you?'

I was hurting. My arms were going to break off.

'Why'd you stop then?'

'Because I want to be able to tell a lover that I love him and I want my lover to love me.'

The girl put her finger in her mouth and bit it. Her eyes looked down at the floor. I felt for just one second how it *was* good between us. I was sorry I had ever hurt her. I wished that she'd told me, right then, I wished she'd told me she loved me.

'Look at you hanging there,' she said quickly. 'Your arms are going to fall off. I've got to let you down now.'

She got up behind me again and untied my arms. She let the pulley out from the hook at the wall. She was acting all of a sudden as if nothing was unusual. I had a circle of burns around both my wrists. My legs weren't steady and I nearly fell to the ground. I put my head between my arms. I heard myself breathing weirdly and heavily.

She touched my shoulder. 'Just take your time getting up. You'll be all right. You can see yourself out, right? I have to go out in a little while. I've got to get ready.'

She left me there in her bedroom. I heard the shower go on. A lump started pulsing in my throat. I didn't know how that had all just happened.

I crawled into her bed. The covers were clumped up. I tried to shake everything straight. My whole body felt strange. My stomach got bloated and I kept farting and farting. I lay there thinking: *Why'd I hit her? Why couldn't I have just been good to her when I had her? Why'd she make me do that? Why'd I do it even if she made me?* If I hit her once, I'd hit her again. That's how it worked, that's how abuse always worked. I knew what she was like. I knew how she was in the world. I couldn't deal with her like that. Especially when she knew how she was in the world too. She'd showed me. She just told me. I didn't think that I could be with her like that. Smelling like pussy. Lips pursed out to kiss me. I would hit her again. In her face, in her lips, and she'd hit me back. She would hit me and fuck me and tie me up like she tied that guy up. I hated her. All that sex she had with me. Her crazed and her open … How when she saw me looking at her she just squeezed her eyes tight. Like she wanted to have her hair in her face and not let me really see her. I didn't believe it! I didn't believe her. I knew all she wanted to do was open her legs and let me see exactly what she was. That body, so warm, but those eyes, that whole face, making me feel like we were both cracking, that we were pressing ourselves together just to pull ourselves apart. When I looked at her when we were having sex I felt like I was looking at the face of all girls cracking open ...

But I still wanted her to love me. I wanted to feel her body, warm at my back, while I slept. The shower turned off. I waited for her to find me.

THREE

Jupiter asked Tiresias: 'In their act of love
Who takes the greater pleasure, man or woman?'

'Woman,' replied Tiresias, 'takes nine-tenths.'
Juno was so angry – angrier
Than is easily understandable –
She struck Tiresias and blinded him.
'You've seen your last pretty snake, for ever.'
But Jove consoled him: 'That same blow,' he said,
'Has opened your inner eye, like a nightscope. See:

'The secrets of the future – they are yours.'

– Ovid, *The Metamorphoses*

know you're still there. Come to me, please. Look at me. I want to tell you what happened. Come to me. Closer. Trust me, please. I want you to hear this. I am telling you this from my innermost parts. Listen. Everything just got so uncontrollable. I feel better now. Okay? Stay with me for a little while longer. I want to be with you. Closer. I'll tell you what I did. Come to me. See, this is what happened:

I decided to stop being with that guy I loved. I knew I had to, I was too twisted up. It got to the point where I barely recognized myself in the mirror. I saw old grey smoke hanging over my skin. And when I'd stare at myself longer, it was like that smoke would fill up my eyes. Squinting, I could see what I'd been doing all that time – on my knees at his hips like a cock-sucking slave, doing it, taking it … Wait, don't go! Please believe me. I wanted to change things, I swear that I did.

It's just that it is almost impossible to untangle yourself when you are in love. It's because you know you've got to find something on the body of that person you are in love with and you know that whatever you have to find is so near, it's right there in front of you, so you're searching for it, sucking and searching, and it doesn't matter what that person does or doesn't do to you, you have to find it.

I'd never cried over any man before. Because every time something ended with a guy, I'd look up and there'd always be another one wanting me. But trying to separate myself from that one felt like vomiting when you can't breathe. That's what my crying was like. I couldn't find that thing on his body and so I couldn't breathe, I couldn't leave. I was stuck on my knees, with his cock down my throat – I was trying to swallow to get closer to the place where I could hear it, swallow to get closer to the place where I could see it, whatever it was that was love there inside him.

But I didn't want to be so close! I wanted to be far away, high away, in the air looking down at my lips and down at his cock, where I could see myself stuck, gasping for air, small and split open, always right there, lost like a slut trying to suck out his love … I know you see how I shouldn't have been there! God, I knew it too. But look at me more, sucking right there and searching, do you see, don't you see how I also look happy?

There was something alive down inside me, murmuring, *Spend your whole, spend your whole life on your knees.*

I had to lock myself in my house to try and separate myself from this! And all I could do was touch myself. I don't know how that sounds to you, but I thought that I could only truly dissolve this thing by touching myself harder and harder. I needed to have a whole other body come out and overtake me.

I did it all over the house. I touched myself in the kitchen and I touched myself in the bathroom. There was this one time when I was doing it in the hallway. I had my back flat against the floor and my legs on the wall in a V. My head was propped up and I could see my fingers moving over my whole lower half like they were powered by fire. Ten fingers squeezing my lips like machine parts. It felt like it wasn't me who was moving my fingers that fast. My chest started moving up and down. My thighs fell open wider. Something started jolting down there, it made my head whip side to side. It was like I had these hard black rods pushing inside me, part of an engine about to blow up! I had fingers above and fingers inside and it was like a tube opened up, a passageway made in the head of a pin. I squeezed another finger up. My pussy was pounding. It wanted me there. The bone curved on top and the walls were sucking, round. I felt like I was going to implode from this touching, fall through the walls, melt down through the floor. I just kept going inside myself faster. I didn't know why I was moaning so much, my body inside me as tight as a rope – I thought I was going to suffocate. Then, though, god, my chest started soaring. I was turning inside something mammoth – oh, how can I tell you? It was an endless dark route folding in on itself.

I closed my eyes and rolled onto my belly. My ass raised itself up. My hands were still under me, moving and poking. I imagined that the guy I loved was right there at my cunt, that he came to my lips, my fool's hanging lips. He was licking me, sucking me, until I went limp. My lips slurred flat on the ground. I felt like a pit all dug out at his feet ...

I opened my eyes, I wanted to stop! I had to remember what I was doing!

I thought that the light from my bedroom was flashing. It looked like there was something in there. I bolted up too fast and ran down the hallway. My head and my neck were stacked on top of each other too loosely, my feet smacked the ground and my limbs were all jerky. I got weird. I gulped air.

In my bedroom I heard people calling my name. I spun around a few times. I kept spinning. My room was a fucking mess that I was whirling through. I started to take off my clothes. I felt like I was dancing, stripping naked on a stage. There I was, glowing underneath the flashing lights. Me shaking my ass in time with the shouts of the crowd, the sounds of their voices shot right through my head: *She is so fucking sexy! Let's take her home!* My body got furnace-hot. Burning wood. I knew that I had enough heat for everyone. *Take me! Take me!* I was touching my breasts and my hips as I danced. My eyes were closed but it was like I could see myself moving. It was like I could see the whole room through the back of my head! I saw all the people looking. I knew that any man would take me right then, my flesh all so loose, my hands in the air. They'd take me from the back, from the front and from the side. They'd swarm me to take me. They'd wait their turn to do it. And when they all got around me, I'd spread open wide, it would all go so fast like a train running through me: my temples, my head and my cunt steaming life.

I felt so heavy. I was down on the floor. I reached for my bed. My tongue hung out. I put my finger on my tongue to calm myself. I climbed into bed, sucking my finger, sucking inconsolably tight.

I knew right then that I'd sucked cocks so much because men gave me themselves when I did it. I mean that I got on my tongue what came out of their body that was white and light and unlike them. When I took in a cock, I knew what a man had hidden inside him. I liked men better when I sucked on their cocks.

Then my lips went soft and my finger slid out. I was coughing, twisting around on the bed. I knew right then that I could not suck that one guy's cock like I loved him because I was sucking a hook, not a cock!

I had the urge to touch myself more, but when I started again it wasn't feeling as good. This time when I pressed my fingers over my clit, it was too raw, impossible. I heard these crows cawing inside my mind. I tried to say my name but it came out all garbled. I heard it coming, I knew it was coming, the crows cawed, *Fool! Fool! Fool! Fool!* Gagging, I stopped, but it started again: *Fool! Fool! Fool! Fool!* Yelling deep in my head all shot through with caws: *You are wrong! Fool! Everything you have done with that man has been wrong! Fool! Since that man mashed your breasts. Since your hand went down your pants! Fool! Fool! Fool! Fool!*

It came out of me. *FOOL!* I lay there, ears open, my throat going numb. I pounded the bed with my fists. Revolted curls in my gut. *FOOL! You're a fool!* God, it wouldn't stop! I hunched over, heaving. I threw up on the floor.

I don't know how long I stayed in that position.

When I finally raised myself up, I staggered off the bed to get over to the window for air, one foot in front of the other. My heart was pounding too loudly. But my feet didn't lead me to the window. I walked into the closet instead, and I started ripping my clothes from the hangers. Then I grabbed for the shoes and the boots that were there at the back and I started throwing them out of the closet. I was shrieking like a hyena each time one cracked against a wall. I wanted to erase all my fucks with the smacks. The sound of those shoes whipped like dead against the wall. Every time I heard a smack I knew there was a reason that man had hit me.

He'd hit me for a reason, yes, a reason so big that it built up inside me. A reason so big that it was shining all over my face!

I went out of my bedroom and into the bathroom. I turned on the shower but I didn't get in. I felt the floor, the blue light, and I stared at myself in the mirror. Under my eyes was so dark. My lips were parted and dirty. I closed my eyes and opened them. I knew right then, I mean, I saw it so clear – I got hit because my need equalled the man's need. Do you see what I am saying? All that time I spent on my knees was this balancing act. I was trying to make something even. I know that might not sound so good, but that is what it was. I got hit to come down to his level. I worshipped the man to bring him to mine. I touched him and stroked him no matter what he did because I was trying to bring up the middle between us.

See, I knew where I was when I was on my knees. When it was like this, I wasn't confused about anything. When I looked at myself in the mirror, I thought I was beautiful.

I still feel beautiful when I walk out of my bathroom and I see his face. He is standing by the window. He has made up the bed. I feel my mouth in the weirdest smile. I know when I see him that I am over nothing.

Our eyes catch like hooks. And for once we are mirrored, for once we are looking at each other with ease. It's the thrilling ease of seeing something you are. It seems funny to me all of a sudden. My smile gapes wider. I see all his teeth.

I know: this time things will be different because this time I am looking straight at him.

We don't say a word. I still don't know where to put all my desire. My desire for him always hurts when it rises. But I am pressing against whatever it is that is coming off him. I keep pressing into that place where I think I am falling, where I brace myself to fall, to come up again, to come and to fall.

I go down on my knees because I want to. I unzip his pants. *I'll take everything you give me*, I am thinking so clearly, *because I know I am taking in every part of you.* With my mouth on his cock and his cock in my mouth I start to really relax. When I am here,

I am right where I am: inside that place where I need to be badly, where he can feel everything, from right where I speak. I'm sucking his hook, I am swallowing whole. His sounds come out like the grunts of forever. I know he will have me, this time for good, love through his hands on the back of my head, I will always suck more to the sounds of this praying. I will always suck more to the end of all ends. I squeeze my whole life into this place, where his love meets my lips, shooting out like a piston. It's the heart that he gives me. Half of a heart, a life full of secrets.

My man stops me and looks. His hand cradles under my chin. His cock is right there, as hard as a horn. Then he slides his arm around my neck, hugging my face tight to his thighs. My whole body instinctively jerks and draws back.

'You love me?' he says, still holding my chin.

I am looking at you.

'I love you.'

We end up lying on the floor face to face. My legs are open wide. His hands stroke my waist. He is coming in naked. He presses on my mouth. His cock is inside me. I pull him all in. Our bodies go fast. It is hot it is hot we are pulsing together.

This is what happens.

Do you see what I see? How I fell back to him? Why I stayed and I stayed near the shield of his chest?

It's because nothing can really die between half-hearted people. We're sharing our hearts and we're down on the ground, where we can confess that there's nothing we know about each other. There we are stuck, beating on each other's chests, where all we know is what we're going to do.

THE WAY
OF THE
WHORE

Sister, the Enchanter
has stolen my heart –
where can I go,
what can I do –
he took the breath from my lungs.
I'd gone to the river,
a jug on my head,
when a figure rose through the darkness.
Sister, it cast a sorcerer's noose
and it bound me.
What the world calls virtue suddenly
    vanished.
I performed a strange rite –
Mira may be a slave, sister,
but she herself
    chose whom to sleep with.

– Mirabai, 1498–1550

MIRE

Things are different in the middle of the night. Rooms, legs, eyes, whatever. The air's so full of static that no one can see, so everyone just acts, because all acts are fine.

The acts that have led me to the middle of the night reveal their inevitable order when I'm stuck. When all my soft and black thoughts slide into a chain.

Until at just the right moment, finally I'm lucid and I know how a cock can complete me. A good hard cock never leaves you alone.

But morning is broken on its way in. I don't care what anyone says about the dawn. Its cracks break me too.

'Men think a woman walking alone at night is a whore,' John said once. He was pulling off my underwear. 'It doesn't even matter what she's wearing or how she's walking. If it's late on the streets and she's all by herself, he's gonna roll down his window and stare at her ass. It's like he's waiting for something, Mira, that one tiny click when he knows that she's going to get in his car.'

John had my underwear down at my feet. I kicked them off and twisted my legs together.

'No girl's going to get in a strange man's car,' I said.

'You would.'

'I would not.'

John laughed as he worked at wrenching my thighs apart. 'Yes you would, Mira.'

'Stop. I would not!'

'You'd get in my car.'

'No!'

'I'd follow you and keep telling you how hot your ass is.'

'Shut up!'

'Oh yeah, I know you. You'd get in my car.'

I rolled my eyes and kept struggling. It was like this every single time we saw each other.

'Come, Mira, come,' John would end up crooning to my pussy. 'Come, baby, come, please come, come, come … '

My mind wandered while he licked me. I scratched my arms and watched his bobbing head. His eyes were slit and heavy between my bent thighs. It didn't feel real. All I could feel was wetness on top of wetness.

I thought of how men were always looking at me. How it happened this one time when I was ten. I was at the supermarket with my father and the guy at the cash said, 'You better keep a close watch on that one.' His eyes squinted down at my chest when he said it, at the two lumps pressing up under my shirt. Then the guy made a noise, a grunt through closed lips. My father looked down at me and laughed quickly, too, but it sounded like he didn't really mean it.

When we got in the car, my father didn't say a word. He just turned up the news and started driving really fast. I put my forehead against the window and watched us pass all the cars. I could still feel that guy looking right through my shirt. For a second I thought my chest had pushed out more when he was staring at it. I heard my father's breathing get loud. Air scratched past the hairs of his moustache. Then something started happening. Between my thighs on the seat I felt hot little beats, like a pulse or a bird was whipping around down there. It started getting louder. I had to squeeze my thighs tight. I was trying not to make any sound from the pulsing, trying not to let it come out in my breaths.

When we finally got home, I kept hearing what that guy had said, how it made them both laugh. *You better keep a close watch on that one*. I didn't really know what it meant. I thought the guy meant – maybe – I was pretty, but when I tried to think more about what he really meant, I felt strange. Lying on my bed, the pulsing wouldn't stop spreading. It filled up my underwear with hot little beats. It felt okay, it felt good, but I didn't want it to keep happening, because I thought my father knew what had happened. I thought, in the car, he could smell it.

Things started to happen more often after that. I would get that feeling around men, older men, men in stores and on the street. It was always when I thought I saw them looking at me, especially the ones I knew I'd never get to meet. The construction men working in crews on the road. The businessmen with their kids and their wives. The guys on the subway who sweat strange perfume. That beating between my legs started happening so much that I thought those men could see right through me. Just from the way I was standing or walking, I thought it meant I wanted them to see. All those beats inside my body, throbbing so loud.

Sometimes I'd imagine a man in my house, a stranger in the bathroom, watching me shower. His two big hands would open a towel when I stepped out. Then he'd dry me, rub me, move the towel really fast back and forth behind my shoulders, behind my back and all the way down. My flesh would shake close to the man's face. My ass red behind me, my eyes blooming wide. The strange man would follow me into my bedroom, his footsteps sounding in time to my beats. He'd stand over my bed while I pretended to sleep, one of my feet sticking out of the covers. Then one arm would fall out, an arm that led to my chest. If I rolled on my side, the man would see more. He would see how my breasts were starting to grow from my body, how my nipples were hard, how my hair down there was getting thick. If I rolled on my back, the sheet would fall off and the man would see straight up between my legs. I'd spread them for him, I knew I would. I was pulsing so much there I'd have to. I thought that if the man could see me naked like that, just silently watch me, then it would all be okay. I'd stay quiet while he touched me anywhere he wanted. I'd want him to come back every single night, too, so he could tell me how much more hair he was seeing on my vagina. How much more stuff he was feeling down there.

I'd never even really touched myself where I imagined a man doing it. Maybe if I had, everything would've been different.

'Mira, you're the sweetest,' John always whispered after licking. He pushed his chin up onto my stomach and wiped his glistening mouth with the sheet. I closed my soaking wet cunt.

Maybe.

I met John when I was fifteen. I was working in this café on the weekends and he started coming in every Saturday, always waiting to order from me. He'd sit there drinking his coffee for at least an hour, looking out the window, then looking at me. One day, he came up to the counter after he finished his coffee.

'I have to tell you something,' he said, leaning in. 'You're a very pretty young woman, you know that?'

My face got hot. I stared down at my hands.

'What's your name?'

My lips were coming apart to speak, but my tongue wasn't there. John read the name tag pinned to my shirt.

'Mira? That's a beautiful name. Mira,' he murmured. 'Are you Spanish?'

I nodded, but I didn't mean yes.

'I'm John, by the way.'

He reached out a hand but I couldn't lift my eyes from the counter. I was staring down at his weird rocky knuckles with little white scratches.

'So, Mira, what do you like to do when you're not here?'

I couldn't believe it – this guy looked as old as my father! There was stubble around his lips and dark skin under his eyes. Didn't he know I was only fifteen? I was squeezing my hands together so hard they were going numb. A creeping smile hooked into my cheek. I felt John looking down at me, waiting for me to say something. I knew he must've known I was embarrassed.

'Well, it was really nice to meet you,' he said quickly. 'I'll see you again, Mira, okay?'

He walked so fast to the door it looked like he was limping. I didn't think he would look back at me from outside, but he did. He turned around and waved. There was this thick feeling under my chin, like his fingers were still there. I was smiling again, that stupid smile that stuck on one side. I didn't like how he'd made me look. *Better keep a close watch on that one.* I didn't like the way he looked, I knew that – his black chin, his thick hair, those scratches on his knuckles – but throughout my whole next week, I couldn't stop thinking about him. I knew he was going to come in the next Saturday. I kept hearing every small thing he'd said to me: *You're a pretty young woman. You're a very pretty young woman, you know that?* No one had ever said anything like that to me before. It made that feeling beat up between my legs, this time more than I'd ever felt it. I had to cross my thighs and put my hands in between them to make it stop. I wanted it to stop because I thought it was going to make me do something with that guy even though I thought he was disgusting!

I told Nadia what happened, because I didn't know what I should do when he came back. She said, 'Go for it, Mira. Older guys know what they're doing.' Nadia cackled, like it was wet inside her throat. Her family was from Russia. I thought it was weird how much older her father was than her mother, who wore makeup and dresses and heels, even in the yard. Her father always sat there in his lawn chair with a newspaper in front of his face and no shirt on, but you knew he was still looking. It seemed like it was a rule of their house that Nadia's mother had to look like that to show all the other women on our street – the mothers who wore sneakers to go shopping or pantsuits to work – that *this* was what a real woman looked like. I'd never seen her dad go to work. Nadia was older than me because she was born in Russia and she came to Canada when she was seven. They put her in my kindergarten class to learn English. I remember how Nadia used to scream in a kind of high-pitched gibberish at recess to make all the other girls freak out. I wanted to be friends with her. She reminded me of a rabbit, the albino kind. Nadia used to make these marks on my arms at the park after school. We'd sit together on the back side of the hill and she'd take my arm and put it in her mouth, sort of suck it, sort of bite it, just to make the marks. I got a pattern of heart-shaped bruises where she did it. I think I worshipped her. Nadia was fancy like her mother, kind of threatening like her dad.

'Finally Mira is going to get laid,' Nadia said, when I told her about John. She'd been having sex since she was twelve. There were always these young, kind of skinny Russian guys with jutted-out jaws trooping through her house. Nadia said they were part of her father's business. I imagined that Nadia lost her virginity with one of those guys. I remember when she was twelve and I was ten, she looked like a woman. She'd strut around in her mother's high heels and braid her hair princess-style. Nadia always talked about sex. She'd say things like: 'I have to come like a guy does, Mira, I just have to freaking come.'

Nadia said that an orgasm was a muscle contraction and that if you didn't have a muscle contraction, you didn't have a real orgasm. Nadia showed me her hand with all the fingers open and said, 'Like this, just like this.' She opened and shut her fingers really quick over and over. 'This is what it feels like. This is how hard it's got to be.'

I knew that that feeling had never happened to me.

John came back to my work the next Saturday. He came back the next week and the one after that. I started to be able to look at him a little more. We never said much after that first time, just the regular 'Hi, how are you?' and 'Fine, how are you?' which was okay, because I still did feel a bit creeped out that maybe he was coming in just because of me. He'd started giving me pretty big tips after buying his coffee, too, at least a dollar in coins, pressing them right into my palm. It always felt like he touched me too long when he did that. I thought maybe it was just me, though, and I was worrying about it for nothing.

Then, one Saturday, John came in to see me three times during my shift. Right before he left the last time, he leaned in really close. He smelled kind of weird, like my mother when she made meat.

John said, 'Do you like Chinese food? Have you ever gone out with your friends for Chinese food? I know a really good restaurant near here.'

I shrugged my shoulders and John touched my arm lightly. 'I'll see you later, okay?'

That was the day he met me outside after I finished work. It was pretty warm out and he was sweating through his T-shirt. I could see the hairs on his chest stuck down in a line. He was shaking his head a bit, smiling at me. I was wearing a purple tank top and a purple skirt that came down to my knees. I wished that I was wearing something over my top.

John touched my arm again. This time he gave it a squeeze. 'I bet you'd like something sweet to drink after work. You must be tired.'

'No, it's okay,' I said quickly.

We started walking down the street and I could feel my thighs rubbing together under my skirt. It made me want to sit down and cross my legs.

John went into a variety store and got me a ginger ale. He bought himself cigarettes. I started drinking too fast straight from the can and I got the hiccups. We both laughed at the high-pitched sounds that were coming out of me.

'I'm going to have to scare you, Mira!'

I couldn't believe I was walking down the street laughing with this guy. I couldn't believe that no one was really looking at us either. I didn't know if John knew I was only fifteen. But I didn't feel like doing anything to stop him when he put his arm all the way around me, or when his fingers started tickling my neck. He kept joking that it was to scare me out of my hiccups.

We turned down a street I'd never been on. There were a few old-looking houses beside this huge apartment building with foil on the windows. I saw two kids waving down at us from a balcony. I was going to wave back, but John shifted my shoulders to turn us off that street. I felt like a car he was steering.

I didn't ask where we were going because John started asking me questions out of the blue, like: 'Are your mother and father still married? Do you have a boyfriend?'

'Yes,' I said, then, 'No.'

John was laughing at me. I kept swallowing instead of changing what I was saying.

'But you probably remember who told you about sex the first time, don't you?'

I shook my head.

John lit a cigarette and looked at me. We were walking pretty fast.

'Listen,' he said. 'The first person who told me about sex was my uncle. He wasn't much older than me, six years or something, we were just kids, you know, but it pretty much scared the shit out of me. He said it like this: "A man gets on top of a woman and opens her up with his dick." I swear that's what he said. I didn't know what he meant but I knew I wanted to, you know – who wouldn't? A man opens a woman up with his dick? I'd never even seen a woman naked, not even my mother, and my uncle just goes: "Watch me. I'll show you." I wasn't saying much back, so he started wrestling with me, the way we always did. I was on the floor, and I remember I was trying to look up at what he was doing but I couldn't really see, you know – I think he was holding his crotch through his pants. Then he was kneeling between my legs and I heard him laughing, going, "Okay, Johnny-John, you're the woman now," and he started spreading my legs – really fucking wide. It felt weird, Mira. It felt all fucked up. I was just a kid who didn't know what was what. So the next thing I know he's pulling off his pants, they're down to his knees and his cock is out, you know, sticking straight out, and the only thing I could think was: *Man, that's big!* What did I know? Fuck, my first hard dick … And I guess it made me get one, too, or something, because I felt like reaching down and putting my hand in my shorts. My uncle was over me, right? He was almost lying on top of me and he started sticking his dick up the little space between my shorts. I could feel it rubbing on my leg. He was pushing it more and more up there and then it squirted – yeah, right up my shorts! I thought it was piss, that I pissed myself or something. But my uncle just jumped off me and I was lying there thinking I wet myself, fuck, why'd that feel so good … '

John stopped. He was rubbing his face with his fingers.

'It's weird to tell you that. That's fucked-up shit, huh, Mira?'

'No.'

'What? You don't think that's weird?'

'No.'

But I *felt* weird, as if there was gas in my chest, trapped.

'Wow. You're the first one then. If I ever tell a woman that story, she just kind of freaks out and thinks I'm gay or something.'

'No,' I said again. Nadia would probably think John was gay and say so to his face. I just wanted to know more – like did it happen again? Did you and your uncle ever actually have sex? John threw his cigarette on the ground in front of us and wrapped his arm tightly around my shoulders. We must've looked like a couple.

'So what happened to you, baby?'

I laughed inside at him calling me that. *Baby!*

'Nothing. Nothing really, my cousin told me something … '

'What? How'd she say it to you?'

'It was nothing. I mean, it was just him and some of his friends in our basement … '

'Sounds interesting.' John laughed. 'Come on, tell me.'

'No, they were just telling me that sex happened between a mother and a father … '

'Yeah? Go on, it's all good.'

I'd never said this to anyone.

'Go on, Mira, you can tell me.' John started rubbing the back of my neck. 'Remember what the fuck I just told you?'

'Well, they told me about sex and it was weird because I'd never really heard anyone talk about it like that before, that's all.'

I shrugged my shoulders. I'd never told anyone, not even Nadia, about this. I didn't want John's arm on me anymore. But he held me harder when I shrugged.

'Yeah, Mira? Come on, how'd they say it?'

Ezrah had shown us pictures from a big softcover book of a mother and father kissing with their tongues. 'The father's tongue makes her take off her clothes,' he'd said. 'Then the father puts his penis in the mother's vagina.' Ezrah had started laughing the second he said *vagina*. 'And when the baby comes out,' he could barely finish his sentence, 'there's a hole in her body the size of a head!' All the other guys had started cracking up too.

'They all started asking me if I wanted a baby,' I said to John.

'And what did you say?'

'No.'

'You didn't want a baby?'

'No! Not from them!'

John laughed and I laughed too. I think my voice finally sounded normal.

Then John turned my shoulders. We were standing in front of an old house with a cracked cement porch. The windows in the front were covered with sheets.

'This is it,' John said, unlocking the gate. 'I want you to come in and see where I live.'

'No, I can't. It's okay, I have to go.'

'Come on, Mira. Just for a minute.'

I told him no again, that I had to go home, but he just kept saying, 'It's okay, we're right here, just for a minute, just a minute.'

I really didn't want to. I didn't want to go inside that house.

John squeezed hard at the back of my neck. His hand felt so big, as if my whole head fit in it. I don't know why I thought that I couldn't just go home – run away from him even. I thought for a second that he might chase me if I ran. Or maybe he would've grabbed me around the neck so I couldn't breathe.

'One minute, come on. Just for a minute,' John whispered. 'I don't say these kinds of things to everyone, you know.' He was shaking me back and forth a little by the shoulders. It made me hiccup one last time.

It smelled like smoke right inside the front door. There was a narrow black staircase that we had to go up. John moved aside so I could go first. I thought he was watching how I walked. I felt my hips move from side to side, even though I didn't usually walk that way.

He was going to touch me. As I climbed the stairs I knew what was going to happen. He was going to touch me.

'Thanks,' John said quietly to the back of my head. 'For coming up.'

I thought again of running, but I was already at the top, waiting for his hands to come around and unlock the door.

It seemed as if the apartment was all in one room. There was a kitchen in one corner, a TV and a couch in another. There were videotapes all over the floor. It smelled as if someone had just been cooking.

I walked over to the window. There was a hole in the screen. I heard some kids screaming and I thought the noise was coming from the huge apartment building with the foil on the windows that we had passed. I could still see it far off, standing like a rock. The sun was orange, just about to disappear.

'So this is where I live, baby.'

John came up behind me and turned me away from the window. He was pointing to a couch. I squinted as I moved toward it. John was smoking again. I knew I should call home, but my parents were probably already out for dinner.

'Why don't you take off your shoes and get comfortable?'

John laid his cigarette in an ashtray on the coffee table. He stood in front of me and gently pushed me down onto the couch. Then he moved the table back a bit so he could kneel on the floor in front of me. Smoke was filling up the room. I squeezed my thighs.

'It's okay,' John said, sliding off my shoes. 'I like you a lot, you know.'

Holding my bare feet in his palms, John started sliding his fingers between my toes. I was sweating. I didn't want him to do that. I curled up my feet and tried to pull them away.

'Okay, okay. Anything you want, Mira,' he said. But he didn't let go. He started kneading the arches of my feet with his thumbs. I let my head lean back and closed my eyes. It made me stop feeling like a sound was going to come out. My hands were on the couch beside my hips. I was bracing myself. It was like he knew something about me.

'You've got beautiful feet, Mira.'

I lifted my head. John was pulling my toes up to his lips. I couldn't believe he wanted to do that! He was smiling, watching me trying to watch him. My eyes kept opening and closing. I couldn't keep them open.

'Relax, baby … '

I felt my feet go all wet with his steam. A suction came down. 'Mmmmmmira … '

His slippery tongue pushed in and out of the cracks. My whole body started to shake. I thought for a second I was laughing with my mouth closed. John stopped and looked at me.

'You're a funny girl, you know,' he said.

John stood up and took off his T-shirt. There was no more sun in the room.

'I know you have a beautiful body under there.'

My teeth were chattering. A beautiful body? I stared down at my smashed thighs. I heard the zipper of John's pants. My fingers were pushing under the elastic of my skirt. I wanted to do it and I didn't. I was wiggling around. My underwear slid off at the same time as my skirt. I knew I should call home.

'Oh man, that's sexy.'

I felt my fingers behind me, unhooking my bra.

The father's tongue makes her take off her clothes. The father puts his penis in the mother's vagina.

'Oh god, yeah. You have beautiful breasts.'

I stared at the hair above John's penis. His penis was starting to jerk around. It moved to the side, looking soft then looking hard. It looked like a worm turning purple in the rain.

I wanted to get rid of the thing that was tightening inside me. I thought that if John just lay on top of me, everything would be fine. I knew what sex was. It was Nadia's fist.

'I could look at you like this forever, Mira.'

My vagina started to feel strange on the couch, like powder dissolving into the ground.

'Aw, baby, why're you cold?'

John's body came down on me quick. His hairy chest pressed into my breasts. He was so heavy I didn't think I could breathe. I felt his penis start to move on my thighs, there was some kind of stuff on it, shiny, lukewarm. I was going to say *stop*, but John put his lips directly over mine. He was kissing me hard. His tongue was in my mouth. I was breathing out the side.

'Mmm, good, you really know how to kiss.'

I started doing it like he was, it seemed like forever. I bit into his lips and he bit my lips back. John's hand wriggled down between both our stomachs. My legs spread wider. His finger poked around.

'Shhhhh, shhhh. Babe, you're so wet … '

I tried to look down between the darkness of our bodies. John's hand was holding the top of his penis. I moaned as he started to push it to my vagina. My moaning was there to keep the tiny space I had left between me and him. John was grimacing, wagging his penis up and down. He was pushing it deeper, then pulling it away. The head of his penis was shining with gloss.

'Open up, baby, open your legs.'

I knew it wasn't right. He was supposed to use a condom. But I felt myself plug. The plug made me mute.

John kept pushing and pushing, he couldn't go in any further. I didn't want the feeling of the tightness inside me. I wanted to break. John forced my knees open and whispered too loudly, 'Open up, come on! Open up! Open up!'

One of my legs suddenly fell off the couch.

'I'm inside you, babe. Come on, babe, come on!'

Bone into bone. The plug was a wall. The only fist I felt was my actual fist.

John lifted his hands to the side of my head, used his hard shining forehead to keep me flat down. My eyelids were grinding.

'Good girl, shhh, good girl … '

I needed to move side to side in my hips. It felt different when I did it, different better. I pushed my hips up into his body. I used my fists to hold myself up.

'That's it. That's the way … '

Something was stuck there inside me, like a log stuck in fire.

'Yeah, baby, fuck, good girl, that's the way … '

It didn't hurt more when I moved a bit faster. There was just something burning, a fever down there. John's hands squeezed my ass, his hands spread me open, spreading until I was bigger, unstuck. Oh god, I was doing it. It! Really It! I was feeling him move faster in and faster out. I was trying to feel every in, every out, but I couldn't keep up, it was going too fast. I didn't even know if I was feeling him or feeling me. I shut my eyes, I tried to relax …

'Yeah, fuck, you're so hot.'

Something flew up inside me. I heard myself grunt. It flooded my insides, flooded my head and I floated, floated, just for a second … Then John's head hit my chest and I was back in the room, back on the couch, knuckles under my bum as John trickled out of me, saying my name.

'Mira! Mira!' The men at the club called me by my real name.

I was doing my trick: lying on the ground with my hands behind my shoulders, then pressing up, my back in an arch. I walked that way to the edge of the stage so that in front of their faces, my cunt touched the pole. It looked like a split-open flower they'd stepped on.

'Oh yeah, baby! Go for it!'

I stood up red-faced and turned around slowly. I imagined their claps slapping right on my ass. I tried to smile backward over my shoulder, but I could only do it for a second. It was a baby's smile, a dog's smile.

I ran downstairs right after I finished. Lani and Coco were smoking in the hallway before they went on. A lot of the girls there never really liked me, so I couldn't ask them for a puff, even though I wanted one. All I ever needed was one puff.

It was disgusting for us down in the basement. Paint was flaking off the ceiling and it smelled like piss because the pipes were too hot. Adi was down there getting ready. I looked at myself beside her in the mirror. My eyes were starting to run. Sometimes I thought I looked like a hot sexy bitch right after I danced – not some pig-breathed, nineteen-year-old thing. But if I kept staring and staring, I saw a smeary-eyed person whose head didn't belong on her body, whose tits hung too low, whose legs were too big.

'Look at me,' I said.

Adi was looking at herself.

'Look. I look disgusting.'

Adi rolled her eyes.

'I look like an elephant.'

'No.' Adi laughed. 'You don't know what it's like to be grey and fat.'

So why was I always looking down when I danced? Why did my tits feel like elephants' trunks?

Adi got up and came behind me. Her long skinny arms roped round my waist. She stared at us both in the mirror and said, 'Up there, on your hands and knees, you put some kind of spell on them. Makes them go crazy!'

Adi could stop me from crying. Well, I wasn't really crying. Adi whispered at my neck, 'You look so good. Everyone sees.'

I sat down and watched Adi finish her makeup. Her straight white-blond hair was tied in two ponytails. She put baby-blue eyeshadow high on her lids. All of it seemed so easy for her. I thought she must've known how to do this stuff forever. Makeup made her look even more beautiful.

Adi gave me a little kiss on the cheek before she left for upstairs. I tried to fix myself up, but I couldn't do it right. I put too much gunk in the grooves around my nose. All I had was a pink skirt and a red tank top in my locker. I never really matched but I didn't care. I didn't think that the men cared either. If they didn't like what I was wearing, so what. I had high heels and big tits.

Adi was the only thing that ever made me get back up there. I wanted to see her dance. The way she moved made it seem like nothing bad had ever happened in her body. Pushing away the floor with her feet, shaking her hips, smiling: *Come with me, come* … Adi's tongue slid in front of her teeth, you had to be quick to see how she did it, first coming out between her two lips, then curling over her teeth, licking: *Come*. When she shook her ass at a guy, it was like she was in love with him. Her pussy out in front of his mouth, she'd hold his chin and practically feed it to him.

It was as if Adi had no fear. The way a vulture has no fear when it's eating the dead.

When I watched her dance, I knew I could do it too. Rush through the beat of those hundred white eyes, plow through the stink of their forced-back come. The men in tight circles, with gritting teeth and short breaths, moving their bottles up to their mouths.

'Mira! Mira!'

It all happened in slow motion. Those men didn't know if what they were looking at was real.

'Hey, I liked your dance, sweetheart,' said the bald one in front of me. His stomach bulged out like a baby's. 'Sweetheart, c'mere.'

The guy tapped his knee. I moved hip to hip toward him and turned myself around. I always showed them my ass right away.

'Yeah. I like that, darlin'.'

I sat on his thigh and wiggled around, pretending to get comfortable.

'Yeah, shit! I like that.'

I arched my back over the guy's gut and pumped my hips in time to the beat. I felt heat from the floor move up to my cunt.

'Name's Bill, darlin'.'

I kept moving myself.

'How much for another?'

'Forty.'

'All right, another. I like how this one moves.'

There was a man at the table with Bill, a skinny guy who'd taken off his glasses. I saw his hands move underneath the table. Two of them, I was getting off the two of them! Bill started snorting behind me, telling me I was a wild girl. I thought for a second that the whole bar was watching my tits move up and down in my top, watching the way that my ass did a grind. I thought all the guys were going to gather around just to witness my cunt glistening.

'Wild, Mira, wild!'

I stood up and braced my hands on the table. I bent my knees deep and pumped back in his face.

'Oh man, shit, she likes that!'

I turned around quickly and raised my hands in the air. I was dancing now, just like Adi. I looked down at Bill's eyes. They were squinty and roaming. I put my hands on his chin and made him look up.

'I'm gonna take this wild one back to the hotel!'

'Don't do that,' I heard the other guy say. 'They have it right upstairs if you want it.'

I'm shaking, I thought. *All I'm doing is shaking.*

'Nah. I want this one back at my place.'

'I don't do that,' I said, smiling.

'Yes you do, darlin'. How much you want?'

'I don't do that.'

'Told you. She doesn't do that.'

'How much?'

'No.'

'Come on … '

'No.'

'She thinks she's better than you, Billy.'

'How much you want, wild one?'

'You can come to the back,' I said.

'Yeah? What's at the back for a young guy like me?'

'Private dance.'

'All right, sweetheart, lead the way.'

'Oh boy, now you're fucked, Billy.'

I turned on my heels, holding on to Bill's hand. It was soft and fat, all the fingers stuck together. I really thought everyone in the club was watching. 'All right, Mira!' they shouted. 'I'm next! I'm next!' The sound of my heels pockmarked the floor. A vulture, no fear, eating the dead.

In the booth at the back, I sat on the table. Bill slid in front of me, eyes at my crotch. Light pricked all over his face in white dots. I inched my panties down to my knees.

'That's it, sweetheart.'

I started rubbing my clit around with two fingers. Bill followed my rhythm on the mound of his pants.

'That's it, Mira. C'mon, how about a kiss?'

Still rubbing myself, I leaned close to Bill's face. He smelled like perfume mixed up with beer. I pursed my lips at his torn-up beard. Then I leaned back and rested my ankles on his shoulders. I gave Bill a view. That's what he wanted, to see: *That's how she opens, that's where I fuck.*

All of a sudden, Bill gripped me hard by the waist. I slid off the table right onto his lap.

'I know you're a wild one!'

With me wedged in between the table and his gut, a tight little spot started to pulse in his crotch.

'Another song, sweetheart.' The music kept pounding. 'Come on, darlin', you know what I like.'

'Sixty,' I said.

Bill breathed like a fool. I was jiggling, splayed open, trying to turn myself around.

'I see your pussy! What a pretty little pussy you got there.'

My skirt was up around my waist. I undid my bra and let him pinch my nipples as I tried to settle on his legs in the right spot.

I was bouncing up and down. I wanted the cash.

'Yeah, lemme feel.'

His hands moved to my ass. It smelled different in the room, like a match had just been blown out.

'There you go, lemme feel.'

His finger was a slug.

'You're wet, sweetheart, yeah … '

'More?' I whispered, looking behind me.

Eyes screwed shut, Bill was nodding his head.

'Ninety.'

'Yeah, just suck it, please.'

His finger fell out of me.

'Kiss it, sweetheart, kiss it, please.'

I slid under the table. Old cigarette butts stuck to my knees. I swam forward an inch through the walls of his thighs. I trickled some juice on him, forming a suck. I looked up at Bill. He was as hard as the floor.

Just a few sudden mouthfuls of cock and I swallowed his cash like a curse down my throat.

'Are you okay?' I remember the way John stroked my forehead after we'd had sex for the first time. It felt repetitive, insistent.

I wanted to hide.

'Mira. C'mon, baby, open your eyes.'

There was a candle making shadows on the ceiling. My back was glued to the couch. John was squeezed in beside me.

'What time is it?' I asked.

'It's okay, Mira. It's not late at all.'

I was covering myself with my arms.

'Why don't you say something?'

'I have to go home.' The whole room was flickering.

'Stay just a few more minutes,' John said. He started drawing circles around my breasts. 'You never finished telling me about your cousin, what's his name?'

'Who?'

'Your cousin?'

'Oh.'

'Well … ?'

'Ezrah.'

John dipped a finger in me. 'Wow, you're still wet.'

'Stop!'

'You want me to stop?'

I felt buzzing in my body. Buzzing through my nipples and all down my legs.

'Okay, baby, okay.'

John reached over me to open a drawer under the coffee table. He took out a thin cigarette and lit it from the candle. He started taking deep puffs. Then he put it between my lips.

I shook my head.

'Trust me, baby, it'll make you feel good.'

I breathed in a bit but started to cough.

'Come on. Just a little more,' he laughed.

I tried but it still wouldn't go all the way down my throat. Marijuana smoke, it smelled like bad cheese.

'Let me do something to you, Mira.'

John looked up to the ceiling and took a deep suck of the joint. Then with his cheeks all puffed out he put his lips over mine. He blew such a huge blast of smoke down my throat that it inflated my stomach and went all the way to my vagina.

'Feel good?' John asked, sounding proud.

It smelled like him inside me.

'God, you look beautiful.'

My mouth gaped wide. My eyelids were boiling.

'I mean it, baby. You look like a princess.'

I started laughing. A Jewish American Princess!

'Shhh … Mira, tell me about your cousin. What was his name again?'

'Ezrah.' I was dizzy.

'Ezzzzraaaaah,' John yawned. 'What kind of name is that? Hey, baby, you okay? What kind of name is that?'

'Hebrew.'

'You're Jewish?'

Tiny sharp prickling erupted in my wrists.

'My family.'

'So you grew up that way?'

I nodded my head up and down too fast. It made me feel sick.

'Wow. Are you religious?'

'No!'

'Hey, hey, sorry, I didn't mean to make you uncomfortable … '

I shifted around on the couch. I thought I might vomit.

'Hey, come on, baby,' John whispered. 'I've just never met anyone Jewish before.'

My body felt like it was buzzing full of bees. They were swarming inside the veins of my wrists, making my skin balloon out all red. I was biting the inside of my mouth to make it stop. Sour stuff coated the walls of my cheeks.

'Hey. Hey, Mira! I said I was sorry.'

John was trying to turn me toward him. I didn't want to move. I shut my lips tight. But then he started stroking my arms softly and I felt a too-loud laughter coming on. It was like he was skinning me.

'What happened to you?' My nipples were raw. 'When was the first time? Come on, forget about it, you're so wet, it's all good … '

My skin was breaking apart like a net. Each time he touched me the holes got so wide. It was hard to breathe right.

'Six. I was six.'

'Really, six?'

'Yeah, six. I was sicks!' I started laughing and laughing. I was all made of holes.

'What happened? God, mmmmbabe, you're so wet.'

John's big hand was a cup under my vagina. His other hand squeezed and squeezed on my tit.

'He and his friends made me go down like their doggy.'

God, it was funny! Did I really say that?

John dropped his mouth to my mouth and pushed his tongue in me. I tightened. I sucked it. Sicks, I was sicks.

'Like the woman on her hands and knees in the pictures ... '

John's fingers went up me.

The Joy of Sex!

'Shhh, babe, what's so funny?'

'All the guys stood around her in a circle.'

John's fingers wiggled. I bucked up my hips.

'Four of them were there.'

Another finger inside.

'Ezrah went first.'

John's hands slid under my ass.

'He did something from behind.'

More. Do it more!

'He felt my tits up under my shirt.'

'Wish I didn't need a fucking rubber here.'

'They all did it after.'

'Mira, spread wider.'

John started moaning. His cock was so hard. He put something on it. My hand was around it – it felt like a doll's leg. The heat split me open. John lifted my hips and turned me over like that. My stomach was down, my ass high behind me.

'How many, baby? How far did they go?'

I heard myself moaning. I felt myself wanting. Something to stop myself from being spread empty wide. Ezrah loved *The Joy of Sex*. He stole it from his parents and hid it in the couch.

'Hey, come on, what's so funny?'

'They go: "Mira, are you a doggy?"'

In the picture for 'orgy,' the woman was drawn on her hands and knees and four guys around her were squeezing her tits, holding her hips, pushing her ass. Ezrah called the woman a doggy. Like I want it now. Doggy! Doggy!

'You love getting fucked on your hands and knees.'

More. Push it more. I want it harder, more! I don't care if it hurts!

'Shit, you know how to move. Sexy little girl. How'd you learn how to move?'

John was splitting my ass and watching me jiggle. Wind screamed through the window screen.

'Yeah, fuck, baby, fuck it.'

Fast up and down. There was thunder behind me. I felt my own body shoot out of my body.

Ezrah knew I was scared of being alone.

In the summers when we were kids we used to walk in the ravine near my house where the darkness of trees made the sun disappear. I'd pick flowers on those paths while Ezrah screamed up at the branches to freak out the birds.

He never wanted to hold my hand. Whenever we held hands it was because I made him pretend. I used to think I would be Ezrah's wife.

One day we walked further than we'd ever been before. I kept saying that we should turn around, that we were going to get lost, that we should turn around now, when suddenly Ezrah bolted away from me, laughing, 'I'm leaving this place! See you, Mir! I'm leaving!'

I was glued to that spot full of mushrooms and leaves. I was scared that he would get lost, that I would get lost, both of us lost in the forest forever. What were my mom and his mom going to do? Flies landed on my shoulders and I swatted them off, going jerky.

I looked down at my feet and started shuffling backward. I went so slowly because I was hoping that Ezrah would come running back toward me. I kept turning my head in case he jumped out behind me. Black rubber branches touched the sides of my face. I realized that my whole body was moving in slow motion because I was waiting for something around me to change.

When I finally made it back to my house, our mothers were stretched out in the sun and Ezrah was there. I couldn't believe it. His arms were draped around his mother's shoulders. He was smiling at me with his top row of teeth. I thought he was saying: 'See, Mir? You see? I know how to get home without you.'

My mother gave me a hug and said, 'Beautiful flowers.' But the stems of the buttercups were squashed in my grip, their tiny heads all looking down, limp.

Ezrah stayed over at our house that night. We slept together on the bed in the den. My stomach hurt. I was still so mad about how he took off on me. I was pretending to sleep when Ezrah snuck out of our bed and got the flashlight from the kitchen. Then he pulled the covers over our heads and shone the light upward.

'This is our new house,' he said, matter-of-factly. 'We'll stay up all night like this.'

Ezrah had grabbed my comic book from the floor and was shoving it in my face. I shrugged and sat up with him. After a few stories, though, I started complaining like I always did about Archie that two girls like Betty and Veronica would never fight so hard over the same guy. Two girls hardly ever want to kiss the same guy.

'Two guys want to kiss one girl,' Ezrah said. 'So what does it matter if two girls want to kiss the same guy?'

'It's not the same thing,' I told him. 'These girls are supposed to be in Grade 9 but look at their tits! No girl in Grade 9 would have tits like this!'

Ezrah snatched my comic book and wrecked our tent. He got on top of me and wrestled my arms over my head.

'What do you know about Grade 9 tits?'

'Stop it! Get off!' I yelled, laughing.

Ezrah put his hand over my mouth. 'They'll hear us! Shut up!' His hand smelled salty and I stopped squirming.

'Tell me you're sorry,' he said.

'Fine,' I said through his hand.

'Tell me. Then I'll get off you.'

'I said I was sorry!'

Ezrah eased up off my gut. His pyjama pants looked weird, like a button was pushed out. He lay down beside me and kept crossing and uncrossing his legs. He pulled the covers up over our heads again and stood the flashlight between our faces.

'Let's stay up all night,' he said.

All I felt like doing was looking at his face. The haze in the blanket made his eyes huge and grey. Ezrah was catching his breath, letting me stare. Right between his eyebrows, his face started changing. First his eyes got bigger, then his eyebrows pointed up. Ezrah looked like a fox. Then he looked like a clown.

Ezrah complained that I'd never stay up all night with him.

'No, I'm awake,' I told him. My eyes were half-open.

It bothered me that I could never remember the second I fell asleep. I wanted to memorize that exact click. I knew people died in their sleep and that meant going to sleep without ever waking up. I thought that if I remembered the exact second before falling asleep, I would know for sure I wasn't ever going to die like that. There was a prayer that I heard some kids say at school that always freaked me out: 'If I should die before I wake, I pray the Lord my soul to take.' Those words kept going over and over in my head. I did not want to die before I woke up.

'Mira, you're falling asleep.'

Ezrah set the flashlight at the top of our heads. A soft yellow circle touched the ceiling through the blanket. I asked Ezrah to tell me what was happening on my face.

Ezrah reached out and touched the spot above my left eye. 'It's okay to go to sleep,' he said. He stroked my eyelid down.

My face felt so hot. I reached out my finger to do the same thing to him: a little, light stroke in the space above his one eye.

We each had one eye open, one eye shut. He kept touching my eyelid and I kept touching his. Our thin purple skins there rippled together.

As I woke up, I felt Ezrah's breathing, humid on my lips. I rolled on my back and took the blanket off my head. From the blueness in the room, I knew it was near morning.

I think I can remember every moment when I touched him or he touched me, because something always happened afterward. It was as if I could feel more things under my skin, as if there were a night light searching inside me. I liked it when Ezrah touched me, but I just didn't always want it to get started. I think maybe the difference between all those times is lost in a pile in my head. Or my thoughts are too lazy to keep my brain clean.

Still, I know the best times happened when nighttime pressed us together, sweating.

Then Ezrah started wanting his friends to hug me, too, and we all started looking at these books, then magazines – two naked people on top of each other, three naked people inside of each other, his head there and her head there, his legs up and her legs down, tits and pussies, cocks and dicks, Ezrah's hands on top of me, more hands underneath. What other girl played these kinds of games? And who else didn't say anything after? I thought I was the only one.

Nadia worked at Carousel's. She'd been there as a bartender since she'd turned eighteen and she always served all of her underage friends. Because of her dad, she said to me, the cops didn't care. I still had no idea what he did. But I'd been hanging out at Carousel's since I was sixteen and Nadia always fed me double rum and Cokes.

The very first time that I met Adi, it was the summer after I graduated from high school. I remember that night how I didn't want to go home because I knew my parents were just going to ask me if I'd gotten a summer job and why didn't I have a job yet.

There were a few cute roadies wandering around with cigarettes and beers, a bunch of kids from our school too. When Nadia saw me come in, she flapped her hand sort of frantically at her nose like something stank. Nadia's hair wasn't braided like it usually was; it was full of static, down to her shoulders, not brushed. She wasn't wearing her silvery lipstick either. She looked so rattled, I thought, because she was drinking too much Coke or something. I knew that my parents would be happy if I just got my old job back at the Second Cup to save money for university. They would never want me to work at Carousel's.

'Mira, fucking help me god,' Nadia whispered, lighting up a cigarette. She grabbed my hand too tight, dug her nails in. 'This girl my dad brought in today is fucking crazy. She's in the bathroom right now. She's here on one of those exotic things.'

'What exotic thing?'

I was thinking about eight hours standing behind steaming coffee pots, the tuna-fish stink of grinding beans. John.

'I mean exotic dancer, come on, the exotic dancer visa thing. What the fuck, I don't need you to jew me out right now.'

'I'm not jewing you out, you Rusky! Who is she, I'm just asking.'

Nadia motioned behind me. The roadies were watching. I turned around in my seat and watched too. The girl strutted out from the bathroom in these fat plastic shoes, Alice in Wonderland shoes, like a cartoon or something. Maybe it was her short white fur coat, too, which was shaggy like a goat. I started to laugh. Nadia hissed at to me to stop. The girl kind of shimmied onto a bar stool. She threw her short white fur coat on the floor.

'Most of them are Romanians,' Nadia whispered. 'But that bitch over there, she's this notorious Volgograd whore.'

I started to laugh again and Nadia couldn't stop me. *Volgograd whore.* It sounded so comedy-ominous. I knew Volgograd was Nadia's hometown and I shouldn't laugh. But that Russian girl who was at the opposite end of Carousel's leather-bumpered trough started laughing too.

'Stop it, I'm serious.' Nadia knifed me harder with her nails. 'I don't know why my dad left her here.'

That girl kind of reminded me of Nadia at twelve: the albino bunny hopping on our sidewalk. Maybe it was her fur coat.

The Volgograd whore was watching me.

'Don't even look at her, Mira. She's a fucking terrorist.'

'Can I get a rum and Coke?' I asked. 'Please? Double-shot me, Rusky.'

Nadia swigged the rest of her Coke. 'Don't fuck with me,' she said.

Nadia always made it seem like the world was going to come down around us, as if everything was just about to go dark. While Nadia was getting my drink, I could see that girl head-on. Her face was as high as a moon off her neck. She had black ink eyeliner painted beyond her eyes. Her hair was bone-blond like Nadia's, but pulled tight in a bun. I knew that Nadia had to help girls from Russia before, when we were younger especially, and I'd always thought it was about learning how to speak English, not some kind of exotic visa thing. I felt stupid right then.

Nadia clipped back with my rum and Coke. 'I need to do something about that bitch.'

'Whatever. My god, Nadia, she seems harmless to me.'

Then the girl yawned, loudly. It was like she was showing us the inside of her mouth on purpose. It was gleaming brown and slimy. I couldn't see any of her teeth.

'Mira, she's an evil horse-fed whore from my hometown and I'm supposed to teach her how to be a Canadian or something?'

'Why doesn't your father do it? Why do you have always do things for him?'

'Oh, for fuck's sake, Mira, you don't understand. You need to get out in the world and grow up. Get a fucking job.'

'Shut up! I am getting a fucking job!'

The Volgograd whore made a choking sound and started spitting on the bar.

'Oh my fucking Christ, do you see what I have to deal with? That girl just spit up on my bar.'

'Sorry.'

I watched Nadia rush to the other side of the bar with a spray bottle and a cloth. The girl started talking to Nadia in Russian. She was flinging her hands around, these bony hands, and her whole body started moving.

When Nadia came back to my side, she was on the verge of tears. 'She's, like, telling me her fucking sob stories about being oppressed. Can you believe that that girl Adi is a fucking mother? She works at the titty club at the end of the road. I feel sorry for her.'

I passed Nadia my empty glass.

'I'll get you another. Jesus, I'm so fucking stressed.'

As Nadia worked I tried not to keep looking across the bar, which was impossible. There's no way that person was a mother! She looked twenty years old, twenty-five at the most. She was wearing one of those shirts with only one arm – it was white and it had a fabric flower on the shoulder. She also had two cigarettes sticking out of her mouth. She tried to hold both cigarettes with her lip muscles and smoke them at the same time with no hands. It was really funny. She was banging the bar with both fists.

'Daddy says you take care of me! Daddy, come!' she yelled in English.

It was witchy. She was witchy. I felt witchy too.

Nadia opened another can of Coke. 'I can't fucking take this tonight, Mira, not tonight. Holy mother of Jesus. Can you help shut Adi up? I just really can't take it tonight. I just need her to shut up. She's been here for hours.'

'Okay.'

'Oh God, thank you, Mir. You're a good girl. Always.'

I jumped off the bar stool. I don't even know if I walked or ran. But now I was standing before Adi's long and tightly crossed thighs.

She handed me one of the cigarettes, which was now half-done. 'Smoke,' she said.

I took it and started smoking. I felt Nadia watching me closely, stressed. I wanted to chop off her bunny head. It's, like, *You asked me to do this, now leave me alone!*

Right away, up close, I knew Adi was something special. I mean she was hard like Nadia but blond-Russian-sexual times ten.

'You know about this titty bar?' Adi asked.

'You mean the one down the street?'

Adi was looking me up and down, thinking.

'You have never come,' she said, smiling.

That shocked me. I mean, I knew she meant that I had never *come*. When I had. I'd come!

'Guys who come to my club know exactly how they come, why they come, you understand?'

I smoked. I looked at the exit sign. I wanted to be friends with this fucked-up Russian girl. I mean, she seemed radical, as if she knew all about men. This girl wouldn't ever be scared of a man. This girl could tell me what I'd been doing with John.

The last time I'd been at Carousel's Nadia had slipped me about five rum and Cokes and I got so drunk I gave some roadie a blow job in the toilet. I cringed at the thought of that. He was disgusting, disgusting.

Adi reached out and grabbed the hand I was smoking with.

'Closer,' she said.

It made me nervous. Heat from the cigarette moved toward my fingers. I shuffled in toward her.

'You have good eyes.'

Then Adi let go of my wrist. Nadia started coughing hysterically, trying to get me back. I couldn't stop staring at Adi, though, how light her eyes were with these star-shaped gold slits. The makeup made her look so dramatic, like a queen. For more than ten seconds we were eye into eye. My face froze. I felt pulled to a stop in the middle of running. How long can a girl keep looking at a girl?

Then the corners of Adi's eyes twitched and she looked away. I think she was surprised that I didn't stop staring at her first. She banged on the bar. She yelled at Nadia in Russian.

Nadia didn't come. She was talking to another girl from our class where I had been with her at the opposite side of the bar. I hated that girl, who wore her hair in these toddler-style pigtails. We were nineteen! We were too old to wear our hair like that.

'Immigrant!' Adi screamed at Nadia.

I laughed in shock. Nadia was totally anxious and fired up as she came over to us. 'If my father hadn't plucked you out of the gutter you would still be there, okay?' Nadia said to Adi.

'Fatherfucker.' Adi spit on the bar again. Her spit was a puddle of foam.

I stood at Adi's side and I felt something for her. Or I felt so different all of a sudden with Adi, as if I were already on her side against Nadia. I felt totally grossed out about Nadia's father. It was like some secret fucked-up childhood thing had just been exposed.

Nadia looked like she was about to cry. 'Mira, come talk to me before you leave, okay?'

Adi let out a mean little laugh. 'Don't worry, Mira's gonna *come.*'

I laughed at that too. Nadia pleaded at me with her eyes. What the fuck was Nadia so scared of? That her father was being outed as a prick?

'I'll call you later, okay?' I said to Nadia.

Adi began to laugh hysterically at what was going on between me and Nadia. It was embarrassing, like she knew everything about our friendship, all its weak parts, its cracks.

Adi jumped off the bar stool and got her goat's fur from the ground. 'Tell your daddy all is good,' she said to Nadia. 'I don't bug you people anymore.'

Adi's body was so skinny but she had too-high tits and a bubble-type ass. I felt like a guy watching her. Adi twisted her shoulders into her coat and I was standing there like a fool, thinking: *But I just got here, don't go!*

'So, you coming or what, baby?'

Baby? Someone else calling me *baby*!

There was something about Adi's neck. It kept tilting to one side. It was thin like a branch that would snap in the wind.

'Okay, that's it. She is coming. She likes us Russian girls. We are smart.'

Adi winked at Nadia. She rubbed two fingers together. Money.

I didn't look back at Nadia and the pigtailed bitch at the bar. I felt like she hated me now. I went with Adi into the night. My chest felt empty. Nadia. Adi grabbed my wrist. Then my hand.

'You make a name for yourself,' Adi said, lighting a joint. 'Not your true name.'

The titty bar was down near the water where all the factories were. Me and Adi shared the joint. We didn't really speak and I didn't know why. I couldn't imagine myself with a different name. Adi sounded real to me. I couldn't believe I was holding her hand. The pot was so strong that my heart started seizing, skipping beats. Cars were double-parked along the sides of the road.

The bar was unmarked – it looked like a factory building. There were silver circled mirrors on the front door.

When Adi pulled me inside, she let go of my hand. What was my name? *Mirat? Mirnot?* It was a dark flashing room, full of mirrors, high ceilings and painted black walls. Girls writhed upward, humping on poles. Inside their mouths it was shining like sirens. I crushed my face into Adi's fur coat. She elbowed me off her. I couldn't breathe. I didn't know who it was in those mirrors: men squatted in circles with beers in their crotches or girls with their nipples pushing through their bras. Those girls looked like wolves with the hair all shaved off them!

'Bitches,' Adi whispered. She took my hand again. Thank god.

I was coughing, but I was with her.

'Hey, Adi, who you got there? Who's your little friend?' I saw this one guy staring at me like a hunter. 'What's her name? You bring her for me?'

My name is not Mira. Call me Sexpot.

The man was so weirdly hot. He had thick eyebrows. He held out his hand. It was massive, with veins jutting up above each knuckle. I squeezed Adi's hand even tighter.

'Tell me, Adi, where'd you find this little hairy one?'

He thought I was disgusting?

'Go fuck yourself, Gio.'

The man stood up, smiling. He was probably six foot five. I stepped backward, away. That *hairy* thing hurt.

Adi was dragging me past him too fast. *Wait a second!* I wanted to scream. I felt suddenly violent and bold from the pot. I wanted to stay and kick his asshole in. I didn't brush my hair, that's true. So fucking what? My legs were unshaved, my armpits too. What did that asshole know about my thighs? *My name is Mira, you asshole. I have only one name.* I tried not to stare back at the guy as Adi yanked me away from him. Suddenly we stopped – Adi bumped into some girl wearing a muzzle and a thong. The music turned into a woman's heavy breathing.

I made myself look back at Gio, that guy. He was watching me with this horrible smile. His eyes were wild, too wide, outlined with black. He looked like a man who could slice a goat's neck and not blink. I really couldn't take it. I let my eyes drop to his legs. His two huge thighs shifted open a bit.

I thought he was telling me: *It's okay. I'm sorry. Come back.*

I hated myself. I was getting wet. I felt tinier and younger than anyone in the room.

Then the man turned both his palms up and showed me the basins of his grip. *Come here*, he signed. I felt the motions in my pussy. *Come over here and sit on my lap.*

I heard Adi getting in some kind of fight with the muzzle-thonged girl. Adi started swearing. She was pulling me away. Sticky wet lines smeared between my thighs.

When I finally looked back up at Gio's face, he had a woman climbing on his lap. He hadn't been motioning to me. Gio's thick-knuckled hands were on the girl's waist and she was writhing around like a puppy in pain.

'Cocksucker,' Adi hissed at the sight of Gio and the girl. 'Fucking bitch, Lani's got his cock in her mouth like a bone.'

It was about fifteen minutes before we closed the next Saturday when John came back to the café. He was carrying flowers and he'd shaved. It was like he thought I was the love of his life.

I hadn't given him my number because I didn't want him to call me at home. I didn't want my parents to ask who he was. I took his number, though, and said I would call. He made me promise I would call. But I didn't. I couldn't. I felt too weird after I left that night. John had called me a cab, he'd even given me money for the ride, and I started hyperventilating the second I got into the car. It was quiet, I mean, the cab driver didn't know, but I couldn't stop thinking: *What'd I just do?* I could still feel John's tongue pushing into my mouth, his tongue making all the noises of sex.

Seeing him standing in front of me, with those flowers, at work, all I could remember was his sandpaper tongue. And his purple hanging cock, how it swung from side to side. I remembered exactly how the whole thing went in me. Over and over, that feeling in my gut, and the second time, too, how I wanted it to happen ... But I knew I didn't want it to happen ever again! I didn't want him as my boyfriend in that house that stunk of meat.

John kissed my forehead. He seemed sheepish. 'Hey, Mira. How about the flowers?'

I took them and put my face in them. Ribbon carnations. Their gross perfume made me think of my period. I'd gotten it in the middle of the night a few days after the sex. I bled so much that it went through the mattress. My mother was mad. 'That was your grandfather's mattress,' she said.

'You're getting off soon, right? I'll wait for you here. We'll go get something to eat.'

John thought I was just going to go with him? That I was his girlfriend or something? He was standing too close to me. I wasn't even off work yet. I had to sweep the floor, mop it and put away the cash.

'I'm still busy,' I said.

My voice sounded mean. I didn't mean for it to be so mean. I left the flowers on a table and started sweeping. My head was saying to him: *Leave, leave, leave.*

'I'll wait.'

John just stood there. I had to sweep around his greasy, fraying jeans. *Fucking leave! Just leave!* I was going to scream it.

'Stop for a second, Mira.'

I looked up.

'What's the problem here, huh? Didn't you have a good time last week?'

John's eye twitched and then widened. I really didn't want him to be here.

'I couldn't stop thinking about you all week. You know that, Mira?'

God! Stop saying my name!

I started sweeping again, moving behind the counter. I wished my boss would come up from the basement. I wished I'd never gone with this person. I wished I'd never done any of it. John was following me. I heard him saying stuff under his breath. 'I thought things had finally changed. I thought some things had finally changed … '

I was looking at his hands, his hands clenched in fists. I wanted to scream for my boss, but I just stood there listening to John's jerky breath.

'You let me have so much of you last week. You can't tell me you didn't like it. Remember how you were kissing me? You loved it. You can't tell me you didn't love it.'

His fingers opened. They were coming out toward me …

John started laughing. 'I'm not going to hit you, fuck! You think I'm going to hit you?'

No! Fuck! You were the one who started all this! You were the one who did everything, god, why'd I let you do all that stuff?

'You don't want to see me again, is that it? Huh? What kind of game you playing? Say something.'

I was watching the floor, still checking his fists. I just didn't want what was next. *How much time does he have to be here? Look. Look what I got myself into …*

'What, you're not going to talk to me? Who do you think you are? Some good girl, huh? Not by a long shot, baby. I've been around and I can tell you that. You gave it to me, Mira. I've seen how most girls are and you were willing, yeah. Other guys are going to want you to go with them too. They can tell you're that kind of girl. They just look at you and know. You know that, too, huh, don't you? Well, no one's gonna do to you what we did, I can tell you that. I've been around. I've seen how things are. You're a rare bird, baby.'

John reached out and stroked my face. I didn't flinch. 'Fuck, you're probably gonna end up sleeping with any guy who says a few nice words to you. You're a real little sex fiend, you know that? Yeah, you know that. Fuck, I've never been with a girl who got as wet and horny as you did, Mira. You could probably take ten guys at once!'

John's hips started moving back and forth. His hands looked like they were holding my ass. 'Yeah, I could get Michael and the guys and we'll come for you after work, follow you home … We can just have you there in your daddy's backyard, yeah, doing the train. And you'd probably moan exactly the way you moaned with me: *Oooh, wait, wait, oooh …* '

'Fuck off! Just fuck off!'

'Mmmm, yeah, all right. Wanna hit me? Is that it? You want to hit me?'

I raised the broom from the floor.

'Yeah, smack me with it. Do it. Smack me.'

John closed his eyes and puffed out his chest. His lips had turned white. I lifted the broom up over my head. I wanted to knock off his head.

'Fuck you! I hate you!'

John's eyes bolted open as the broom whacked his head. It scratched into his ear and onto his face. He started swatting me away but I just kept on smacking. I heard weird grunts from the back of my throat. I was breaking through skin. I wanted to do more.

But I stopped when I saw he was cradling his face. Light red blood was dripping through his middle fingers. When John saw the blood, it was like he got happy. He started laughing with his jaw open and was practically singing: 'A slut, a slut, a good-time fuck, the kind of fuck that's yours for free … '

We heard my boss coming back upstairs. John looked at me and smiled and ran.

I'd been there for a month before I finally went onstage. The titty bar was full of exotic-dancer-visa Russians, and Nadia had been right, Romanians. There were a few girls from the Philippines, too, like Lani, who'd defected from her nannying gig. Everyone was tarted up like poodles or something and poodles hated me because I was a mutt. I'd been hanging out with the DJ and walking around the bar in a bra and skirt and heels for a month. I shaved my underarms and my thighs. Adi had to almost force me onstage the first time.

'I started out like this at home,' she said as she made up my face with too much blush. 'I was born with a thong on, girlfriend.'

I could never tell if she was serious or not.

I ignored Nadia every time she called me. It was like I thought talking to her would mess up my act, like it would cut the thing that I'd started between me and Adi. I told my parents that I was at the Second Cup in Union Station and that I was staying at Nadia's most nights.

In the basement dressing room, girls were running around under fluorescent lights. They stopped to look at me getting ready for the stage. Lani started laughing her sharp birdy laugh. Adi kept me wired on her pot while she handed me things: a short dress, shiny shoes. I raised my arms, dizzy for a second.

When I told Adi that I wasn't going to make up any stage name for myself, she was surprised. She said, 'So this is Canadian brave?'

I stared at myself in the mirror. I didn't feel brave. The dress was too small. My tits rubbed together, my thighs rubbed together, my lips rubbed together. I was fucked.

'This is what they like, Mira.' Adi slathered lipstick on my lips. 'This is how they like you.' She brushed my hair, pinched my cheeks.

I just wanted to stay down there with her. Lie on the floor. Turn off the lights. Lie down and not move.

That was when she told me that all the girls want to dance naked for men. All girls would do it. Every last one.

'Not every one!' I got high again laughing. I knew so many who would never do this, wouldn't even think it. They'd never show their tits.

'Listen,' Adi said. 'You find me a girl who won't take off her clothes after you tell her what you like, there's no girl like that. A girl who won't strip after some guy tells her he wants to see her tits moving around in the air and tells her all he wants is her ass to get shaking. Then you'll see how she wants it, how she'll do it for your friends.'

I was thinking about Ezrah, me and Ezrah and his friends.

'You just tell a girl how you like her sexy hot body, that you like how it moves, that you like what it does, you tell a girl this and you'll see how she'll do it.' I felt Adi's breath steam up my forehead. 'A beautiful girl like you, though, you've really got something, Mira.'

Nadia was always the beautiful one between us. I was the plain one, fleshy and hairy and brown.

Me and Adi held hands as we went back upstairs. Sweat from her palm wet the middle of mine. Now I felt more relaxed as I walked with her like that. Our hips were moving at exactly the same time.

Adi led me up near the stage and talked to the DJ. He winked at me; I mean, he'd been encouraging me the whole month. 'You'd be good at it too,' he always said as we watched the girls dance. The DJ let his tongue out of his mouth panting like a dog when he saw me all made up. It made me feel good that he thought I was hot.

The girl onstage was Lani's best friend, Coco, a Romanian, and she was folding herself in half. Coco peered backward at the crowd through the slit in her thighs, tensing her ass cheeks open and closed. It was like she was talking to the men through her ass. I thought she was telling them: *I'll squeeze you in my cheeks. It'll be the best feeling any one of you ever had! My asshole's strong, fuckers! Come on! I dare you!*

'DJ said you could go after,' Adi whispered, her lips near my neck.

It felt good with her there so I leaned back. 'I know,' I said.

Adi laughed as she took my weight. 'You're a funny girl, Mira.'

I turned around and wrapped my arms around her. 'I can't!' I moaned. My hands slid down her skirt.

I didn't want to tell her I was scared of that man being in the audience. I meant Gio, who was there almost every other night. He didn't think I was hot. He always ignored me. He took dances from Coco and Lani and I didn't know why them, what did he like about them? Adi told me to stay away from him. She wouldn't say anything about him but that.

Adi kissed me on the lips. Coco whipped by us.

'Go. Go ahead.'

There was blood in my ears, I felt blood down my neck.

'Go, Mira! Go!' Adi gave me a shove.

After Coco's dance, the room was always ready. I was taking Adi's normal spot.

There I was. Standing over the men. Including *him*. And his horrible eyes.

I was watching my toes all crushed up in the shoes. I hated those shoes. I kicked them off. I heard clapping below me. Strong lights overhead. I felt myself moving. My hips were too loose. I felt my breasts bouncing bunched tight in the dress. God, I was stoned, with my hair in my face. I wanted it to stop. Pull my tits from my body ...

'What's her name?' someone shouted.

'That's Mira.'

'Go on, Mira!'

The dress was clumped like rubber at my hips. I was twirling around, reaching behind me.

'Jesus, check out the hooters on that little babe.'

I was taking it off.

Then my hands hit the floor. My hands and my knees. I saw the dress under me black as a rag. Sweating, I'm sweating. My bra and my panties. I looked down between me, crawling away. Hundreds of eyes were watching my ass. Animal, animal.

'Look at that ass!'

Beats shook the floor. I put my ear down. They all want to fuck me. Mira. Fuck Mira.

My ass tilted higher for Gio's mean eyes. I hated that *he* didn't want me. *Butcher-man, why do you hate me?* The shame of that helped me. I was pulling my underwear tight up the crack.

'Spank yourself, Mira!'

My hand made my ass red. Flat on my face, humping the floor …

'Kinky little chick.'

I don't know how long I was down there like that for him, spanking myself for hateful him. I was licking my lips when the thumps started changing. I pressed up to stand with the dress tight against my chest. There was wetness on my thighs, splinters in my face.

'When's she coming down here?'

'Yeah, I want a piece!'

I looked for Gio out there in the pit. I wanted to jump straight down through the fire, throw myself to the lion …

But Gio wasn't sitting where he was before. Maybe he'd left in the middle of my act. I stood there, dumb, thinking: *I am the lion.*

I ran off the stage and right into Adi.

'I'm not what those guys are used to, I'm not!' All of my breaths started to pour out at once.

'Fuck you, yeah you are! That was fucking hot!'

Suddenly Adi kissed me, longer than before. My underwear was soaking wet. I felt myself opening, my tongue on her lips. I heard her sink a little moan into my mouth. We started frenching, our saliva was sticking. It felt really good just to play with her tongue. Adi's hands were sliding toward my ass. I was too wet. My teeth dug in her lips. She tasted like smoke.

'But Gio didn't stay,' I whispered. I felt for a second like I was going to cry.

'Good,' Adi said. 'I told you to leave him alone.'

Then I bit down so hard on Adi's lip that she pushed me away. I think she was shocked, she was covering her mouth, but I just started laughing. Laughing instead of crying.

When Adi realized that a few guys were watching us, she grabbed me by the waist hard and pulled me back close. She was going to forgive me. I opened my mouth on her neck and I felt us shuffling over toward their table. Then we were kissing again, full-on making out, this time grinding ourselves into each other. Adi squeezed the sides of my breasts. I think a few guys got closer around us. Someone undid the string of her bikini-top bra. Adi pulled down my dress from the neck. She pressed and rubbed her nipples into mine. She forgave me for thinking about Gio. I held her naked back. We were stepping on money, sliding on bills. Then Adi's hot nipple hit my mouth. She held my face down as I licked and sucked hard.

I wish it could've stayed like that longer. When I knew Adi liked me and I liked her too.

Everyone believed me when I told them I worked at the twenty-four-hour Second Cup at Union Station. My family did, anyway. I told them I liked the people I worked with and that the money was better when you worked the night shift. I mean, how much does anyone really want to know anyway?

The only one I ever told the truth to was Ezrah.

We hadn't seen each other in a while because he was away at school. I hadn't seen him that much since the first year of high school, actually, because his family had moved up north and we'd stayed downtown. We just saw each other on holidays. It was Yom Kippur when I told him. We were in the back seat of his brand new white car.

I'd stayed inside synagogue longer than Ezrah because sometimes I liked hearing the people singing, that wailing coming out of their nostrils.

Ezrah always made fun of me for wanting to stay. 'Being a good little Jew?' he asked when I got in the back seat with him.

'No. I don't understand what they're saying.'

'Yeah? That's because it's in Hebrew.'

'I know, Stupid, but it still bugs me. You'd think I would understand something after all this time.'

'Why?'

Ezrah was staring at my dress.

'Because what's the point of being there if you don't understand anything? What's the point of standing up and sitting down if you don't understand what the rabbi says?'

'You're not supposed to.'

'You are too. People understand a priest when they go to church.'

'Whatever, Mira. You want to go to church?'

'I would understand it at least.'

'No you wouldn't. You're Jewish.'

'Because our family is.'

'No, because you are.'

'Well, I'm not. I don't feel it.'

'That's really fucked up, Mira. You know what the Jews have been through to survive? You know how amazing our religion is? Don't say that.'

Ezrah always acted the same. Ezrah always looked the same. It was something about his eyes – he always scrunched them up to sound moral. I wasn't going to be Jewish just because he made me feel guilty. I knew there was something I was really supposed to feel. What was the point of doing it all if I didn't ever feel a thing?

I assumed everyone felt something when they were in the temple. I remember how proud Nadia looked when she went to church with her mother. In a taffeta skirt that was black blood red and high heels, she looked like God was going to personally inspect her. She told me once that her mother said that they had to dress up for God so that God could feel their respect. I'd never even imagined that God could be in a man shape, with man thoughts. I thought God was more like a bird than a man, whipping and trapped up at the rafters.

'All Jews believe in God,' said Ezrah. 'It's totally different than believing in God if you're Christian. God, for Jews, in case you care, is a moral force.'

That was fucking funny. I imagined moral God as some light-sabre Luke who whispered in people's ears as they stood up and sang. *Keep singing for me, Sir. Keep singing for me, Miss.* Moral God's voice would be deep and fulfilling: *I'll watch you, Man. I'll protect you, Woman. Just keep rocking back and forth.* Isn't this the only reason people would do it every Saturday? Because they felt God as a moral force breathing inside them, because they could feel some real presence worming into their heads? I knew that the feeling of God would have to exaggerate things like this. Until there was some kind of needy hole in your system – like the beak of a baby bird waiting for its mama, shrieking until she drops nourishment through. If you prayed every day you developed this hole and God would stick his little moral tongue through.

Ezrah reached into the front seat and put on the radio. 'I want you to come and visit me at Thanksgiving. You should really meet some of my friends, Mir.'

The song was on loud, something about a baby shaking conga.

'Will you shut that off,' I snapped.

Ezrah turned the radio off and looked at me. 'What's wrong with you?'

'Nothing.'

Then silence.

'What the fuck is up, Mira?'

'You look like you're working hard these days,' I said, changing the subject. 'What's up? You a doctor yet?'

'What's up, you have a boyfriend yet?'

'Fuck off. None of your business.'

'So what are you doing then? My mother said the Second Cup still?'

'Yeah. So what are you doing these days besides studying?'

'Studying.'

'That's it?'

'Yep.'

'No girls?'

'No girls.'

'I don't believe you.'

'It's true.'

'I bet there's some good-looking girls in your class.'

'They're all right.'

'What? No one you like?'

'No one like you.'

'Oh, come on!' I was smiling at him. His legs looked too long for the back of the car. I was uncomfortable in my dress. It was low-cut. I had a shawl wrapped around me.

'Let me see you.'

'No.'

'Why not?'

I let the shawl fall down my shoulders. I shifted a bit on the seat so that my body was facing him.

'You look good.'

I looked down.

'So what are you really doing now?'

'I feel weirded out telling you.'

'Why?'

'I don't know. Just do.'

'Why?'

'Stripping.'

'What?' Ezrah turned his body away from me. 'Fuck!'

Both of us went silent. I could tell he was thinking of what to say next without making things worse. But his lips were shut so tight it was hard for him to get it out.

I wanted to touch his arm or something. 'Don't be like that, come on.'

'Why the fuck are you doing that?'

'I don't know.'

'No. You don't know? Fuck, how can you do that?' He was disgusted with me. It was sliding out of him more easily now.

'It's what I'm doing right now. I don't know. It's not a big deal.'

'What the fuck, Mira, it is a big deal. How can you actually do that?'

'Because, I don't know, it's in me. I don't know. That's how I can do it.'

'What are you talking about?'

'I mean … I don't know. I mean, maybe I was meant to do it.'

'No. You really fucking believe that?'

'I don't know. Yeah. Maybe it was something people always said to me.'

'Who? Who said it? Guys said that to you?'

'No. Sometimes … ' *Were you always this disgusted with me?*

'That's embarrassing, fuck. I don't know how you can do that.'

I didn't want to talk to him anymore. I didn't want to say another word. Suddenly Ezrah turned around and stared at me. He was looking at my cleavage.

'I'm going to come and see you.'

'No you're not.'

'Yes I am.'

'No you're fucking not!'

'Any dumb bastard can go see you naked? So? So can I.'

'Fuck off.' *Fuck you. Ever since we were kids. Fuck you.*

Our breaths were filling up the car. I opened the window and heard a song coming out of the synagogue. I knew it was the last one. A bunch of people all crying together, not wanting to die.

'It's almost over in there,' I said.

Ezrah got out of the car and left me. I watched him walk through the big wooden doors of the temple.

I felt like laughing for a second. I didn't even tell him the whole thing. That after a while I didn't even think the men were that bad. That I'd had their fingers up me. That I let them kiss my breasts. That they'd sucked me, stroked my head. That I wanted this one man, Gio, to fuck me so bad.

I stayed in the car until I saw my family come out of the synagogue with the crowd. My father and mother had circles under their eyes. Ezrah was there, talking to my mother. I didn't care. I hated him then. He looked tired and mean, just like his dad. As I watched him I was thinking about later that night, about getting stoned and dancing at the club with Adi. I wondered what she would think of Ezrah. Of me sitting in the car with him, atoning for my sins.

Adi made all the arrangements for us to move upstairs. I did it because I wanted to get out of my parents' place for good. After a few months at the club, I'd made pretty good money and Adi said that we'd make a lot more if we lived up there. I usually made at least $150 per shift and always extra if I did stuff in the back. Adi said that the girls who took guys up to their rooms could make over $800 a night! Management took 35 percent at the end of the week, plus $150 for laundry and phone. I thought that was a lot, but Adi said we could stiff them a bit, pretend like our tips were smaller than they were and just give 35 percent on the standard fees: $75 for a blow job, $150 for full service.

I didn't think so much about what it would be like living up there when I said yes. Making big tips was part of the thrill of the whole thing.

The day we moved in, I waited in a little area outside the office with my stuff while Adi got our keys. I wanted to know how she got into dancing, but it always seemed like a stupid question right before I was going to ask. I mean, I knew it was probably complicated because of immigration. I'd seen Nadia's disgusting father once at the club, with this young Russian girl who looked almost skeletal. I went downstairs the second I saw him and stayed for two hours.

After a few minutes, this guy stuck his head out of the office. He looked at me like something was wrong with my clothes. I'd never seen that guy at the club before. He was short and thin, with brushed-back black hair. I opened my mouth to say something or smile, but he just turned and closed the door.

I heard Adi speaking Russian. I didn't want to meet that asshole. I was glad she knew what to say to him.

But when she came out of the office, she wasn't looking at my eyes. She just linked her arm through mine and we headed up the stairs. I noticed Lani and Coco hovering up at the top, but they had disappeared into their rooms by the time we got up there.

I didn't expect that it was going to be so much like a regular hotel, a regular shithole. The stucco walls were grey with dirt. Sheets were heaped knee-high outside the doors. Our rooms were right beside each other: 221 and 223.

'Don't worry,' Adi said to me as she handed me the key. 'We'll be out of here in a few months. Make the cash and then leave.'

'Where are we going?' I asked.

'Jamaica. Good weed.'

I thought for a second about living with Adi in a bikini, stoned on the beach in Negril. I wanted to go by myself to Japan.

Everything in this craphole hotel was right away worse than I'd imagined. It smelled like bourbon and beer. I could hear a radio through the walls. I felt like I'd just arrived at a place where girls were carcasses packed together in a freezer.

It didn't smell so bad inside my room, though. Someone must have just sprayed perfume. But in the bathroom there was a clump of black hair down the drain of the sink. The plant in the bathroom had wilted brown vines. I unhooked it and gave it some water. The soil was filled with tiny white balls.

In the bedroom, two mirrors faced the bed. One of them was full-length. My window overlooked the parking lot. There were a few trucks out back. For the first time I noticed that there was a park down the street from the club, at the end of all the factories. It looked like a high green hill with trees on top. I couldn't tell how far it went back. I was standing there staring when the street lights turned on.

I went over to Adi's room. She was putting her stuff away in the drawers. I'd told my parents I was moving into a friend's apartment, so I didn't really bring that much stuff. Just two big bags of clothes, some books and some shoes.

'You're already finished unpacking?' Adi asked without turning around.

When I didn't say anything back, she said, 'Don't worry, Mira. Everything is fine.'

I sat down on the edge of her bed. She still hadn't looked at me. For the first time I felt like she wasn't telling the truth, that nothing was fine.

'What'd that guy downstairs say about me having a room?'

Adi kept wiping her hands off on the bedspread in between unpacking her clothes, which were all folded expertly. It occurred to me at that moment that maybe she did really have kids.

'You have the room, don't you?'

Adi was setting up her makeup by the table and mirror. When she finished, she turned on the TV. Then she propped herself up against a pillow at the top of the bed. I climbed in beside her. I felt like talking but I didn't know what to say. I didn't know if I felt bad or if she felt bad or which of us was worse. I took her hand. It was cold. I kept moving my fingers around, squeezing, trying to say something about the place, or ask something about her, her life, but it wouldn't come out. We just stayed on her bed like that, eyes glazed over, watching TV. I fell asleep on top of the covers.

When I woke up, I didn't know where I was. My neck was twisted and my muscles hurt. I turned to look over at Adi. She was still sitting up. The TV was on but she'd turned off the sound. Her eyes were wide open but it looked like she was sleeping.

I slowly rolled my head until it was straight. I just wanted to be still. I wanted to keep my body still.

I remember how after I hit him with the broom, three weeks later, John came back. I couldn't believe it. I guess I felt a bit strange about what happened. I mean, at first I was relieved when I thought I'd never see him again, but then I felt bad. I thought: *What if I was wrong? What if I was wrong to be so upset?* I couldn't believe I'd hit him with the broom! Why exactly had I been so mad?

John didn't look at me when he ordered a coffee. He didn't give me a tip either.

I thought: *Just be nice to him even if he isn't nice to you.*

I went to clean off the table where he was sitting to say hi. John didn't look good. He was smoking and looking out the window. I felt like I had to make things better.

'Come on, John. How are you?'

He looked up at me with soupy eyes. For a second I thought for sure he was going to cry. I had to make it better right away.

'John … '

'What?'

It wouldn't come out of my mouth.

'What, Mira?'

'I don't know … '

'Yeah? What do you want to say?'

'Nothing. I mean, I feel bad about last time.'

John reached for my little finger and squeezed it. He butted out his cigarette and then took my whole hand.

'We're gonna be okay. It's all going to be okay.'

I didn't want him to say that. That's not what I meant. I just wanted to make sure he was okay. God, I didn't want him to say that! I smelled the smoke and the coffee wafting off him.

John waited for me outside after work that day. He was standing there grinning with his hands behind his back. I thought: *I am the one who's done it this time. I didn't leave it alone. I made this happen.*

We walked back to his place in silence. My stomach was a mess. He'd cleaned up a bit in there. It didn't smell as meaty as the last time either. I sat on the couch. John sat down beside me right away.

'I've got to say it, Mira.'

I was staring out the window.

'You look beautiful. I mean it. You are a beautiful, sexy girl.'

'Stop.'

'What? Hasn't anyone ever told you that?'

'Not like that.'

'Like what?'

I glanced over at him. 'Looking like you do and saying that.'

'You mean looking at you like I want to kiss you?' he asked.

I squeezed my lips together. I couldn't stop them from turning into a smile.

John slid closer to me and took my face with his hands. His skin was dotted with sharp black hairs. Suddenly his tongue was everywhere in my mouth. I tensed my thighs. I was letting this happen all over again.

John pulled away first. Our lips came apart with a loud pop. My mouth felt like it was hanging from my face.

'Now you look even more … You really look like a princess. Look, I'll show you how beautiful you are, just wait.'

John jumped up and turned on the TV. He got out a video camera that was behind it. I just sat there staring. My body was beating from that kiss. I didn't want to be on this couch again.

John was hunched down behind the video camera. It was a bit easier to look at him when his face was covered. 'You see yourself, Mira?'

I was on the TV, leaning back against the couch. I'd never seen my face on a TV screen before. My cheeks were red. My lips were kind of open. That was what I looked like? That was how he saw me?

'See how beautiful, baby? Look.' John told me to shift to the left and relax my legs a little. 'I'm not taping this, okay? I'm just showing you how pretty you look.'

I didn't recognize myself. I thought I looked older than fifteen. I put my finger in my mouth and bit it to stop myself from saying out loud: *Do I really look like that?*

'Yeah, baby, like that, that's good,' John was focusing in with the camera so that my head was at the top of the screen and my knees were at the bottom. The back of the couch was shining black behind me. I didn't believe him that he wasn't taping.

'Mira, you're a natural.' I saw John's cock pushing up inside his pants. 'I gotta show this to Mikey. He's going to love this.'

I watched my legs shifting on the screen. *Am I sexy? Does every guy think so?*

'Why don't you take something off and get comfortable?'

'Who's Mikey?'

'My uncle. Michael. Take off your shirt.'

My fingers were moving in between my buttons.

'Why's your uncle going to love this?'

'Because he's smart. He's going to love it, don't worry, he's going to love you.'

I thought right then that I was at John's so that something would happen to me, something I couldn't ever do by myself.

'That's it, Mira, that's the way.'

I wanted him to keep talking.

'That's sexy, baby. Just a bit more, take off some more.'

I was out of my shirt. I sat there in my bra. The straps were making red marks on my shoulders. I touched the top of my breasts and dropped my finger down the crack. I kept wanting to see my finger disappear. My nipples got hard. John started going in close-up on my stroking.

'Look how pretty your tits are. Look.'

My nipples were itching inside my bra. They looked so big. I'd never seen them that big. I rubbed them through the fabric. I thought I would put them in my mouth.

'That's it, touch them. Pinch them. Fuck, that's good.'

I had one in each hand. I was squeezing and twisting. I heard John breathing behind the camera. 'Move your hand now, babe.' He was telling me what to do. 'Touch yourself lower. Touch your pussy. Look at yourself.'

I saw my face changing, my mouth getting bigger. I couldn't stop licking the corners of my lips.

'You look so fucking sexy.'

My bra was hanging from my arm.

'That's it, take it off. Good girl, take off your skirt.'

I didn't know if I wanted to see what it looked like down there. Everything felt so big and rushing.

'You are a fucking sexy girl.'

Hairs in thick strokes were covering my vagina. A dark brown line separated the two parts that were sticking softly to each other.

'Hang on.'

John took his face away from the camera. He was setting up a tripod, taking off his pants.

'I gotta show you something.'

Crouched behind the camera again, I watched his big stomach, the beef of his legs. John started focusing in on my vagina.

'Stop it. Don't!' My voice got high-pitched. I covered myself with my hands.

'Easy.' John laughed. 'Just wait. You'll see how pretty it is. You'll see what I see.'

'No. I don't want to.'

'Yeah you do, baby. You've got the prettiest pussy. All I can see is that pussy in front of me. I dream of it at night, growing over my face.'

There on the screen were my thighs, all that hair … John came over and kneeled on the ground. I wanted to slam my legs shut and put my hands over each other. I turned my head to the side and held hard.

'Open your eyes.'

Slowly, squinting, I looked at the screen. John's thick fingers moved my slippery hand. He was trying to spread me. The whole screen was moving with red and pink dots.

'See it? You've got such a beautiful wet pussy, Mira.'

I strained my eyes. A beautiful pussy? I wanted to hurl like a brick through the screen!

'I want to show you how it looks.'

No! I'll never get used to what that looks like.

I was holding his fingers right where they were sliding. I couldn't help looking down. My vagina stuck onto the fingers of a man.

'Your pretty wet pussy.'

There was foam on John's hand. I looked up at the screen. There was something about all the skin, pink and stretched – it looked like a bat hanging upside down.

Quickly, John leaned in and placed his head between my thighs. He stuck his tongue deep up in me and started really frenching me there. I watched the back of his head on the screen: I felt him pushing in, licking me all around the hole. The muscles of his lips were curling inside me. I couldn't stay still. He was sucking all my wetness. It was making me sweat.

'Stop, stop … ' I heard myself moaning.

John spread my legs wider, then he stopped and pulled away. He looked back at the screen.

'Don't you see how sexy that is?'

Still watching the screen, John pushed his finger up me. I was so wet that his finger disappeared. He was holding my thighs, making my lips flare. Another finger went in. Then there were three. It wasn't going to stop. This was never going to stop. Heat rose between my shoulder blades, two red-hot rods. I stared at the screen. All of his fingers were pushing inside me. I bucked my hips up into his thrusting. It was never going to stop. It was never going to stop.

'That's it, Mira, watch yourself fuck.'

The hips of me fucking. I couldn't stop fucking! I couldn't stop moving in time to his jabs. I felt more, I felt more, god, just one second more filled up on his fucking, all of me there …

'Look at you, baby. Look at yourself.'

I stared at my pussy, his hand was inside it, stretching me naked, fucking me harder. I watched myself shaking, my pretty wet pussy, his thick fingers jabbing so hard I was huge.

'God!' I screamed, and sucked in. I felt the great fist.

Shuddering, I was shuddering.

I imaged that she was the mother and I was the daughter, with all those eyes on us, calling our names. We both wore red dresses with white around the edges. I licked her breasts. She stroked my head. She was the mother and I was the daughter. Her arms wrapped around me.

'Suck her, Mira, suck her!'

We got down on the floor. I was lying on my back. Adi was above me, shaking her hips. She was spreading herself open under her dress and I saw for a second a wheel at my eyes. It was a bright red circle that was rusted inside: that was her pussy. It was nothing like mine.

Adi told me she never wanted to have children. Just after I thought she maybe actually had children. But maybe she was lying. Or maybe Nadia had lied. I didn't believe it when Adi told me she was thirty-one. She was doing all this stuff at thirty-one? I raised my arms. I held on to her waist. I wanted her to come down to sit on my face and shut up my thinking. Fuck, I didn't believe it, thirty-one! Her cunt was a wheel spinning out from her centre. I wanted to stick my tongue through the spokes.

But Adi just kept hovering over my mouth, dipping down for a second, then shaking up.

'Sit on her face, Adi! Squash Mira's face!'

The needs of old men and lights circling above us. It tasted like crying inside my mouth.

Adi's back-and-forth ass, her back-and-forth hips. She finally split open, sank hard on me there. A cunt full of pieces was stuck in my mouth. I just wanted to keep doing it, I wanted to take the weird pain from her there, suck it all dry so she couldn't wail. I wanted her to know that she still felt good. We were showing a roomful of men what sex really was.

Sex is the animals licking and cleaning, sister and sister in front of a crowd, making each other come, tears sliding down their throats, going and humping and groaning from their guts: *This is love! It doesn't matter how we got it!*

Me and Adi never talked after shows – one of us was usually busy with a guy. We talked around noon, when we got up. But Adi came to my door later that night. She was wearing a light purple slip. I knew she'd just smoked. She didn't bring any for me.

Adi lay down on top of the covers, close to me. 'I've never done that before,' she said.

'Done what?'

'You know.'

I'd brushed my teeth but she was still there.

'I'm not right down there.'

My eye kept steady on a crack on the wall.

'No …'

I said no to protest, but I said it wrong. Adi knew. The skin of her lips was swollen and raw. The smell of her body dripped down wrong. I was licking so much, though, I didn't care. I was an animal trying to help another animal.

'I didn't think anything bad was going to happen,' Adi said slowly. 'He just told me I was going to dance. I knew what dancing was. He said, "You'll do well. You are a sexy girl." People have told you that, too, I know …'

She was finally speaking about Gio. I tried not to move so she would say more.

'I knew who he was. He was always around – well, always leaving, always coming back. Doing business deals, bad business, I knew. Everyone loved him in Volgograd even though he was bad – all the parents loved him, all the girls too. But not this time when he came back, talking shit about American cash, American this, Israeli that. We were Christians in Volgograd. Everyone hated America and Israel. Nobody trusted him after he'd been to Israel. We knew that he was going to cross over to the Jews.'

Adi looked at me. She had purple smearing under her eyes. She didn't know I was Jewish.

'So me and Gio end up playing pool this one night, I'm seventeen, just a fun little girl, and he tells me I am someone who can go somewhere with my life. He says most of my jackshit friends won't ever do anything, they'll never leave Volgograd.' Adi started laughing. 'So I was thinking he thinks I'm going to go to Israel with him. I'm going to pretend to be a Jew, some honorary Jew!'

'What's his last name?' I asked stupidly.

'Mogilevich. King of the Jews. Israel is a torture chamber, Mira. They treat Russians bad unless they have cash. I don't know how he'd managed to set up things there. He kept me, seventeen years old, in a room in some Jewish torture fucking chamber!'

Adi started laughing hysterically. I touched her shoulder. But it made her laugh even more.

'So he takes me to the land of the Jews and he's some hot-shit pimp man or something over there and he makes all this money and I've been fucking for him and now he wants me to be his wife? My mother told me all Jews are corrupt.'

Adi rolled away from me, choking down her laughs. She got up and started pacing at the foot of the bed.

'Uh, how long were you in Israel for?'

'Ten fucking years. Two fucking kids!'

'Wait … '

Adi's neck had turned red. 'You know how bad that motherfucker Jew fucked me? On the way to this city we stopped at some old factory where they used to make paper. I am an old woman by this point, twenty-seven, right? And he just takes me and we leave the kids and it's all business, right, and his friend meets us there. You know this friend, too, that bitch Nadia's dad. So Gio and this daddy talk about the visas and then daddy tells me to lie down on my back, spread my legs. He points to the floor, covered with the soggy stuff that they turn into paper, and then he makes Gio watch as he fucks me. It's a fucking blood sport! No condom, nothing. I just lay there and waited, this pulpy crap under my shirt.'

God, why does every girl have to get fucked?

'We got here in the middle of the night. Daddy puts me in a room with one other girl, kitchen down the hall. I stayed for two years. Gio came every day at the end to get my money. You know, I thought Canada was not like Israel … '

'Why didn't you run away from him?'

'Mira, why the hell ask me that?' Adi stopped pacing. Her voice suddenly went low like a man's. 'He is a liar. Gio Mogilevich is a liar.'

Adi held her slip bunched up at her stomach. 'Now that fucking two-timing Jew comes and looks for other girls to make me jealous. To make me want to die.'

Blotches of sweat spread under her breasts in moon shapes. Adi's smell was stinging me.

'Let's go away, okay, Mira? Let's just get out of here. Just us. Jamaica.'

'We should go to the doctor.'

'Doctor?' Adi began coughing uncontrollably and fell back on my bed. 'You think I'm going to a doctor?'

I reached out and touched her shoulder. 'My father's a doctor. We could go to his nurse. She's a good nurse … '

'Your father? Your father? Your father wants to stick his hands in my pussy? Your father probably already sticks his hands in my pussy!'

Adi got up again, clutching her gut.

'You have any pot?' she asked.

I shook my head.

'Hey, come on, you have pot.'

I rolled over and faced the window. I didn't know why I had brought up my father.

'Sorry,' I said quietly. 'I think Lani has some.'

After a few seconds, Adi slammed my door.

Gio Mogilevich was an amoral Jew. I had never known an evil man Jew.

He grabbed my waist and smacked the back of my ass. He started moving his knee between my wet thighs. I knew Michael wasn't watching my breasts onscreen. They were jiggling out of my nightgown. I was hot on his lap. He placed one hand on my thigh and one hand on my breast.

'Where'd Johnny-John find a treasure like you?'

I felt like laughing so hard when Michael said that. I knew he didn't like it. Michael was gay! I only did stuff with him because I knew he was smart.

'Mira is creative,' he'd said to John after he met me and watched me on tape. 'She is the maker and you are the taker.'

I felt his big knee coming up through my panties. I slid myself forward, tried to let myself melt. It felt like a glass was spinning on my chest. Michael had to be rough, otherwise he couldn't come. He yanked my wrists behind my back and never let up with the bounce of his knee.

'I swear it's relaxing. To see a young girl fucking is a totally relaxing thing.'

'Shut up!' I said.

His cock was a lump. I really knew Michael was gay from the second I'd met him.

'Mira, that's good,' I heard John saying. 'Look up at the camera.'

Michael was grunting, he only took a few minutes to come and he never actually went inside me. He sat there afterward, hunched over his dick. Michael really made me laugh. I couldn't believe he was John's uncle. He was twenty-nine but he looked like an old man. He was going prematurely bald. Three long black wrinkles were stuck in his forehead, as if his whole life had been gouged up in there.

I tried to imagine the story that John had told me about Michael, how Michael stuck his cock up John's shorts when they were kids. The reason I couldn't really see it was that I couldn't imagine Michael ever being young. I kept imagining a skinny little boy's body with his man-sized bald head.

The three of us used to sit around drinking beer after shooting and Michael would talk about all the books he used to read in university: Genet, Ginsberg, Ferlinghetti. This one time I started going off about Genet. I'd just read the book *Our Lady of the Flowers*, or most of it, on Michael's recommendation, and by my third beer I was ranting that I didn't think it was such an 'erotic masterpiece.'

'Genet was the best thing that ever happened to literature, Mira,' Michael said flatly. 'He writes for people like me – "a child-roughneck whom chance had given gold."' Michael recited those words with his eyes closed.

John agreed, he was nodding his head vigorously, but I knew that John had never read Genet. He barely read any books. He just wrote, which was so stupid. How can you write and not read?

'Fuck you, Johnny-John, you don't really know how to read!' Michael said that the second after I thought it.

I thought it was amazing that Genet wrote *Our Lady of the Flowers* twice. He was in prison for stealing and he wrote the entire manuscript out on the paper bags they had to make there. When some guard figured out what he was doing, he stole the manuscript and destroyed it. But Genet just started it all over again.

'Only fucked-up people are truly great in this world,' Michael said. 'Genet was a fucked-up, masturbating genius.'

I told Michael that the part I liked best in *Our Lady* was when one of the characters kills his girlfriend by banging her head against the brass bed, then just looks out the window and thinks the sun is malevolent. I didn't know how Genet did that, made me follow that exact train of thought: 'To love a murderer,' he wrote. 'I want to sing murder, for I love murderers!'

I started an *Our Lady* game with Michael. The next time he came to John's and we were all drinking, I stared at him, really seriously, and quoted from the book. 'Your dead man is inside you,' I said. 'Mingled with your blood. He flows in your veins, oozes out through your pores, and your heart lives on him, as cemetery flowers sprout from corpses ... '

'Yeah, that's good,' Michael laughed. 'You're smarter than I thought, Mira.'

'It's the part that reminded me of you.'

John looked hurt.

I rolled my eyes. 'It reminds me of all of us, John. *Our Lady of the Flowers* is going to vomit out all our carcasses!'

Michael smirked, so I continued quoting from the book. I knew it was kind of dramatic: 'The night, which has come on, does not bring terror. The room smells of whore. Stinks and smells fragrant. To escape from horror, as we have said, bury yourself in it.'

I don't know why that passage made me and Michael crack up. I think because we both knew that John didn't really get it, I mean that him and Michael held their dead men inside them and I was the stinky fragrant whore!

Our game happened a few more times. Michael quoted something to me about me from the book and I quoted something back to him about him. But then I didn't see him for a while, a few weeks, and the next time he came over, it was strange, it was like we'd never even had the *Our Lady* game, or the inside joke that we were both smarter than John.

If I asked John where Michael was when he wasn't around, John would get mad. He'd say: 'Mikey's a businessman, Mira. He can't always come over and educate you.'

I missed Michael though. Being with John was boring without him.

But Michael never came over alone again. He brought some big weird guy once who drank beer with us. I felt nervous because Michael was acting like a completely different person. He didn't say anything smart or talk about books. He just kept drinking and smoking and scratching his arms.

The only thing he said to me was: 'You're always making Johnny jealous, Mira.'

I didn't get why Michael and John were acting like they were friends with this disgusting new guy. They were all flicking their bottle caps into the middle of the table, cheering when they hit each other.

I was pissed off that Michael was acting so stupid. As the night went on I kept waiting for him to change. But he didn't change, he just got more drunk.

It was three in the morning when he finally told John to set up the camera. 'Take Joel with you, Johnny, show him how it's done.' Then Michael leaned over the table to me and said, 'Joel likes you. He wants to do it with you.'

'Why are you so into this dirty-video thing?' I asked.

Michael stared at me with his heavy pink eyes. Then he spoke very slowly: 'Because I am a bum. If you do this tonight, I will not be.'

That big Joel guy had thick yellow hands. I made myself fall from his crooked lap before anything happened. I started screaming at John to turn the camera off. He didn't do it right away. That guy was disgusting. I didn't have my underwear on.

'Turn it off! Please! Turn it off, turn it off, turn it off!'

'Fuck, Johnny, she's freaking out,' I heard Michael say nervously. I looked at the screen. My vicious red face. My cunt was a monkey's ass hanging behind me.

'Turn it off! Turn it off!'

'Okay, shhh, it's okay. It's off, baby, look, it's off.'

My palms were nailed to the ground. John came down quick, crouching around me. 'I'm sorry, Mira, baby, I love you, come on.' John's arms were tight around my shoulders. 'Guys, I think you should go … '

Hurting black fluid was filling my nose. John's arms were sweltering. I couldn't stop crying. I realized that Michael didn't give two shits about me.

But he did quote me back from *Our Lady of the Flowers*. After another month away, he gave John a note to give to me. His handwriting was slanted and bunched-up like some psychotic person's scrawl.

'Her life stopped,' the note said. 'But around her life continued to flow. She felt as if she was going backward in time, and wild with fright at the idea of it – the rapidity of it – reaching the beginning, the Cause, she finally released a gesture that very quickly set her heart beating again.'

Adi wasn't in her room when I banged on the door. I went downstairs to the change rooms to ask the girls if they had seen her. It was six o'clock in the evening. We had to work in a few hours and I'd slept most of the day. Lani was down there, smoking and looking fucked up on coke or something.

'Looking for your girlfriend, Meeeera?'

'You're not going to find her here, cocksucker.' Coco was in a bikini top and plucking pubic hairs from her moustache patch.

They both knew that I started living upstairs only because I was friends with Adi, that only the visa girls were supposed to live upstairs. I thought that Coco must've come here like Adi, fucked and fucked and fucked in small rooms.

I started walking toward the washrooms. Lani ran up and blocked me. She turned me around. I smelled her rancid breath, salted skin.

'You think Gio wants you?'

Her spit sprayed my lips.

'He can't even look at you!'

Coco came up and joined Lani the bitch. 'Who gets your money, huh? How much you give him?'

'How much you give, Mira? How much you give downstairs?'

'I bet she sucks his crap dick so she doesn't have to give thirty.'

'She'd suck a pig!'

I hadn't ever given my money to anyone but Adi.

'What? Tongue only comes out when there's cock?'

'Why are you so fucking mean?' I finally said.

Lani passed me the butt of her joint. I took it from her and sucked the burnt end. Lani and Coco returned to their preening. The sides of my throat felt like they were glued.

I don't know how or why I stayed with John for so long. I was fifteen. Maybe I was just new to the game. I broke it off for good the night John told me he wanted us to be together forever. He said he'd felt a space open up in him the very first time he ever saw me. He told me that he always wanted to know me. *Forever, Mira*. He actually said those words. And that possibility of eternity made me remember all the things I'd ever done with him when I'd thought I was okay, when I'd thought I was being myself – when I realized that I was acting like an automaton. Thank god he used condoms.

I'd let him lick me for hours. John went down on me even when I was bleeding. He always wanted to be between my legs. He liked it even when I wasn't clean. He made me spread my legs, saying, 'Please, please.' He wouldn't take no even if I really didn't want it. Sometimes it was the first thing he'd do when I came over. He'd get straight down on his knees, pull off my underwear and stay there for an hour.

It started taking me longer and longer to get into it, to get any kind of feeling down there. Sometimes I imagined that it wasn't John's head. I pretended it was some guy I didn't know, that I was sitting at a table and some stranger was reaching under there, eating me. A few times, I even imagined that John was Ezrah.

I knew John didn't care about my fantasies. It got to the point where he was like, 'I just want to be your dog, Mira.'

But I didn't need a dog. I cared for him, sure, and there were times when we had fun. John told me everything about him and Michael growing up, how their families lived down the street from each other near the slaughterhouse, and how they used to have these contests to see who could get closest to a dead cow. Once, some guy stopped and let Michael touch the still-warm skin of a carcass through the fence. That was when Michael said it was barbaric, John said, and stopped eating hamburgers.

Sometimes neither of their families had heat in the house, and there were times when they couldn't wash for a few weeks because the shower was too cold. John's mom kicked him out when he was eighteen because she just wanted him to get a job. No one in either of their families had ever been to university. John lived on the street for a while after high school until Michael convinced him that he wanted to go to university. John didn't make it past the first year. He didn't like all the reading, he said. But Michael had stayed, on loans, for three and a half years before it got to be too much.

'Michael hated all the bureaucracy,' John said. 'I mean, all the fucking administration. He had to pay to take his exams. Total bullshit. And then it was like karma or something, seriously. The day after he quits school he meets the guy who's exporting our tapes at a bar … '

'That's how you guys got into porno?' I interrupted.

'We don't call it porno, Mira,' John said, offended.

'What is it then?'

'It's erotic entertainment. Porno is illegal.'

'It is not!' I said, laughing at him. 'There's porn in every single video store, in every single country, in every single city, on every single screen! How the fuck is it illegal?'

John looked at me skeptically. Sometimes he could be so dumb. John used to talk about the theatre company he wanted to open to produce the plays that he and Michael wrote. John sometimes let me read his stuff – it was always typed out with no breaks between the words. I didn't understand all of it, but I sort of liked it. John was actually funny when he wrote.

'Ilovethe/manwhotakesthebusinhisunderwear/andswears/ thathewillneverhaveawife/ortellalie.' That was the name of his first play. It was about a man who falls in love with a woman he always sees on the bus. It turns out she's the head of the big electricity corporation that has just turned off his heat.

John could talk about his writing forever. He always held it to his chest after I read it and asked, 'You liked it, you really liked it?'

I told him I did. But I would've rather read Michael's stuff. If I ever asked John what Michael wrote about, John wouldn't tell me. He said that Michael's plays were genius, though, because Michael was a genius.

'Have you read them?' I asked.

John shook his head. 'He's waiting for a big audience, you know? He doesn't want to waste his time on any community theatre shit.'

'Why doesn't he ever come back to see me?'

'I think he's working on something big. He'll come back soon, don't worry, Mira.'

Maybe I stayed with John because he seemed okay in the world. I mean, that he was okay considering everything he'd been through. I'd never been through any of that stuff. I didn't want to *be* with him though. I knew that. Especially not the way he wanted to be with me. I remember thinking it was okay if I did it for a little while, but after that time they tried to film me with that guy Joel, I really just wanted to spit it all out. I knew Michael wasn't coming back. And I hated John's smoke-and-beer smell. It was always there now, as if it were my smell too.

The night we broke up, I really didn't want him to go down on me again, and when he started to anyway, I pushed his head away.

'Let me, babe!' John begged. 'Come on, let me eat your pussy. I love it so much, it tastes so good.'

I started coughing uncontrollably. John lifted his head and got up off his knees. He went to the bathroom to get me some water. When I didn't want the water, he said, 'What's the problem here, Mira?'

I was thinking: *How does anything ever really end?*

'What? What's wrong with you, Mira?'

'I don't want to do this anymore,' I said.

John's eyes sagged down. 'Hey, I just want to be your dog. How many times have I told you that, babe?'

'But I don't want to anymore.'

John got an old joint from the table beside the bed. He started smoking it and didn't offer me any. He was really angry. The room started to shrink. 'You don't want to see me anymore, is that it?'

I was sitting on the edge of the bed with my back to him. I was looking around for my bra.

'Why? Huh, Mira? You tell me.'

'I don't feel anything.'

'Aw, fuck.'

'I'm sorr– '

'Don't say that. Just don't say that. After everything we've been through together. Fuck it, I don't fucking believe you.'

'I'm sorry, I just – '

'I said, don't say that!' John was pacing around in front of me. He started pulling at his chin.

'John … '

'No. Shut up. If that's what you want, Mira, then just go.'

'Go? Go where?'

'Goddammit. Just go. Get out!'

'But it's too late right now.'

'So?'

'How am I going to get home?'

'I don't know. A smart girl like you will think of something.'

John grabbed the sheet off the bed from behind me and wound it around himself. He was blinking wildly. 'What're you worried about? Get that look off your face. C'mon, they'll think you're a whore. All men think a woman alone at night is a whore. For fuck's sake. You gonna cry now? Don't be a baby. Fuck. You're not a baby anymore. You're the one who wants this.'

'Does the bus run all night?'

John started laughing. 'You'll find a way home! Go back to your mommy and daddy. Go back to your little life.'

John poked my shoulder to get me moving. I heard him exhaling hard. I was looking around on the floor for my bag.

When I finally got all my stuff together and was walking to the door, John stayed close behind me. He was making pissed-off breathing sounds. For a second I was worried he was going to push me down the stairs.

'She thinks it's all just going to end when she wants it to?' John opened the front door so hard that it banged the wall and sprayed plaster. 'You finally getting the fuck out of here, huh?'

I didn't want to cry. I didn't look at John's face. I ran down the stairs and heard the door slam behind me. I stood outside on the porch for a few seconds, swallowing hard, sweating under my hair. I heard a huge crash upstairs. I thought John must've kicked in the TV.

Fleeing through the dark streets, I kept hearing his voice: 'All men think that a woman alone at night is a whore.'

I thought she was brave in the dark in her high heels, standing tall while I was running. She could face the thing that wanted to lodge itself inside her.

Adi was sitting on my bed like a man.

'You scared me! Where were you?' I'd been getting myself ready in the bathroom. Red cheeks, red lips, hair in pigtails. 'You were here the whole time? Aren't we working? What are you doing? You're not dressed. It's late.'

Adi was hunched over. Her foot was sticking out over the straps of her shoe. The top part, the bridge, was swollen like a little anthill.

'I have to go home.'

'What? To Volgograd?'

'No, Jamaica.' Adi started laughing. Her foot looked infected. I don't know why I hadn't noticed it before.

'No. Where are you going? Tell me.'

'Israel. Wanna come screw some Hasids with me? They like the Russian pussy.' Adi shoved her hands in her lap. 'Fuck, I always forget you're not Russian, Mirushka!'

Adi was shaking, she was white, that anthill on her foot.

'What's going on, Adi? Come on, can't you just tell me?'

'Exodus.'

'Is *he* going with you?'

'I told you to stay away from him!' Adi shouted. 'He hates you because he still hates me.'

I got nervous. Adi was grinding her teeth.

'Gio said to me, Mira, that you are a Jew.'

Adi looked at her feet. The hurt one wouldn't move.

'Yeah? So what?'

A car beeped outside. Adi dragged herself to the window.

'You are a Jew.' She was grinding her teeth and cracking her jaw. 'I can't believe it!'

Then Adi turned from the window without looking at me. She hobbled toward the door past me, shifting her weight from the bad foot to the good. I tried to stop her but she used her elbow in my chest.

'You stay away from me, Jews,' she hissed, and limped out my door.

After six weeks of hanging out with her every single fucking night she was dissing me now because I was Jewish? Fucking God.

I went to the window and waited to see her in the lot. After a few seconds, Adi stumbled out the back door. Her arms were rigid by her sides. There was no car. No one was waiting.

God, it made me sad that she was so fucked up. Adi swayed side to side, picking at something on her cheek.

Then a small white car drove past the club. I watched Adi wave her arms and run to it. She ran like a goat, dragging her clod. She leaned down into the driver's window.

'Adi!' I screamed through the screen. 'Wait! Don't go!'

But Adi had already skipped around the car to the passenger side. The car flashed its headlights up at my window.

'Wait!'

I couldn't see Adi and I couldn't see who was with her.

I raced out of my room past the heaps of old sheets. I thought maybe Adi and Gio were actually going somewhere together. Even though I didn't believe she had ever been to Israel. And I didn't believe she had ever had kids. I knew she wasn't going home either.

A few cars in the lot of the club were idling, soft: regulars wanting to be the first inside.

Adi and the white car were gone. I stood alone. Someone beeped at me.

There was this slimy low voice in my head that was saying without thinking: *Love will be different for you.*

It will be different between a Jew and a Jew.

HALLUCINATION

After my second shift of the night, when I was already undressed and ready for bed, a guy started banging on my door. It was the guy I hadn't seen since the day me and Adi moved in, that landlord with the brushed-back hair.

'Famous Mira,' he said as he entered my room.

My tongue felt thick and full of sleep.

'No comment?' The guy laughed. He had the accent of Adi, of Gio, of everyone here. I would've kicked him if I'd been wearing something under my nightshirt. 'Now that your best friend's gone, you find out how things work around here.'

I crossed my arms over my chest. I looked on the floor for some leggings or a skirt. I had wondered when someone was going to say something to me about living upstairs without Adi. I'd always given her my money for the month and I hadn't paid yet since she had gone. It had been just a week. I wanted this Russian lord out of my room. I couldn't find anything to cover myself.

'Thirty percent goes to the office each time you bring a fuck to your room. I don't care how much the fuck's given you either. You get a hundred and you bring down your thirty.'

I thought it was thirty-five. Adi told me it was thirty-five.

'What about the hundred and fifty for phone and laundry?' I asked.

The guy started laughing through his nose. 'Me and that crazy bitch go a long way back but she got you good, all right.'

The guy scratched his scalp and stared at my crotch. 'What's a girl like you's doing here anyway, I've got no idea. But they seem to like you. Thirty percent and you stay as long as you like. Keep the one-fifty, princess.'

My breath smelled and I opened my mouth. The guy made sure I smelled his too. The stench of us together was milky.

I barely felt myself running to the bed. Cream thickened down the walls of my throat. Why'd Adi do that? Why'd she steal my fucking cash? *I* did that sucking. I earned my fucking keep!

Adi, fuck you. Fuck you, Adi.

The door clicked and he left. Finally I was crying.

It was that time of night when light wants to break but dark wants to stay. There were hundreds of bugs flapping in circles on my screen. My hands and feet were still tingling from fucking. That last guy did it so hard my cunt was pulsing like a phantom. I had to go outside and get some air.

I'd never really walked around the club at night. I knew people were hiding all over, screwing in the parking lots and the spaces between the buildings. I knew that they looked for each other in the park at the end of the road, past the lit-up parts, in the darkness that smelled green.

I veered left and walked up a steep little hill. Old sperm was growing like spores in the grass. I passed rustling, a grunt. I walked into the forest. My eyes turned to pins through the rows of thick trees. There was someone behind me. I crouched down and rested in front of a trunk.

I knew it would happen.

'Working?' a voice asked.

'Yeah.'

'How much?'

'Sixty.'

'Suck and fuck?'

'Yeah.'

The guy stuffed some crumpled-up money in my hand. I knew it wasn't enough. Sixty? This is what I'm good for? This is how I work?

The guy pulled me up. He took me jogging through trees.

Leaves were ripping down all around us. I was trying to breathe, I was skipping to run. The tree trunks were gleaming with dark purple glaze.

'Here. Stop here.'

I didn't see his face. He was pushing me forward. I banged into wood. Fuck! I should've said more. His hands on my shoulders, his weight from behind. My teeth grazed the bark and my knees sank in mud.

The man was holding his cock at my neck. He was trying to turn me around by the chin. I could see him, I swear, from the back of my head. He was chubby, some father, a bull with a beard.

'Take it. Come on.'

Oh god, this guy had the funniest dick in the world! A stubby old mushroom with a soft wilted head. He was tapping it downward, trying to paste with it back and forth on my lips.

'Bareback,' he grunted. 'Gimme bareback. Please.'

'Condom,' I said, shutting my lips.

My neck stayed arched while the guy searched his pockets. The sky was the colour of bruises, the feeling of him. I promised myself: this was the last time.

But the guy started getting pissed. He couldn't find a condom. He was swearing and he started pushing his naked cock into my face all over again. This time, he grabbed under my jaw. I whipped my head from side to side, but he kept smashing the mushroom into my lips.

A growl was spreading through my chest.

I was seething. Blowing. My brain disappeared. I scratched my fingers down the guy's legs. I pulled at his hairs, tried to rip his flesh.

'You little cat! You scratching me up?'

The guy's pants lay in a pool at his feet. I was stuffed in the mouth and my fingers were scurrying, digging inside his thick leather slit. I picked the whole wad. Took plastic too. Buried it under the dirt of my knees. His balls were slapping like jelly on my chin. I tensed up to keep him from going so fast. But I couldn't get tense, something made me loose. I kept feeling this strangeness blow up through my body, up from the mud, up to my throat. It made my saliva start tasting like tin. I was sucking to swallow, to keep myself breathing, his thickness, his cock, his stale white drops.

For a second I thought that someone else was there, or something behind me, around me, a swell of warm air. Something was telling me to take his body, suck out his energy – take him from him.

I heard myself moan. The guy let go of my head. My eyes flew high to the grid of the branches where darkness was being sucked by the whole sky.

'Say *fuck me*, please. Say *fuck me, fuck me* … '

My hands held tight on to the columns of his thighs.

'*Fuck me.* Say it: *Fuck me, fuck me* … '

'Fuck me.' *God! Are you there in the tree?*

The man shot into the back of my mouth. He collapsed to his knees. 'Sorry … Sorry.'

I spit out his grains. I didn't say a word.

The guy stood up quickly. I watched him from the ground. A body loomed over me, a floating head and bulbous gut. He was pulling up his pants, zipping, trying to say something.

'It's okay,' I shrugged. I didn't care if men hated me, I didn't care that Adi was gone.

This time burned its shit knowledge in.

Light was sinking down slowly through the branches. It turned the trees into spotty grey poles. I watched the guy walk away until his back disappeared. When I dug out his fold, I was smiling.

There, from my window in the middle of the day, walking through the parking lot away from the club, there in the middle of the shining concrete – he looked like a man walking out of the desert.

I lifted the screen and stuck my head out. I started waving my arms from side to side in the air.

'You! Wait!'

I flung myself halfway out the window. He didn't stop.

'Gio! Look!'

He turned to face me. I put my hands on my breasts and squeezed them together.

'Come up here, you fucking asshole!'

Gio used his hand over his eyes to shelter them from the sun. I unbuttoned my shirt and took off my bra. I let my tits hang out in the air. Gio's head tilted sideways.

'Come up here! Come! I need to talk to you!'

Gio's body rocked from side to side. I pinched my nipples between my fingers. I was keeping him there, watching me. For the very first time in my life it felt like what I wanted and what I was doing was exactly the same thing.

Gio raised his free hand in the air. First it was a fist. Then it was a finger, the pointing one.

One second? One minute? What the fuck did that mean?

'I can't wait anymore, come on!' I pressed the brick window ledge to fly out even more.

Gio moved his first finger from side to side. *Tsk-tsk,* it was saying. *Don't be a bad girl.*

'Fuck off! I'm not scared of you!'

A sluggish smile spread across his lips. His white shirt billowed behind him like a sail.

'I need you right now!' I shrieked into the wind.

But Gio turned away from me. His finger was still pointed up in the air. One minute? One year? One hundred fucks more? I'd be a good girl. I wanted him.

One week from the window scene, from Gio's one finger held like a match in the air, I'd made almost one thousand dollars. I stretched one finger up from my fist when I took off my clothes and shook it onstage. Code meant: *Fuck me. Fuck me, Man. I will fuck you and you will fuck me.*

The smallest dicks were always the meanest. They jutted in too fast and they never slid out, just in, in, in ... Big dicks were kinder. Little-dicked men wanted to kill. They made me suck their horns with my hands behind my back. Some men who came to me couldn't even fuck. They'd just sit there and sob, stroke their soft pack of veins. God, I saw so many cocks. They came to my door in one long line.

I didn't believe that I'd ever get dry. I thought: *How can a woman ever get dry?* But sometimes my cunt really hurt when I fucked, like a space getting carved from a heap that's too thin. But then, other times, it felt like a monster! It would get so fat, all the juices ganged up. When Gio came back after one week to see me, god, the first time, I swear, my cunt was like a buggy banging up and down on a rough, potholed road, being dragged by four horses, horses pulling on my lips, horses stretching the skin from my cunt over holes, so that each time I bumped up and down it was – god! – pouring love from my holes, bumping over more holes.

I danced all for him. I was a one-pointed light.

Nighttime, nighttime. Flies on the screen.

My door was unlocked. I met Gio open with my legs already spread. My see-through panties were barely a screen.

Gio stared at me hard. He was wearing a suit. I wanted him to take it off. He stood at the foot of my bed. I writhed on it, stoned.

'Do you know who I am?'

I nodded. I knew. It was like Adi threw him to me.

'When did you first know that we were going to do this?' Gio asked.

'Right now,' I lied.

I wanted him to take me any way he wanted.

Gio kneeled down at the end of my bed. He was so tall that I could see his whole chest. I thought he was smirking at the fabric of my panties because my hair came through its tiny holes. His eyes looked metallic. I heard Gio letting out breaths through his nose. I propped myself up and stared at him. My breasts felt heavy. It was like he was going to pray to my pussy. Gio grabbed my ankles and started stroking lightly. He was murmuring something. I couldn't hear what it was. Then he licked his lips and slid in like a drone.

I was waiting to be touched. Beating through my panties, I let out a groan. I couldn't take more. I wanted his mouth.

Gio gripped my thighs and launched himself forward. His lips pushed against the tissue of my panties. He licked once up and down with his whole entire face. God, just that once, pressing on my slit, he got me to the point where I was already gone. He finally moved my panties to one side. My black space opened up and his breath poured inside me. He stared at me there. I was too swollen to care.

Breathing from my cunt, talking from my cunt, I was bulging forth from hairy lips.

I know it's terrifying if you look it in the eyes.

Gio used his knuckles, dipping into my wetness to stretch me and rub me. He pinched my lips with his rough-tipped thumbs. He stretched me even wider. I wanted his tongue. All I wanted was his face. He was pulling and stretching, he could've bit down and I would've spurted come. I was going to come, my breathing was fast, I was gonna come out, I was just about to come ...

Gio slithered up over my belly. His face dripped with sweat. He took his shirt off and leaned on one hand. His chest was one huge smooth rock of hide. He unzipped his pants. He yanked down my panties. His cock was so big it hung over my breasts.

Adi's been here, I thought. *She's been where I am.*

Gio was like the king of the forest, the beast who had the right to lord over his bitch. This is a man, a Russian evil man Jew! I was anxious, too ready, and I grabbed for his cock. But he took my hands and stuck them onto his back. I held on to the curve where his muscles started bucking. I had to suck in my breath. Gio didn't take time. He kneed my legs open and pushed himself up, plowing through my thickness, my blackness, all wet. I felt my head roll over to the side. I shut my eyes and just let the juice gush. My cunt felt like the shape of a boat where wood gets squeezed into points from each shuddering side. The force of his thrusts carried shocks through my chest. I wanted his come, right at the back of me, right at the end. With Gio on top of me, moving and fucking, I felt myself being forced through the bed. He was fucking so hard that my body hit earth.

'I always knew,' I said between his thrusts. 'I always knew me and you were going to do this.'

Then Gio pulled out and spurted on the rise of my gut. One short sound fell out of his throat.

He stared at his stuff on my belly, trembling on me there. Then he wiped me off with the sheet. He left the bed and went into the bathroom. I heard the shower run.

I flapped around on the bed still feeling his cock in my cunt. I was like a fish needing water, more salt in her gills!

And I still hadn't recovered when he came out of the bathroom. He was fully dressed. I was flat on my back. Gio leaned down to kiss me. 'I'll be back,' he said.

I didn't make him pay.

I swear it was like he'd just given me something. Something I wanted that I couldn't say out loud. When he was in me, I didn't want to come. I just wanted him to stick me, over and over, because with each of his thrusts, my pussy got tighter. My pussy got hotter and stronger so it could hold him in there. Each second we were fucking, a voice in my head breathed: *I want you, I see you, I know who you are.*

I felt that the very first time that we fucked. Gio was someone I already loved. So what is love but already loving?

God, why do I love him more than he loves me? Why do I love his body so much more than he loves mine? It's like he is the woman and I am the man. He's the indifferent one and I'm the one ravishing!

I know the way the flesh feels on his stomach, animal thick. I love the way his back rounds at the top. I know the width of his neck and the mark on his forehead, the mark that I think is from praying on the ground. Why do I imagine Gio religious? Is it because I'm the religious one now?

I think of him praying with me, us praying together, our foreheads down on some scuffed tiled ground surrounded by smoke, weird orthodox smoke.

Hey, Ezrah, would God accept me with my fist in the air? My moral fist in the air and all this sperm in my brain? Would God accept us in the temple together?

I don't know who God is. I felt Ezrah's hate, I knew Gio moved money and women around.

It had been just over two weeks since Adi got into that white car and never came back. I thought about calling the cops and filing a report, but almost all of the girls at the club had overstayed their visas and I knew I couldn't do that to them.

I also had no idea what Gio had to do with Adi being gone.

Mostly I knew that I wanted Gio all to myself. I wanted Gio Mogilevich mine. Because something came out from his heart that was dark and alive, some kind of ray that pierced through my weak protection.

And Gio came back for me seven days later. Fucking bastard, it took seven long days! I made a measly $200 because I was only thinking about him. To get myself to sleep I imagined Gio and me in Japan, drinking like gangsters, praying like slugs.

It was noon when he came and I was just getting up. He was wearing a grey suit jacket, which was strange because it was hot out even though it was September. Gio sat beside me on the edge of the bed and started tickling my ribs with his fingertips. I had to choke back my laughs. Then he did the same thing up near my throat. That made me yell, louder than I meant to. My head was lifting off the bed and slamming back down and Gio began tickling me even harder from throat to waist, throat to waist, until the whole bed was moving and I was spinning. I squeezed my eyes and let myself go …

'Shhh, Mira! Stop breathing so heavily.'

My eyes opened up. Stop laughing? Stop breathing? Gio's lips were pressed together. He was staring at my neck. He thought he was looking at my face, but he wasn't. I knew that look from other guys. The glazed eyes that meant: *I want to be with someone I don't feel guilty about right now.*

'Hey, why're you wearing that jacket?' I asked loudly. 'Where were you? Where are you coming from?'

Gio wasn't going to tell me where he had been. He sat there vacantly, like I'd ruined the moment or something.

'Is something wrong?' I asked. 'Did something just happen?'

'No.' Gio took off his jacket and arranged himself over my body. His thighs locked like walls at my sides. He scooped his hands under my neck and brought me up to the big lump in his crotch. The smell of sweat charged the creases in his pants. I wanted to rub my face down there, burrow.

'You're hungry, yes?' Gio asked. 'Tell me you're hungry.'

I was mute. Hungry.

'You want to put it in your mouth?'

Yes. Up and down, up and down like a fool!

'Why do you like putting things in your mouth?'

I don't know. Just give it to me!

As my mouth opened, Gio's zipper came down. He let out his cock. I couldn't look at his face. His cock was the only thing I could look at: the thickening root, the slit like an eye. His cock was the part that already loved me.

Put it in my mouth, gimme, gimme, gimme, please …

'If you don't speak, we'll do it like this then.'

Holding the back of my head, Gio shifted toward my face. He placed his hard flesh on the groove of my tongue. I was stunned. I got hot. I dropped into his cradling. I was sucking his body in gulps down my throat. I wanted to swallow to see how we fit. A suctioning clasp. Forever. No key.

With my mouth on his cock and his cock in my mouth, I didn't remember any other man I'd ever been with. No other man had ever been inside me. I was a bud, sprouting fresh from the mud.

Ezrah, maybe you think that's dumb female essentialism, but it's not.

It was daytime when I went back to the park. I walked to the top of the hill, up a set of wooden stairs. I hadn't realized that there was a clear way up – that what looked like a forest at night was just a bunch of crooked trees. I could see the club down at the end of the street: the silver door where the men came in and the brick part at the back where all of us lived. The buildings of the city were packed together in the distance. The sky hung above them like a heavy white sheet.

Lani and Coco sat together on the grass. They were passing a bottle back and forth, waving me over.

'Come, Mira!' Coco shouted, almost standing.

For a second I thought she might start being nicer to me. Lani shoved her cigarette butt into the grass. The patch they were sitting in was yellowish, flat. When I got up close, I saw they'd both been crying.

Coco passed me the bottle. I sat down and took a swig.

'What is this?' I coughed. It was fizzy and off.

Lani started laughing. 'It's to clean out your mouth!'

That one mouthful made me feel sick. It prickled in my throat like an acid or something. I put my head on the ground. An old cigarette touched my cheek.

'Adi's not coming back,' Coco said.

'What are you talking about?' I said into the grass.

There was a push in my gut then my throat, as if I were really going to vomit.

'She's dead,' Coco said. Lani started to laugh, her sharp birdy laugh.

I closed my eyes, totally repulsed. Deep in my head I heard something snapping, one tiny wishbone broke in each ear.

I sat up, dizzy. Coco lit up. Lani was as blank as the clouds.

'You guys, she's not dead. She called me two days ago. Maybe three, I don't remember.'

'Oh my god, what'd she say?' Coco passed me the joint. Lani perked up.

I sucked in harder than I'd ever sucked a joint. That toxic drink still crawled on my tongue.

'She said she was, uh, sorry that she left, but she was trying to make a go of it somewhere else. I don't know. I didn't hear where. I wanted to know but I didn't catch where she was. She said I shouldn't tell anyone.'

'That's it?'

Coco took back the joint. Lani poked the dry ground.

'Uh, she asked about Gio. She asked if I'd seen him.'

Lani and Coco stared at me. They knew he'd been to my room. My heart started beating too fast.

'You should not have fucked him, Mira. That was fucking, fucking wrong!'

I rolled my eyes. I fucked her old lover. So what? She stole from me.

Coco helped Lani up from the grass, clutching her fat arm. They left linked together, whispering. I realized right then as I watched them go back to the club that Adi was more like them than like me. I saw right then the biggest difference between us. Adi wasn't ever going to go home and neither would Lani or Coco. They wouldn't leave here like I would one day. This was their life, their stuck, money-making lives. I knew that some girls could do things like fucking for cash and they could always go home, they could always feel new, but some girls do things and never escape – they fuck up their bodies, take drugs, sit in shit.

This was the line between me and Adi: the revolting line of inequality.

I put my forehead on the dead grass. Shame explored my shit-flung face.

It was early in the morning the next time Gio came.

'Morning has broken,' he said, at the bottom of my bed. He had a strange look. His eyelids were flickering.

God, why did I want to be with him so badly? Why did I wish that he would just climb into bed and get naked with me?

It sounded like Gio was humming for a second, like he was some old man letting it come out through his nose.

'I'll see you then, Mira … '

'You're leaving?'

Gio walked to the door. 'I will if you're not downstairs in five.'

I didn't have time to dress in anything good. I didn't put on makeup and I didn't brush my hair.

When I ran out back, Gio was standing beside a smallish white car. He opened the passenger door for me. I didn't want to link up his car with that car.

The seats were covered with burlap and it smelled like gas inside. It had a bit of trouble starting, but once we got out onto the highway, everything seemed all right. We were driving east, away from the city. Both of us were quiet for a long time. I kept trying to think of something to say, but nothing seemed right. Maybe I felt Adi's body sitting in my seat.

'Where is your family, Mira?'

A low scraping noise suddenly started running with the engine. I looked behind us. Gio accelerated.

'What's that?' I asked.

'Don't you speak with them?'

'Who?'

'Your mother, your father.'

'Not really,' I said.

I wasn't going to talk about my family with him. I didn't even want to think about my family with him. My family meant nothing inside this car. Even my Ezrah shit disappeared.

'What does your father do?'

'Why are you asking me?'

'Why don't you answer?'

'He's a doctor.'

'A rich doctor?'

'No. He has enough.'

Why the fuck was he asking me this? I was betting his next question would be: *Why are you doing this?*

Well, sir, Mr. Mogilevich, since you asked, I am prostituting myself so that I can go to Japan, so that I can travel and see the whole world, in fact, so that I can make money quickly and not be in debt to my family, the government or amorphous men. I don't care about having some predictable good job at twenty-two so my mummy and daddy will pat me on the head.

'What about your brothers?'

'Brothers?'

'Yes, what about the brothers.'

'I don't have any brothers.'

'No brothers? Poor father!'

I snorted.

'And Mother?'

'My mother?'

'Who is your mother?'

'She's a teacher. What do you mean?'

'She teaches *what*?'

'Religion.'

'Religion?' Gio started coughing. 'What kind of religion?'

'I don't know, my god. All kinds.'

'Your mother teaches "all kinds" of religion? You think there's "all kinds"?'

I was glad he was hacking. What did he really want to know about my family? How much money we made? How I was sheltered from life? Did he want to know how my mother taught kids the Hebrew alphabet? Gio knew I was Jewish! Adi told me that he knew.

'We have a long way to go,' Gio said abruptly. 'Why don't you sleep now.'

Sleep? For fuck's sake. I was too anxious to sleep.

'Adi told me you were from Russia too.'

'I *said* go to sleep!'

Who did he think he was talking to me like that? Like I was dumb? In a way, I felt more Jewish than I'd ever felt in my life. I felt fucking persecuted!

I stared out the window. The clouds were all withered. I felt myself getting tired, even though I didn't want to. My grandfather who'd died when I was ten used to sing me this song in Yiddish when I sat on his lap. I was trying to remember it, something about names and rhyming names, when my chin dropped onto my chest. Then my eyes popped open. I mean, I felt like I was dreaming but my eyes were wide open. I saw me and Gio still driving on the highway, but in the distance I saw all these people running toward the car. There were fifty of them or hundreds of them, coming closer, throwing rocks at us, plates at us, garbage, rats … The highway got narrower and the people smashed their faces on the glass.

They were flat-lipped, screaming, *Let us in!*

I was trying to scream too, *Keep driving! Keep driving!* But nothing came out. We must've run over something. There was a dragging sound. I turned and I saw there was blood on the road printed behind the tires. Air bubbles started popping in my chest. I knew there was someone dying underneath us. *God, get away!* I was trying to wake up. *Get away! Get away!*

'Shhh!' Gio was gripping my shoulder.

'Where are we going?'

'Calm down. You're okay.'

Gio took his hand off me and slowly rubbed his face and chin. I was trying to focus on his face, the hairy outline of a man. He reminded me of John, of Ezrah, of Michael, my dad – the way all men's cheeks are rough and black.

'I sent the children out a few months ago,' Gio said. 'I knew it was going to get worse in the city.'

'What?'

Gio glanced over at me. 'I have a woman at the house who takes care of them when I'm not there.'

I realized that Gio had draped a coat around me while I was sleeping. The coat had slipped down to my waist. Gio kept turning his head to look at my tits. I stared straight ahead and slit my eyes. I felt my nipples through my shirt. I wanted to make myself feel them even more. His staring was making heat flash through my tits.

'I had to take my children from the city. Their mother left them alone in this wasteland.'

I just wanted him to keep staring at me, I wanted these feelings in my breasts to continue. I wanted liquid to spurt out of them. I was with a man who had come to my bed twice. A man I didn't make pay. The man who fucked Adi up. Who brought her here. Who sold her here. God, what exactly was I trying to find out about a man? I felt like a man myself, a compartment – amoral.

The trees beside the road were getting thicker, all the trunks stacked in the same darkened lines.

'She was a little like you, their mother.'

I didn't know why I thought I was in love with this fuck!

'Relax, Mira,' Gio said softly.

I closed my eyes. My stomach was made of soft shit. We drove on in silence, the trucks, the trains and us.

I started thinking about Ezrah. It was his birthday soon, the tenth of October. I thought I might call him. I just wanted him to know that I remembered. But I was too embarrassed to call or too mad to call, maybe too gone, too amoral to call. I didn't even know which thing I was more.

Why couldn't Ezrah like me no matter what I did? What if I cleaned trash from the streets for a living? What if I was legless, leprous, contagious? Why couldn't he love me just because I worked at the club? Just because I had sex with strange men, is that a reason he shouldn't love me? I could say it over and over, every which way: *Why don't you love me with come on my hands? Why don't you love me legs spread for the crowd?*

I don't love you, Ezrah would say to me, *because this isn't you.*

Yeah? Who am I? You tell me who I am.

The Mira I knew when I was a kid, the Mira I want when I'm feeling alone.

So what's the problem?

There's shit on your knees, it's all over your knees.

Fuck you, Ezrah. There's no shit on my knees.

Only I can see it. You can't see that genre of shit.

I knew he would say something like this.

Or: *Jism is not invisible, Mira.*

Oh, go fuck yourself, Ezrah. And fuck your jism-flecked birthday!

'Who do you pray to, Mira?'

Gio's voice woke me.

'Nobody,' I said.

'That's not true.'

'It is. I hate God.'

'Don't say that. Don't ever say that.'

My eardrums beat blood.

'While you were asleep, you were crying for God.'

'I was not.'

'Yes you were. You were crying, "God, God!"' Gio imitated my voice. He seemed to be getting more comfortable with me or something.

I stared at the road. The road never changed. 'Look, I'm not religious,' I said.

Gio laughed. 'Do you know how the Christians pray?'

I remembered Nadia Russian Orthodox in her taffeta skirt. They dress up for God to respect him, she'd said.

'Yes or no?'

'No.'

Gio rolled down the window to let in some air. It started whistling over our heads.

'The Christians pray,' he said slowly, 'to believe in the flesh of Jesus Christ: the real man, with real blood.'

I felt weird that he'd just said *Jesus Christ*. The heat in my body had all gone away.

Gio shifted around on his seat. It was like he was trying to scratch inside his back. 'When a Christian girl kneels before the priest,' he said, 'the body of Jesus is put in her mouth. She says: *Hoc est enim corpus meum*. You know what that means? Come, say it with me.'

I thought he was joking. Nadia would've told me about that! A girl on her knees before the priest who puts Jesus' body inside her mouth?

'*Hoc est enim corpus meum*. Come, say: *Hoc est enim corpus meum*.'

'No.'

'Mira.'

Gio was so stern that I laughed.

'Okay, okay. *Hoc est enim corpus meum*.'

'Good. "This is my body." Say it.'

'This is my body.'

I looked down at my chest. My nipples were big again.

'And when the priest holds up the goblet of wine, he says, *Hic est enim calix sanguinis mei*. Say it.'

'*Hic est enim calix sanguinis … ?*'

'*Mei.*'

'*Mei.*'

'"This is my blood." Say it.'

'This is my blood.' My gut rumbled.

'"Except you who eat the flesh of the Son of Man and drink his blood, you have no life in you." John 6:53.'

Gio looked at me and nodded, as if I knew what he was saying. But I'd never heard this kind of thing before. I didn't know anything about Jesus Christ.

'The Christians pray,' Gio continued, 'because Jesus was a real man. He had a real body and real blood. The Christians pray because Jesus showed them his body, his unclothed body pierced with nails, so that they could look at his wounds and remember their own.'

Gio stretched his huge fingers over the steering wheel. Yeah, Jesus was crucified, that much I knew.

'The very first time I met the mother of my children,' Gio said, looking over at me briefly, 'she wanted to kiss me, she wanted to "do it." But I knew that I would be an animal with her. I didn't want to be an animal with her. I was going to grip her neck and sink my teeth in … '

Something was changing inside the car. There was this electricity between us again. I reached out and touched Gio's neck. Soft baby hairs flattened down on the skin.

'I couldn't stand that she was doing the same thing to all those other animals.'

We turned off onto a smaller highway. Gio stopped talking. He let me work out the kinks in his neck. I felt him start to relax in my grip. When we were kids – of course I remembered this now – Nadia told me that Jesus was killed by the Jews. Suddenly Gio twitched and something cracked in his neck. My hand flew off and stuck to my lap.

'You, as a Jewish girl, cannot so easily be a whore, am I correct?'

Oh my god. Why the fuck was he so shocked about me? *He* was the one who came to my room. *He* was the one who was a smuggler pimp!

'It has nothing to do with being Jewish,' I said.

Gio ignored me. He took out a handkerchief from his pocket. He pressed it to his open mouth. It looked like he licked something off it.

'Do you know why God told the prophet Hosea to marry a whore?'

'I think I should get out,' I said. 'I just told you I was not a whore.'

Gio accelerated.

'Why would God tell the prophet Hosea to marry a whore? Would many men want to marry a whore?'

'I don't care, okay? I want to get out!'

Gio swallowed, his throat bulged. 'They'd be disgusted. Why?'

'Fuck off, fuck off, fuck off,' I muttered.

'God forced Hosea to marry a whore,' Gio said, 'because being with a woman who'd slept with so many was the only way to show him the real way to love.'

Hate, I thought. *Hate*.

'You think this is easy for a man, Mira?' Gio went on. '"For she is not my wife," said Hosea, "neither am I her husband: let her therefore put her whoredoms out of her sight, and her adulteries from between her breasts, lest I strip her naked, and set her as in the day that she was born, and make her as a wilderness, and set her like a dry land, and slay her with thirst ... "'

'Fuck off! I don't care about Hosea. A man is the one who helps a woman be a whore!' I screamed.

Gio smiled and attacked the road. 'You're right. And Hosea was obeying God by taking the whore as his wife. Her name was Gomer. Hosea and Gomer.'

I imagined Adi and Gio twisted around each other. Gio and Adi on the seats of this car.

'"I will discover her lewdness in the sight of her lovers," said Hosea, "and none shall deliver her out of mine hand."'

Gio gripped the steering wheel so hard now that his knuckles had turned white.

'Hosea had to pay another man to get Gomer back. He loved her and still she kept on being a whore. He loved her and *still* she didn't want to be with him forever. The Hebrews need to know these things about their Bible.'

I realized the car was veering onto the shoulder. We'd slowed down too quickly and dust was rising all around us. Gio got out of the car and slammed the door hard. He walked to my side and started knocking on the window. His eyelids seemed peeled back, his white eyes were bulging. He was struggling to open my door, but I was holding it tight.

'Get out. Open up! You wanted to get out!'

I didn't know him. I didn't know this man at all.

Gio stormed around to the back of the car and opened the trunk. His shirt was soaking under the arms. All of a sudden, I let the door swing.

Gio was back in front of me now, breathing hard.

'Get out, I said.'

It got cold inside my forehead. Why was he yelling? I thought my face was showing I was afraid.

'Just get out of the bloody car!'

A pearly white dress unfolded from his fist. It was swinging between us. Still I couldn't move. Gio's hand came down for my wrist. The second he touched me, I flew up, I don't know how.

'That's better, Mira.'

I was standing there in front of him. My horrified breaths. Gio lifted my shirt up over my head. His thick fingers reached behind me and unhooked my bra.

'I don't know why you always wear this thing. I like it better when your breasts hang loose.'

Gio watched my nipples stick out in the air. Then he slid the dress onto me, arm into armhole, neck into head.

'Now you look right.'

The dress was shiny, too tight at my sides. And I was itchy suddenly, as if there were hairs at my nipples.

'Take off your panties.'

I stood there for a second, still breathing too hard. Then I started to turn away from him. I was slow, so slow that he probably couldn't see I was moving. I was aiming to put my hands on the roof of the car.

Gio grabbed me roughly and spun me around. He jerked down my pants and underwear in one tug. The door handle was stuck between my legs. It was making me pulse. I felt him staring at the tilt of my ass. I pushed it out a little. It was the only thing on me that could move. Maybe I'd been waiting all day to fuck him. Maybe my body was dumb and it was telling me what to do. I flattened my breasts down hard on the window. The silky dress made me slide on the glass. I heard Gio's zipper and a car racing by. Then he lifted the skirt of the dress. He felt between my legs. I was wet.

Gio pushed my panties to my ankles. I was stuck there dripping with them stretched and tied around me. Then the head of his cock hit the line of my ass. I wanted to tell him to just put it inside me, split me open, right open, fuck me right now. I bent my knees down to try and tell him to just do it, but Gio leaned his massive chest down, a big slab on top of me, pinning my wrists.

He breathed in my ear, 'You're the next. You're the next.'

I got hotter and wetter. *Next, you're the next.* I wanted to reach out and spread it, spread my ass wide, but my hands were locked tight. *Next, you're the next.*

I thought right then that he was going to be my husband and I was going to be his wife. I'd be a good wife, a great wife, a hot Jewish wife! I'd be the woman he'd been waiting for forever. The one he'd come home to every single day! I'd love him at home and suck him at home, bathe him and feed him and fill him at home …

Gio stuck his tongue in my ear. 'Mira, Mira, you're the next.'

I thought he was in love with me. We were in love. *He's in love, he's in love and I'm in love too!*

But it was only for a second, both of us like that.

Love is so strange it can hardly bear more. It's a nightmare vine, a plant with a face, wood with the veins ripping through, squirting come. Love is one second inside these dark folds.

'Fuck me, please fuck me.' *I want your come!*

'Mira, you've got a hungry little pussy.'

I wanted to be like Adi when she was dancing.

'Mira, little pussy, little cub, little whore.'

I wanted to be the next whore that he saved. I would give up my money. I would give up my life and shove it in the ground.

We were struggling and humping. My fingers stretched out. Gio turned me around by the chin. He pushed his tongue in and out of my mouth. I was a sponge. I'd take anything from him. I thought I was going to come in a second, just from us kissing, just from the wind, just from my hips banging into the car. Clenching my cunt, I squeezed and let go. The rushing, the fucking, my ass got all split. My legs were all locked. The sides of the road extended forever. Then his cock was inside me. His cock pushed so hard. His cock went up through my ass like a rock. There was nothing between us. This was how I loved. Hot on his stone, oiling it down, I was holding it inside me, squeezing it inside me. My ass loved his cock. I wasn't letting him go, he was fucking me harder so I could take more. His cock pushed in behind me all the way to my clit and my clit flowered open, a bulb from inside. I choked, I came, I heard it in my throat, his tongue through my lips, and I came and I came! His pulsing fat dick pushed the come into me.

God, wait, don't stop!

Gio's cock left me.

I collapsed inside the car. I was wet on the seat. I was going to cry. I wanted to cry. I wanted more! I wanted him back. I'd wanted him from the first time I saw him: eyes like a hunter's, eyebrows all in one line. I wanted to go back to right where we just were, where my ass was so strong that I was showing it off. As strong as him, I was as strong as him and I wanted to do it again and again, get stronger than him, zap him and kill him just like a leech sucking blood from the bone. I hid my eye in my shoulder to stop myself from crying. A hard pain shot through my body and lodged itself inside me.

Gio got back into the car carrying a small beanbag pillow from the trunk. He wedged the thing between my face and the window. He said, 'Sleep for a bit now. Go back to sleep.'

I didn't want to be asleep again. The feeling of fucking was too strong inside me, but when I closed my eyes for a second, the lids stuck together.

The next thing I heard was Gio saying my name.

He stood outside the car. I was holding my stomach. I thought I was bleeding. I shoved both my hands down there: thick, fuck, I got it.

'Rise and shine,' Gio said.

We were at the bottom of a driveway that curled up a small hill. Gio's palm was in front of my face. He was holding the handkerchief that he'd pushed to his face in the car. It was filled with little cream-coloured pills. It almost looked like they were homemade. White dust was coming off them.

'Take one.'

'What is it?'

'Take it.'

'I got my period.'

'For that.'

'Is it good?'

Gio nodded. I didn't move.

He took one of the pills and wedged his fingers between my lips. I opened my mouth and it fell on my tongue. It tasted mouldy and came apart fast. I just wanted to run and get to a bathroom, but Gio was staring between my legs. Blotches of brown and bright red dyed the creases of the white dress. My gut felt like it was being scalped.

'I've got to go clean up,' I said. My period always started really strong, blood all over my legs for a day.

'There's the creek out back. Do it there. Wash the dress too.'

I was bleeding and he wouldn't let me into his house? Gio leaned down inside the car. Above his lip were clear drops of sweat. I thought for a second he was going to kiss me, but instead he gripped me by the arm and lifted me out of the car.

My toes were clenched. I knew I was leaking. I held the beanbag pillow at my crotch.

'Come on,' Gio said. He was irritated again.

The ground was made of sharp white stones. Just a little way down from the driveway was a still brown pond in the middle of a creek. It looked like a place where people washed pots, threw stones.

'Go,' Gio said as we walked toward the water. 'Go on, get in there.'

'Will you come in with me?' I asked.

Gio's eyes roamed up and down my legs. He stared, revolted, at the stains on the dress where I held the pillow, where the dress was a clump.

He poked my ass. 'Clean yourself.'

I walked in tiny steps. I held the beanbag between my legs. I was thinking maybe we could stay here awhile. I'd even hang out with his kids. I didn't want to be in this freezing, this cold! I wanted to lie between sheets with Gio beside me.

'Go on! Get in there!'

I was right at the edge where water was lapping. I moved bit by bit down into the pool that had turned black and blue as I got closer. My thighs, then my stomach, then my breasts disappeared. Long weeds were floating on the surface of the water. I scrubbed the dress between my fists and let it flare out as big as a blossom.

So this is my body. *Hoc est enim corpus meum.*

Red smoke rose from between my thighs and settled like scum on the surface of the pond. I felt like laughing for a second – so this is my blood!

When I looked up, I saw that Gio had walked to the edge of the water. His hands were lifted as high as his heart. Trees waved around his head in a circle. He was watching me, patting the air in downward strokes. I imagined his hands were touching my shoulders, pushing me down to where everything was ice. *Go under*, it was like he was saying, *dunk yourself clean.* Breathing fast through my nose, skin turning to scales, I disappeared underneath the freezing cold plane. Gio's hands pushed me down. Oh fish. Oh god. I thought God was in the ice water with me. Adi, are you down here too?

'Mirrrrrra!'

I shot up for breath. Gio's body, chest bare, was coming in toward me. I was dizzy from gasping, dizzy from swallowing, I was walking sideways in short jerky steps. Who was this man who was walking in toward me?

'Fuck, what did you give me? I feel dizzy. I'm stoned ... '

Gio looked different in the water. His hair was tighter to his skull and his skull seemed thinner than his neck. The bones above his cheeks protruded, temples beating.

'I had sex the first time with an illusion,' he said.

Gio looked like Jesus fucking Christ.

I glided toward him. My body felt suddenly good, all sucked in the dress. He had come in for me! I was not an illusion.

'I stared at a girl in a porn magazine. There was no hair on her vagina.'

'Was it Adi?' I asked.

'You need to repent for your thoughts,' Gio answered. He put his hand on my forehead. He was going to push me backward and I tried to resist.

Gio had this disdain for me. Adi and Coco and Lani had suffered. They'd been fucked and fucked and fucked in small rooms. I reached through the water for Gio's tail. He had unzipped his pants and I found his dick, all waxy and limp. My grip kept slipping off its head. I liked it when a cock was soft and I was the one who made it hard. Gio braced himself on my shoulder as I pulled on his cock underneath the pond. His cock was getting a bit harder in my grip. I rubbed faster and faster, looking up at the sky. Then I saw the house up behind him. It was a white painted house with a spire. That house was a church? No, the house was a nunnery! A man with the nuns! I started laughing hysterically. I couldn't help myself.

'You live up there with the nuns?'

Gio took my hand off his dick, lifted it out of the water and spread it flatly on his chest. His heart felt like some kind of frog: cold, deliberate, rasping. He lifted my arms and started twirling me around.

'Lift up your arms, Mira. High, higher. Don't forget your legs, lift them too! Lift your legs, stand on your head! In happiness, too, there are heavy animals!'

I was dancing and splashing. This creek was a swamp! The sky started turning purply red. I saw rain in the clouds before rain came down, vibrating holes from the tiniest grids. I knew rain would squirt through those clouds and pour out, dissolve like glass splinters into our skin.

'Let's get out of the water!' I splashed Gio's chest. 'Let's go and lie down in the stone room and fuck!'

But Gio didn't budge. I stopped my wet dance.

'All Jews must go to Israel,' he said.

My feet sank into the clay of the creek. I felt a big clot of my blood release.

Gloom settled over Gio's face. I wanted to pull us in toward the shore, but I couldn't feel my feet. Everything was numb. I had no desire to go to Israel. I wanted to get lost in Japan.

Suddenly Gio got down on his knees. His chin bobbed just over the surface of the water. He closed his eyes. His bottom lip was turning blue.

'What does it mean, Mira, when a rabbi says that Truth is all over the world?'

I looked down at Gio's square-shaped Jesus-like skull. 'I've never heard a rabbi say anything like that.'

Gio opened his eyes and looked up at me. 'It means that Truth is driven out of one place after another, and must wander on and on and on.'

'Maybe the rabbi meant the Jews are driven out of one place after another and that's their search for the truth, right?'

'Yes. We wander. You wander too.'

Light filtered through my stoned daze. I understood now. We wander through the wilderness. Being with Gio is wilderness. The titty club is wilderness. Maybe my room is the wildest place I'll ever be.

The sequence in this freezing creek in front of Jewish Jesus on his knees was all of a sudden clear to me: I met a man named John, then I met a man named Michael, then I met a girl named Adi and I followed her to him. To Gio, Jesus. I did what Adi did, she left and I left with him. Now I remembered, I knew how I was who I was. A wandering Jew! Struck dumb. On her knees. Truth is driven out of one place after another and wanders on and on and on …

Gio held my legs together under the water. 'I've called all the other girls,' he whispered. 'But they don't respond. It was you who knew who I was even though I tried to confuse you. You saw what I wanted from you and your want responded. You are a Jew who can save needy souls.'

'Amen!' I said.

That felt so funny I wanted to say it again but Jews don't shout *amen*, they wail to Adonai.

'Amen! Amen!' I screamed, bleeding in the water near his chest.

'Yes, Mira, you hear the requests of unworthy men' – Gio was stroking my thighs up and down, up and down – 'and you pray to God for the whole world and them that their wandering through the desert should not be without fruit. You are the one who can do this, Mira. I know you are the one, the only one.'

I put my hand on Gio's head. I was above him and it felt right, yes, Jesus Christ.

'Gio,' I whispered. 'Will you, will you marry me?'

'Fuck no, Mira.'

Gio let go of my legs. His face went blank. He stood up and walked out of the water. I heard him say no again.

I took off the pearly white dress. I pushed it down to the bottom of the creek. I got naked. Amen. I squirted fresh blood. Amen. I stomped the white dress into the pond's slimy ground.

All of a sudden I felt ready for something. Fuck becoming a stupid wife! I was ready for every kind of game in the world! I felt a restlessness spread through my body, itching and rushing, fluorescent waves. I remembered how Ezrah and his friends had huddled around me when I was young, when I was down like a blob on my stomach and back. The magazine was spread so we could do it how they did. Those guys made the rules until someone's finger pushed in me. Until I felt how big I was there and how small the finger was, how nervous it was.

I wanted Gio to see me bloody and naked. But he was walking, up toward his house.

Alone, alone, I was at the edge of the water. It felt strangely lukewarm. The foaming edge of it squelched between my toes. I started going forward. My foot didn't sink. I was skimming it forward: my foot did not sink! The arches of my feet were like the sails of a boat and underneath my soles was warm air. It was like my legs swelled into balloons. Steady in my pelvis was a helicopter pulse. I was a body made up of water. All of my blood was softer than water. I could walk on this, fly on this, skim or dissolve. I walked forward on the water. I was walking on water like Jesus fucking Christ. This was real, not a dream, everyone could do this. Lift up and move with the pulse in your ass, spray from your heart. Everyone should feel this!

'Daddy! Daddy!'

I spun and I fell. Shit! Two little bodies were running down the hill, heading straight for Gio's legs. I plunged through the water, hid myself under. Gio scooped his girl in the middle of her dash, and threw her high up into the air. Shrieking, she was as thin as Adi. The boy raised his arms, he wanted up, too, but Gio wouldn't stop twirling his girl.

I crouched underwater now, up to my chest. My heart was making sounds like the frog. The boy saw me first, a boy with a paunch. He was staring at me with dark eyes and dark lips.

'Is that the new one? Is she going to stay?'

Gio put his girl down and frowned at his son.

The girl started jumping up and down and pointing at me. 'Is she gonna come out of the water? Daddy, tell us that story with the woman from the water!'

Gio touched the girl's chin. 'Like water, love clings when you hold it loosely. Like water, love goes when you grip it too hard.'

The girl clapped her hands, laughing, looking up at her father. Then she smashed her smile into his thigh.

'Is she going to stay?' the boy asked again.

'No. She's too wet to come inside now.'

Gio's daughter was staring at me strangely. She put her finger in her mouth and started wiggling it back and forth. I tried to smile but I couldn't.

Those were Adi's kids, I knew.

Gio put his arm around the girl's shoulders and they started walking up the hill. The boy followed, but he was looking back at me. *Like water, love clings when you hold it loosely. Like water, love goes when you grip it too hard.* But truth wanders on and on and on …

'Daddy, can I have that?' I heard the girl say.

My bloody beanbag pillow was on the sand.

'No. Leave it. It's dirty.'

'But that was Mommy's special pillow!'

'I said to leave it.'

'Why is there blood on it?'

'Leave it!'

Gio slapped the back of the girl's head. She let out a yelp and she left it alone. The pillow was like an organ on the ground.

I watched them walk up toward the house. The boy picked up stones from the driveway and threw them back at me. Gio put his arms around both his children and ushered them inside.

I walked out of the water and got my clothes from the car. I shoved my T-shirt into my underwear. Then I crashed down in a small patch of sand. I hugged Adi's pillow between my legs.

The sun hit my throat. I was bloody. Why was I alone? Is this what happens to amoral Jews?

Ezrah, everyone's path is from pure to disgusting. There's some moment that wrenches our nice things away. There are only a few years in our lives when our mothers will keep cleaning us, there are only a few years before our mothers put us down. But still we want to get picked up and thrown in the air! Our mothers say no and our fathers say no. They say children have to walk and learn to clean themselves. So how do we learn to clean ourselves? How can we love each other when we are so filthy?

Ezrah, this is about a secret. You still loved me, I'm telling you, when I was fifteen, when I was out every night with Michael and John. When I was silent, constipated, stuffed up with rags. You still loved me, even though you didn't know it. You were always so smart. You never got in trouble. You told your parents lies when you drank with your friends, when you drove their car blasted out of your brain. They still bought you your own car when you were eighteen, they still paid for your school, they still thought you were good. Yeah, you've always been so smooth. Your lies and my lies should be the same. But I guess what happens when we grow up is that some of us swelter and pour forth the goods and some of us freeze and dive into the cracks. I'm female, right? I went into myself.

You know, I saw this couple the other day walking hand in hand on the street and I knew exactly how they had sex. It's my talent, Ezrah, I have X-ray vision. I can see how people fuck. And I saw that these two fucked so well, even in hatred, because she was the lock and he was the key. It sounds stupid, I know, but it really works like that! Cunts and cocks have to fit – if they don't then they're doomed. You know how people fuck when they're in love? They each give up their sex for the other. They say: *You have my pussy, you take my clit.* And: *You take my balls, you take my cock.* One lover volunteers to be neutered if the other lover can be doubled with sex – full of the power of the pussy and the dick!

Yeah, real lovers are magnets, not attracted to shit. Shit makes you tired. Shit really smells. Fucking's for parasites who feed off shit! I clean the shit, you understand, Ezrah? It's a compulsion I have. I'm confessing my compulsion to deal with shit. The shit in the well, at the bottom of the well, the shit in the cold pool and the shit in the creek …

Listen to me. What I'm saying is this: fear is my realm. I'm waiting for fear. Because before anyone comes in, from the moment I'm wet, fear's stooped beside me, it's inside my gut. When I'm with a strange man, I'm waiting for fear. It feels really good to meet with this fear.

I heard Gio's steps crackling down the path. The sun was almost down. I waited until his body cast a shadow over mine.

'We have to go now,' he said.

Gio leaned down and tapped my head. The ends of my hair were still wet, all sticking together. Gio took my hand and helped me stand up. He walked over to his car. He motioned for me to follow – *Come on, girl, come here. Good girl.* I stood there and looked up toward the house. It still looked like a church. Gio had already started the car. I picked up Adi's bloodied pillow from the ground. I climbed into the car beside him. The muscles on the backs of my legs started spasming. We pulled out of the driveway. I thought I saw the kids waving from the porch.

At first we drove down a narrow mud path. Branches scraped the sides of the windows. We turned left onto an empty paved street before we got back, too soon, to the highway.

I opened my window to get some fresh air. Why the fuck was Gio acting like everything was okay?

'Roll up your window, please.'

'No. I need air.'

'Roll up the window, I said.'

I did it so hard I though the crank would crank off.

'Is this why Adi left you? She couldn't take how you spoke?'

Gio cleared his throat. He was mad. I leaned my head into the glass.

'When did you become a whore, Mira?'

'Oh, for fuck's sake, Gio. I was twelve years old. On the cusp of womanhood.'

I started laughing. Then I stopped. It occurred to me, some girls really have to do this at twelve …

Gio looked at me like he could taste my guilt. It was the first time that I saw all his teeth. They gleamed like bluish pieces of snow.

'All great whores become pure,' Gio said. 'Even the foam on her lips becomes pure.'

The air in the car was bacterial, unbearable.

'Mira, do you know how a whore becomes pure?'

She swallows buckets of come? She fucks up the ass? I wanted to say that and burst out laughing again.

'Mira, my God, in the name of our God, Adonai, for whose sake you have wasted your flesh this way – you can't hide who you are or where you came from, or when and how you came to be in this place. You are a Jew like the great whore of Babylon. The woman is Sodom, she is Egypt, she is the River of Blood.'

'I *know*! Oh my *god*! And you just fucked the Jewishest River of Blood on the way here at the side of the road, right? Am I not right? Jesus, Gio. What the fuck is your trip?'

Gio started to drive insanely fast.

'Mary of Egypt was only twelve years old, like you, when she left her parents to travel with a man. And once she did this, she kept on travelling, alone, city after city, to let all the other men take her the same way. Mary did this out of insatiable desire. She wanted to wallow in the trough, Mira. That, to her, was life.'

'I had sex the first time at fifteen with a scumbag named John,' I said. 'He and his uncle used to film me wallowing too … '

'One day, when Mary was walking at night, she saw a great crowd of men, Egyptians and Libyans, going down to the sea. She stopped one of them and asked where they were going. "We are all going to Jerusalem for the exaltation of the Holy Cross," they told her. "Do you think they would take me, if I wanted to go?" Mary asked. "Anyone who has the fare can go," the man replied. "Indeed, Brother," Mary said, "I have neither the fare nor any food, but I will go and get into one of the ships and they will take me even if they do not want to. I have a body that will serve as both fare and food for me!" Mary wanted to go, you see, Mira, so that she might experience more lovers, so that crowds of men could watch her.'

'Once a carload of guys drove by me. They were hooting at me, late at night on the street. All men think that a woman walking alone at night is a whore.'

'Mira.'

I was silent.

'Do you know how to repent?'

A grunt.

'Tell me how you will repent.'

'Fuck till I'm sore.'

Gio ground his teeth together like Adi used to grind her teeth together. 'You must learn how to repent,' he said.

I let out another grunt plus a snort. 'Jews wander on and on and on … '

'Think about where your mouth has been. Think about where your hands have been, your open legs. Don't you know what you have absorbed? You have sucked men's sinning, their filth, Mira, right up inside you. These guys have sex with you. They watch you. They watch how you move. They do not think good thoughts about you, Mira.'

'That's not true! They do. I know they do.'

'No. The whore is the woman he beats out of his body.'

I remembered Ezrah in his car with me when I first told him what I was doing, Ezrah in the car with me outside the temple during Yom Kippur, slamming the door. When he left me alone I pulled the shawl I was wearing up over my head and I covered my face. I slid my hand under my dress, into my underwear, and I lifted my leg. I stuck a finger inside my ass. The first time I ever felt there. A dark, tight, unloved inside.

This was how I atoned for our sins.

'I knew it was from the very first time you came near me,' Gio said. 'You are an open furnace, able to feel anything. I'm telling you this for a reason.'

My throat constricted. I put my hands over my eyes.

'If you repent for your sins, Adonai will take you back. God promised the whore His undying love. God sings to the whore His saddest love song. "And I will betroth thee unto me forever," He sings, "I will betroth thee unto me in righteousness." I am telling you, Mira, that there are whores who have been wandering in the desert for thirty years. They are the ones who truly know the Lord, our God, Adonai … '

I took my hands from my eyes and looked out the window. God was not watching. He was not watching as I fucked!

We were back on the busy part of the highway, speeding by gas stops, bright cubes selling food.

'After having sex with as many men as she could on the boat, Mary finally made it to Jerusalem for the Festival of the Cross.'

I wanted to blow this car up and die in the fire.

'But she found that the church would not let her in. She tried to go in with the swell of the crowd, but as soon as she set foot at the threshold of the church, something repelled her, Mira, some kind of force.' Gio paused. He kept checking on me. 'Mary suffered this way five or six times, watching all the other people enter the building easily. And yet she could not go. There was some kind of force field repelling her. She felt it all over her body, inside herself too. Eventually, Mary gave up and stood in a corner of the court. And just when she gave up … ' Gio paused again. He enunciated every word. 'Mary knew it was the conscience of her uncontrollable lust that prevented her from going inside the church.'

I was leaking through the T-shirt in my underwear, sitting in blood on his white car seat.

'Mary needed the Mother of God. She wept and grieved and beat her breast. "Help me," she prayed to the Mother of God. "It is not a man that I need anymore!" She got down on her knees and this is what she prayed: "Virgin and Lady who gave birth to the Word, I see that it is not suitable or decent for me, defiled as I am, to look upon you, you who always kept your body and soul clean. It would be right for you in your purity to reject and loathe my impurity … "'

Gio was making his voice high and girlish.

"'But help me, please," he continued, "for I am alone. Receive my confession, woman to woman, and let me enter the church. Do not deprive me of the sight of that most precious wood upon which was fixed God-made-man whom you carried and bore as a Virgin!"'

I started laughing at Gio's performance as the whore. I sat through the rest of it, hating him.

"'Oh Lady, let the doors be open to me so that I may adore the divine cross! He showed us how to die to the world – how to die in our heads, not in our bodies; how to let ourselves die by burying ourselves in horror, to die to the world but to rise and live again. I beg you, Mother, from whom God became flesh, to guarantee my promise and I will never again defile my flesh by immersing myself in horrifying lusts!"'

'My lusts are not horrific,' I said.

God, I am not religious. God, let my vagina melt into the seat. God, let my two feet descend to the highway, through sudden holes in the floor of this car. Let me make sparks with my flesh on concrete.

'I can feel every cock that has ever been inside me.'

Buildings grew up ahead. We were back in the city, back near the club.

'When she promised to never again defile herself,' Gio said, in his normal voice, 'Mary was finally let into the church. Mary was ready to be led to salvation. The voice of the Mother of God came to her and said, "Cross the river Jordan and there you will find rest."'

'I think I'm going to be sick.'

'When I met her, Mira, Adi had already been wandering for years. She was a naked girl with no hair on her vagina who had not eaten for years.'

I was swallowing, fighting the vomit back down. I closed my eyes to shut up my throat.

Gio's whole body was shaking strangely. I wanted to curl far away from him. I had the bloody pillow behind my back. I took it and hugged it: *Mommy's special pillow.*

God, get me out of this fucking white car. Get me to a toilet quick.

'Jesus said that we must bring forth what is within us or else it will destroy us.'

'But I've welcomed every cock, every dirty, hot and cursed one.'

'We must bring forth what is inside us … '

I felt myself smiling, my lips shut with shame.

'We must bring forth what is inside us, Mira … '

'We must bring forth what is inside us, Mira … ' I mimicked.

'Or else it will destroy us.'

'Or else it will destroy us.'

Stopped at some tracks with my eyes flashing red, I took Adi's pillow and opened the car door. Gio didn't stop me. I stepped out bleeding and slammed the fucking door hard. Gio waited for the lights to turn green. He drove over the tracks. I walked on water.

VIGOUR

I spat on the gravel. I was limping, bloody, heading toward the park, thinking what made me be with a strange older guy for my very first time and then never say a word? I spit on the gravel. What made me be some freakish escapee like Mary, Gio's twelve-year-old whore? I lurched toward the lights. I could still hear his white car squealing away. Gio had flipped some kind of switch in my chest that made me horny for him while he hated me! I worshipped his body without my consent.

Fuck, what made me think that I could handle grown men, fucked-up ones like Gio and John, and then just reject them, X them out of my life? Why didn't I call the police?

I could not handle a man or a woman. I could not be trusted with anything.

I had actually seen John again – he'd come to the club one night about a month ago with Michael, just before Adi left. I was totally freaked out when I saw them at first because it had been almost four years and I had no fucking idea how they knew I was there. I mean, they didn't know I was there, but I was scared when they saw me they might want me back. I wanted to get high when I saw them, fucked up and high. Adi told me, though, to go over and surprise them. *Fuck them*, she said. *Fuck what happened, past is past. Go, Mira, go be a mirror to them!*

Adi was braver than me, she was always braver than me.

From the black-lit side of the room, I could see that Michael was sick. I mean, he was green, and his clothes were practically falling off him. I thought: *He has AIDS*. John looked like some kind of gorilla beside him.

They were drinking beer and chain-smoking. John was overexcited, eyeing all the writhing things.

'So, it's fifty a song, big boy,' I said, leaning on their table, my tits in John's face. I felt like a businessman mirror.

John immediately pulled away like he was scared of me. I started laughing at the expression on his face. I couldn't help it. He looked like someone had just sliced off his fingertip or something. He was swallowing and swallowing, pushing his chin into his throat.

Michael started laughing like me. 'You still watch the Mira tapes every week, don't you, Johnny?'

It was like John couldn't take the sight of me so close to him. He kept retreating his head like a turtle does. I had on my pink cut-off T-shirt, the one that was so short you could see the bottoms of my tits. I was standing above John with my hands on my hips.

Me and Michael seriously couldn't stop laughing. Michael's eyes were the same, but everything else on his skull was shrunken.

'What's going on with you?' I asked.

Michael coughed so hard he had to put out his cigarette.

'Nothing,' he finally got out.

'You look like a ghost,' I said. Then quickly added, 'Sorry.'

'No, Mira, it's you that looks like shit.' John was angry. He lit another cigarette.

'Shut up, Johnny,' Michael snapped. 'Mira looks hot. You look a fuck of a lot hotter as a lady, Mirabella.'

'Just get rid of those tapes already, will you?' I yelled at John, feeling half-embarrassed, half-proud from what Michael had just said. 'I'm not your fucking eternal release.'

John nodded. He closed his eyes. Michael crack-toothed smiled at me. Lights flashed over his face, red and green.

'Our Lady,' Michael said, suddenly sitting up tall and looking around the club. 'If I were to put on a play in which women had roles, I would insist that these roles be performed by adolescent boys and I would so inform the audience by means of a placard, which would remain nailed to the right or left of the sets throughout the performance.'

I leaned down toward Michael and put my lips on his temple.

'Our Lady,' I whispered. Michael's blood beat visibly there. He nodded and chewed on his bottom lip. 'It's really okay,' I said. 'Our good wishes are furtive and whispered, as, among others, those of proud servants and lepers must be.'

I turned to John, but he still wouldn't look at me. He was sucking so hard on his cigarette that the filter got wrinkled.

Michael grabbed on to my wrist and dug his fingers in. It reminded me of Nadia grabbing my arm at the bar with Adi, so long ago.

Michael said my name desperately. 'Mira, let's read together, okay?'

I tried to smile. 'I have to work,' I said.

Then I went straight over to Adi, who welcomed me into her humping. I knew John would take a good look at me now. Me and Adi were fearsome, a tower, me pulling my shirt up, tits bare and jiggling, her squeezing me on top of a guy. I felt myself as pure sex power – hard and soft and completely plugged in. Adi's rules of engagement had worked: I'd been a mirror with them, finally hard-edged and *clear*.

The next time I looked over, John and Michael were gone.

I climbed the rotting wooden stairs to the field where I'd been with Lani and Coco. I took off my shoes. Blood had run into them. I needed a patch wet with muddiness or dew. I got down on my knees and I dug through the grass. I got past the gravelly part until I struck mud, raking bugs, wrecking ant holes. I dug the ditch until I could feel up to my wrists, then my elbows, and I dug to my shoulder. Until I could've fallen in. I dropped Adi's pillow in there. *Mommy's special pillow.* I threw the ant-holed mud-wrecked earth on top. It was Adi who told me that all girls are whores. But only those who stay whores die.

I knew Michael lived in one of those massive high-rise buildings downtown. I'd gone with John to visit him once on the twenty-second floor. I remembered how his place had a mustard-coloured shag carpet and cubic glass fixtures from the seventies. It had smelled like John's at Michael's place, too, that one time we'd been: burnt vegetable oil and smoke on top of smoke.

I found Michael's name on the directory, but it didn't say the number of his place. I waited until a woman came out from the lobby. It was late but there was no security guard.

I took the elevator to the twenty-second floor. It smelled like pepperoni in the hallway. I heard an electronic beat, so many tvs.

I didn't remember which door was his. The floor was a maze of brown and gold doors. I walked into dead ends, then retraced my steps. I passed the elevators at least three times.

When Gio had stopped the car in the middle of the road, before he pulled me out and after he'd yelled, it felt like this time with my father when I was twelve, when he'd picked me up from a sleepover at Nadia's aunt's place up north. I'd called him to get me because I felt so stressed out from the night that I just needed to be at home. But when we'd arrived, I wouldn't get out of the car. It was early in the morning on a Sunday and I'd made it through the night, but I remember how my father yelled at me when I wouldn't get out of the car; he used the same voice that he used with the dog. He was this strange man in our driveway yelling for my mother: 'She won't get out of the car! She won't get out of the bloody car!' My father's dull body with his face full of hair, hair around his lips and a voice full of spite. He was a person with skin red from yelling. That was what I knew inside the car, with my legs squeezed together, with my mother running out in her bathrobe, at the car, leaning in: 'What's wrong with you, Mira?'

My mother spoke to my father with hoarseness in her throat. She said, 'Go in the house. Everything's fine.'

My mother told my father I was fine.

With my mother's head poking back into the car, her coffee breath, it was easy enough to get out.

'What is it, Mira?' She said something like that. 'What is wrong with you?' Sighing. 'I'm sure there's a reason for this.'

My mother put her arm around me even though I felt too old for hugs. We walked slowly to the house. We walked slowly up the stairs. It was all too gloomy between my mother and me, when I should have laughed, I was on the verge.

Nadia's aunt and boyfriend had been having sex through the walls all night. Her aunt was an alcoholic who had given me and Nadia our first beers. There was this choked sound or a pop. I'd never heard sounds like the sounds that she made that night, all night, and I thought she could've been dead and I wanted to wake Nadia up but I was too scared. I wanted to go home, I just wanted my home.

Back at home, though, when I was twelve, when my father yelled for my mother because I wouldn't get out of the car, I knew for certain that something was wrong. Something was fucked between women and men. I knew it because of the way that Nadia's aunt acted like nothing was wrong in the morning light. I knew it when Nadia joked with her aunt. I knew because of how my mother looked at me after she told my father that everything was fine. I knew that both of them believed now that something wasn't fine but neither of them knew exactly what it was. Or exactly how to talk to me ever again.

The problem with my father yelling and the problem with my mother's gloom and the fucked-up problem between men and women, between me and Ezrah and every man I'd ever known, was that I knew right now – the problem was mine.

I slid away like a snake from my home. Because what my parents thought about me was true. What your parents think about you is true! What your father thinks, what your mother thinks, all of it is perfectly true. Your body is helpless so far from the ground as you grow. You're see-through and flimsy and if you don't slide away, slither, then you'll stay and you'll lie and have your head filled with their shit.

When a girl's body is just starting to be formed, people teach her to ignore the men in the street. Just ignore and ignore and all will be fine. If there's a buzzing in your pants, don't say a word.

Even if something cracks loudly in your head, some rotting fence about to fall over, don't say a word, because everything's fine.

But sometimes some things need to be said!

All great whores become pure, Gio said.

I knocked on Michael's brown painted door with key scratches in the centre. I had to knock ten times, loud, because of the drum noise pounding.

'Mirabella,' the skeleton smiled.

Michael shivered under his stained robe. He had long grey hairs growing out of his chin. An unlit cigarette stuck to his lip.

'Hi,' I said. Then I started to cry.

Michael turned away from me and lurched headfirst into the noise. I locked the door behind me. It sounded like AC/DC or something. There was a chemical stink that mixed with the smell of my blood. Michael's place was a mess of teacups and blankets in tents on the floor, bottles on their sides and books off the shelves – split open and stuck in the shape of brooms.

I didn't want to sit and I didn't want to stand.

Michael teetered and dropped down on his black couch, moaning as he dropped.

'Stop crying, Mirabella. I want to watch you dance.'

'Why?' I screamed, trying to stop myself from more crying when he was the one sick. 'I can't move to this!'

'It's Swedish – Dead Korinthians,' Michael said. He didn't have to scream. 'I can't read anymore.'

I stood there in front of him, pooling blood. I couldn't move. The sound was male howling.

'Dance, Mira!' the skeleton said. He raised his purple-knuck-led fist in the air.

I started moving my hips in tiny circles on top of my legs. The music ramped up and Michael fisted along. His hand turned into a V sign, then back to a fist.

I gyrated and spun. Me and Michael entered the obliteration of open men's throats. The backs of my legs started spasming in pain, the way they had in Gio's car.

I heard Michael chanting. I let my head hang. I let my arms hang. I realized that all I'd really done in the past year for exercise or anything else was dance at the club, dance in high heels. My legs felt dead. I hung my head down to that sound. Almost all of my body had turned into static. I felt blood in my eyes. I started to get used to the hanging, this feeling of trying to feel through the numbness.

I looked through my hair at Michael. He was smiling at me, perfect in midnight light.

This near-dead man wanted the truth out of me.

Between my head and the carpet, I felt hot little beats. I wrapped my arms around my legs, hugged my chest to my thighs. It felt so good to have my stomach in a fold. My whole body spiralled in on itself.

Michael's face seemed thicker, suddenly pink. The song finished so abruptly that the silence rang in my ears. I stood up, unsteady. I rubbed my hands on my face.

'You dance like a warrior woman now. How'd that happen, Mirabella?'

I felt proud and then embarrassed.

'Uh, there was this guy that I was seeing at the club and he said that the first time he saw me dancing he felt ashamed for me. He said I was up there because of men's longings. Like, that all men wanted me to be their whore. And that reminded me of you and John, like how I grew up with you guys or something. But Gio said he didn't know if I could handle that yet. He said he didn't know if I knew how to soothe a man yet. How to let all these strange men love me for their own release. Gio said that the other girls forgot what they did – grabbing on to men's cocks for a living. Gio said I was different. All the great whores become pure, Gio said.'

I felt pins and needles all over my body.

'And do you align yourself philosophically with this guy?' Michael stared at me, pointing the remote at the stereo. A new song cut through, screams about Lucifer.

'I think maybe I do,' I said.

My Russian evil man Jew was the Bringer of Light.

'Maybe you should reconsider,' said Michael. 'The so-called purity of the great whore.'

I bent my knees deep and reached my hands to the ground to sit down, but I lost my balance and fell into the carpet.

'Rahab,' said Michael, 'was the political whore.'

Michael lit a cigarette and immediately began to hack. His robe came open and I saw his chest. It was lined with purple holes.

Michael passed me his cigarette. I sat up and I smoked it.

'Rahab was a harlot, as they called her, a woman of the night – a totally great whore in other words, totally impure – who took these spies in, Jewish spies, and she hid them in bundles of flax on her roof when the enemy was looking for them all over the village. After the enemy left, the Jewish spies marked Rahab's house with a red string, they made her a Jew, in fact, so that when their army came in the next day to loot and pillage and kill, Rahab and her house were saved. "Don't touch the righteous whore's house," said the Jewish spies. "She collaborated with us."'

Michael started to shake. I got up from the floor and sat beside him. I put my arm around him. I closed his robe and gave him a puff of his cigarette.

'All religion is a total mind-fuck manipulation, Mira, but I think you're a woman of faith, I really do.'

Michael started horking and wracking. The music was like a black-sun Nordic war.

I put out the cigarette in the mustard-coloured shag, which I realized was pockmarked with burns. I took Michael's hand and he took mine. He put his head on my shoulder.

'I'm staying here to be your nurse,' I said.

'I have one already. John's a very good nurse.'

I started to cry again. A woman of faith. I wanted to tell Michael that I'd walked on the water.

Michael attempted to turn his head to look at me but he was stiff and white. I saw that some of his teeth had fallen out.

'I think this whore-purifying fascist nonsense is the key to your fucked-up issues with men.'

I started to laugh. Michael turned the music off.

'Don't be a pussy, Rahab,' he slurred.

I slapped his arm. Silence.

Michael had fallen asleep. I waited a few moments. I somehow manoeuvred to hold him, digging under his armpits. I dragged this horrible stick man down the hallway and into his bedroom. I hadn't been in there before. Michael's bedroom was pink, with these buffoonish kinds of curtains, I mean a *Gone with the Wind* kind of deal; the whole room was a little girl's love of ribbons and bows. He had stuffed animals lined up all along the windowsill, these fluffy white dogs and rabbits and bears.

The clock shone green: 3:13.

I heaved Michael up onto his bed. I put him under the covers. I kissed his skull goodbye.

The second I lay down on the couch back in the living room I fell asleep.

When I woke up it was five in the morning. Heavy blood. I lit a fresh cigarette. I looked for the phone. I held it between my hands for a bit.

'Ezrah?'

Silence.

'It's me, it's Mira.'

I heard a gurgling.

'Hey, Ezrah, come on. It's early, I know … '

'What do you want?' It sounded like Ezrah's mouth was full. 'Why are you calling me in the middle of the night?'

I took the phone away from my cheek. Dusk was coming in through the blinds.

'Wait,' Ezrah said, swallowing constantly. 'Wait, it's just late, all right?'

'No, you're right. I shouldn't have called.'

'Where are you?'

'Not sure.'

'What the fuck do you mean you're not sure? No one's heard from you in months. My mom said your mom hasn't heard from you in months! They don't even have a phone number for you, Mira. Your mom's mad. At first she was worried, but now she's just mad. I don't even know if she's going to talk to you when you call. You're gonna call her, right? Do it now. You have to call her.'

'I called *you*, Ezrah. I don't want to talk to my mother right now.'

'Fuck! They just keep asking me if I've talked to you. I say, yeah I have and you're doing fine, you just don't feel like talking right now. But I can't do that anymore. It's been months, for fuck's sake! Some girl *died* around there. Did you know that, Mira? I was freaking out and I couldn't tell anyone, you hear me? I was freaking out. They found a girl's body, she was completely naked, they knew she was a sex worker. Whatever, that's what they called her in the papers … '

'I haven't read the papers.'

'I went down to the fucking police station, I drove all the way to the morgue with the police to see this poor girl. You know why I did that, huh?'

I didn't ever call the police.

'Because I thought it was you. Because I thought it was you. Because I fucking thought it was you!'

'Sorry … '

'No. The cops told me they found saliva in her – not semen, just saliva. They don't even think she's from here, they think she's from Russia somewhere, or Poland. No one's come to get her. No one knows anything about her. All the girls at your club are Russian or something, aren't they? It's disgusting. She was so skinny. Her face was black around the eyes. She looked like a crow. I was the only fucking one who'd come down to see her! The police took a swab from my mouth, they said they knew it wasn't me, but no one had come to get her. No one!'

I steadied my breath.

'Did you know her? Mira?'

'Yes.'

I closed my eyes and this is what I saw: on an empty highway with marked-up poles and drooping wires, Adi's head at the side of the road. It was stuck in the gravel, neck trimmed, no gore. I crouched down close. I wasn't afraid. Because I saw there were words etched into her forehead. Green and black letters that had bled through the skin.

It was written: *This one lived according to my wishes.*

I was a woman of faith.

'It's okay,' I whispered, wanting to throw up. My mouth felt full, full of white cud.

'I want to come get you. It doesn't matter where you are. I'll drive and come get you. Where are you, Mir? Just tell me.'

Ezrah's voice had changed for a moment. But still I couldn't tell him where or how I was. I pressed my forehead into the receiver.

'How's school?' I asked.

'Why the fuck are you asking me that now?'

'Just tell me how you are. That's why I called.'

'Just tell me where you are!'

'I left, okay? That's it. That's all.'

'Oh god. Thank god.'

Ezrah was excited. Why was he so excited?

'God, Mir, that's good. That's amazing. I'm so relieved. That's amazing.'

'Okay.'

'I'm so happy, Mira. That stuff wasn't for you. You know that now, don't you?'

What I know is that you are exactly the same.

'Hey, Mir?'

'What.'

'Why don't you come stay with me for a while? I don't have my exams until December. I'm just here, studying, whatever. We can hang out for a few weeks. Or you can stay longer, it doesn't matter. Why don't you come and stay with me? My room's all right, it's big enough … '

'I'm just calling to say hi, Ezrah.'

'I want us to hang out again.'

'Why?'

'Come on, don't do this … '

'No, tell me why.'

'I don't know, because I want you to be happy … '

'I am happy.' I am a woman of faith.

'Come on, that's not true. Your voice sounds all weird.'

The cud in my mouth now was lining the walls.

'Mira, I thought you were dead. Do you actually understand that?'

I was about to hang up.

'Wait, Mira, just wait where you are. I'm going to come get you. Just stay where you are and I'm going to come right over there and get you.'

I held the phone far away from my face.

'Don't go yet, Mira!'

'Why?'

'Because I miss you. I mean, I really, really miss you.'

The phone cord was wrapped three times around my wrist.

'Mira?'

'Look, Ezrah, I'll see you soon, I just think I should be alone right now … '

'No, you shouldn't! Why haven't you called me all this time?'

'Come on, you know why.'

'No, I don't.'

'Because I didn't want to talk to you.'

'Don't say that. I don't want to hear you saying that.'

Now I was the one starting to get mad.

'Fuck it, Ezrah! How can you forget?'

'Forget what?'

'You were disgusted.'

'No … '

'You were.'

'I was not … '

– 208 –

'Yes, you were. You still are. In fact, you've always been kind of disgusted by me.'

'Look, Mira, I just couldn't be okay with all that … You in that place, all those guys, doing that … I'm sorry. I love you, okay? I couldn't help it. It just wasn't for me. Come on, I think most people would understand that.'

But love comes from disgust. Trusting disgust.

'Mira? I said I'm sorry. Don't you understand? Fuck, I thought you were dead … '

'I get it.'

'It's just that I know you can do something better with your life, that's it. That's all. Believe me.'

'Yeah.'

'Talk to me. Just keep talking to me, okay?'

'Okay.'

'Mira?'

'Okay. I'll keep talking.'

Silence.

'Please.'

'Okay. That girl you saw dead? Well, she was in love. And the guy she was in love with? Well, he was the one who told me what I was doing there, what men were doing with me … '

'What are you talking about?'

'Being there. Me being at the club.'

'Okay … '

'It made sense.'

'What made sense?'

'It's hard to explain.'

'Try.'

'Okay. Just wait.' I took a deep breath. 'There's this story in the Bible about Hosea, he's a prophet.'

'Yeah, I know that.'

'Okay, so Hosea marries a whore because God tells him to, because God wants to show him the meaning of love, because

God will always love the whore. God loves the whore! Rahab, you know her? She was a Jewish whore, a political whore.'

'A Jewish whore? Mira, who is this guy? Just some fucking bastard that you danced for?'

'No.'

'What? Was he your boyfriend too? You fucked that dead girl's boyfriend?'

'Shut up!'

Silence numbed the line again.

'I shouldn't have called.'

'Fuck it, Mira, just go on. What about Hosea and his whore? What about Rahab?'

'I shouldn't have called you.'

'You're frustrating me.'

'Yeah?'

'Look, I want to understand, but you're frustrating me. Let me come and get you now, that's all I want to do. Okay?'

'It's not a good idea.'

'Fuck!'

'I should be telling someone else. I should be telling everyone else.'

'What? Telling them what?'

'That Hosea loves his whore, no matter what she's done. The whore knows how to collaborate.'

I heard Ezrah's breathing slow right down. I kept talking into the sudden space.

'I've felt all these things from what I've been doing. I mean, it was a whole other world in that place, in that club, everyone had different weight to their feet, everyone was heavier and we were all attached to each other. If someone was slimy, I had the same slime. It wasn't the law of opposites attracting: the girls were like the girls and the slime was like the slime. It's good to be a pig rolling in the slime sometimes, Ezrah. Because now I know what everyone pays for, now I know whose body pays more. I've been there trying to clean it all up. I have been trying to organize people's unbearable needs because I see their unbearable forms. All I want is for things to be equal.'

Ezrah was about to protest.

'All the feelings I had there have rebounded and hit me in the chest. Shame is just everything that hit me in the chest before the feeling came full circle.'

'I don't understand,' Ezrah said slowly.

'I had these moments in the dark in that crappy little room when I could literally see from the back of my head … '

'Stop, Mira, please … '

'And there was this gluey white thread there, floating in the air, it was about halfway between the bed and the ceiling. I knew that this cord had been whipped around the earth … '

I heard Ezrah snort back to life, a nervous reaction in his nose.

'I want to wait for more of these feelings, Ezrah, I want to wait every night, ruined or not. It feels good to see these kinds of things, like your brain's practically dripping from the walls, like your brain can act outside your head, moving without static, like everything is equal, I can understand myself and all men … ' My voice suddenly got hoarse. 'Will you tell my mom that I called?' I heard myself asking. 'Tell her I'm okay. Tell her I'll call her.'

'No.'

'Please, Ezrah. Just tell her I'll call her. I've got to go now.'

I heard Michael coughing awake.

'I'm coming there. I'm going there right now. The police told me where that dead girl worked. I don't care who's there with you, I'm going to pound his face in. You happy now, Mira? I bet you're there anyway. I bet you never left that fucking shithole.'

'Don't you dare go there. I am not there.'

'I don't believe you. I'm going. Getting my shoes on. Getting my car keys … '

'Ezrah, I mean it. Don't go. I'm not there!'

'I'm leaving in two minutes, coming to get you. I don't believe a word that comes out of your mouth. It'll take me a half-hour. See you.'

'Don't!'

'What? Is your boyfriend sleeping there? Is that it? I'll pound his face in if he's there.'

'Ezrah, fuck!'

'Ezrah fuck what?'

It was the last thing I heard. My fingers were bright red. I ran out of Michael's apartment, shot down twenty-two flights and out into the world of light and its rising.

They were waiting for me on the opposite sides of the room. I walked to my window and leaned my head against the glass. Gio was at the edge of my bed and Ezrah had his arms crossed over his chest at the wall. I turned on the light and they both flinched the same face. The difference between family and stranger was erased. Killer equalled cousin equalled father equalled pimp. And Jew equalled Jew equalled Jew.

Gio said: 'You have to rid yourself of this man.'

Red patches rose up and flushed Ezrah's face. 'Just fuck off, man, okay?'

My bottom lip started to shake. I had to remember: *collaborate*.

'You're coming home with me, Mira. Just come now, okay?'

Ezrah was walking right toward me. I had to move away.

I walked to the window, leaned my head against the glass. God, what is this place that it can break people in half? This place where men come to fuck their own daughters. This maze where fathers and daughters meet up ...

'Excuse me,' Gio said. 'I think I can explain. Nothing is wrong here. What has taken place here isn't wrong.'

'Wait,' I warned Gio, without looking behind me. How was I supposed to collaborate with them?

'Why doesn't *she* tell me to leave then, you asshole? Mira? Why don't you tell me to leave? Just tell me to go and I'll go, okay?'

'But it's not you who has to go, it's Mira who has to stay,' Gio answered. 'She still has work to do tonight.'

'Hang on,' I said. My throat felt caked with mud. I turned around to face them. 'I don't want to be here but I don't want to leave. I want to finish my job at this place and move on.

'I want to talk to you both, but one at a time. Maybe, later, I can talk to the two of you together. Maybe, one day, I can talk to a room full of men. Maybe one day I'll be the Lord of all men. Maybe the Mother of God was a whore. Maybe one day I'll be naked and shining and you won't have to worship me or any young girl anymore. Maybe one day we'll all have holes at the top of our heads and be programmed for God. And women will fuck men instead of men fucking them. And then this place can be burned to the ground.'

I smiled. They were both listening to me.

AFTERWORD

remember the embarrassment I felt when *Lie with Me* came out over ten years ago. There was no good way for me to explain why I shot fiction with pornography, hoping for the best. That initial public embarrassment was likely a kind of useless repression. Because I had no big truth to tell about myself. Now, though, in retrospect, I know why I wrote *Lie with Me*. It was to sustain this perfect, merciless feeling I first had while spitting art's extremity into the suckhole of porn. And it's not embarrassing for me to admit anymore that I was desperate to find meaning in this action.

Unfortunately, by the end of two books I didn't know any more about female sexuality than when I'd started out. My mercilessness had not blossomed into compassion either.

Is untapped sexual energy in women even still a problem these days? In 1999, I felt that problem as acutely as my shame. And it was this push-pull of pressures that made me transcribe and complicate the getting-fucked female voice – a voice that I found in porn, a voice that was utterly wasted by porn.

Porn *needed* fiction, I felt. I needed the fight.

Significant visions are not always easy to remember. But memory, sometimes, functions all right. This one feels loaded: 1982, in the basement closet of a girl in my class I saw a bronze naked man projected onto the wall, guffawing and walking toward a very high bed. This bronze naked man had a rod sticking off him. I had never seen a thing like that, I'd only ever seen them mottled and soft and hiding like purses between hairy legs. This one was a workshop utensil! This one was pointing and leading to something airtight. What I got from my first vision of cock: cock was a tool, you had to use that thing right.

The girl's mother called her name from upstairs.

The bronze king honed in on the very high bed where there were two women waiting with soft boobs and flipped hair. Those two were like chipmunks, fawning on their knees.

Something was about to happen, something I knew I had to see.

The girl's mother yelled, 'What on earth are you two doing down there?'

The king's rod was about to be taken, or hung off or fed to the fat-cheeked females! I felt something freeze inside my gut. The girl's mother was walking down the basement stairs. My friend knew when to stop. The film caught and snapped dark; light got suddenly sliced up inside our closet. I heard my friend laughing and I ran upstairs after her, confused and coughing, past her mom. We burst out the front door onto shining concrete. My laughs were dry yelps. That girl's mother knew. Her lips were down-turned. I knew it wasn't the first time that the girl had done this, i.e., shared the miraculous inevitable.

I hung out with that girl for at least another year, but I never thought about what happened to her that night. Did she get in trouble with her mother? Did her mother go into the closet after we'd left? Did she rewind the film that her daughter stole from her drawer? Was a kid supposed to get in trouble for seeing this?

I didn't contemplate any consequences for seeing a cock and two girls put to work – nearly. What I understood was that adults were very powerful creatures. Sex was their secret and inborn pact. That circle-edged, soft-core minute of film pushed at the edges of my growing girl mind. It shouldn't be nightmarish to admit this as true. People today seem terrified of the effects of precociousness in girls. But after the bronze cock vision in the closet, I did not go out and start to fuck. Porn did not shut my mind down. It ripped and stained my mind's eye, maybe, but I don't even think it's as ominous as that. I had a truck load of shame to tar and feather myself with yet. A dream is a dream. A kid is a kid. Some dreams get trampled, some thrive, some expire.

Enter James Deen, L.A. porn-boy-next-door. It's 2013. James Deen hadn't even been born when I was indoctrinated in that closet. James Deen is the pre-eminent sign that the 'chipmunk-cheeked' don't have to feel shame anymore. James Deen says that he will not have sex with a woman on camera who does not want to have sex with him. James Deen reverses the poetic violence of the porn I first saw, read and wrote, because he's so transparent, so puppy-like; because he does it *with* the girls, not *to* them at all.

Sex is like soccer, says Deen. It's fun and athletic, and you should do it with your friends.

It's possible, though, that shame is essential for growing a spine. Maybe humans are just all mutations of shame. Maybe James Deen is the devil in disguise and porn today is an apolitical trick. Ariel Levy wrote the book *Female Chauvinist Pigs* about the misogynistic impulses in and around porn, porn that is often full of sexually traumatized subjects.

It's true that porn is full of misapprehension. Porn ill-advisedly too often gets rid of our shames.

It seems fitting, regardless, that a man should put us chipmunks at ease. James Deen, the sweet metafictional entertainer, takes my decade-old, shame-laced, porn problematic – how can a fucked woman speak clearly? – and he turns me to look in the mirror while doing me up the ass.

Speak up, he implores. Don't rest there dammed-up, hiding or weak!

Okay, James, Motherfucker:

Porn's a non-functioning hologram where men and women are equally fucked, each according to their wishes, each according to their need. This alleged egalitarian space in real life is a particular *Deenian* paradox – the naked and the public are slut-loving and safe; it's the end of being born female as a receptacle for shame. And if our current, steady Canadian existence is threatened by juiced-up females roaming and fucking in packs, in my opinion, there will still be empathy.

Notes and Acknowledgements

Reference is made to the following authors and works:

Acker, Kathy. *In Memoriam to Identity*. New York: Pantheon, 1990.

Buber, Martin. *Tales of the Hasidim*. New York: Schocken Books, 1975.

Genet, Jean. *Our Lady of the Flowers*. New York: Grove Press, 1963.

Mirabai. *For Love of the Dark One: Songs of Mirabai*. Trans. Andrew Schelling. Boston: Shambhala Publications, 1993.

Nietzsche, Friedrich. *Thus Spoke Zarathustra*, Fourth Part, 19. *The Portable Nietzsche*. New York: Viking Press, 1968.

Reines, Ariana. http://canopycanopycanopy.com/16/preliminary_materials_for_a_theory_of_the_young_girl

'The Life of Saint Mary of Egypt as told by Sophronious.' *Medieval Saints: A Reader*. Ed. Mary-Ann Stouck. Canada: Broadview Press, 1999.

Thank you, Alana Wilcox, little cat! Thank you, Evan Munday, and thank you, Leigh Nash and Heidi Waechtler of Coach House Books.

About the Author

Tamara Faith Berger was born in Toronto. She wrote porn stories for a living and attempted to make dirty films before publishing her first book, *Lie with Me*, in 1999. In 2001, *The Way of the Whore* (*A Women Alone at Night* in the U.S.), her second book, was published. Her third book, *Maidenhead*, came out in 2012. *Little Cat* is a re-release of her first two novels in substantially revised form.

Typeset in Whitman and Trade Gothic

Printed at the old Coach House on bpNichol Lane in Toronto, Ontario, on Zephyr Antique Laid paper, which was manufactured, acid-free, in Saint-Jérôme, Quebec, from second-growth forests. This book was printed with vegetable-based ink on a 1965 Heidelberg KORD offset litho press. Its pages were folded on a Baumfolder, gathered by hand, bound on a Sulby Auto-Minabinda and trimmed on a Polar single-knife cutter.

Edited and designed by Alana Wilcox
Cover design and hand-lettering by Ingrid Paulson
Author photograph by Christine Davis

Coach House Books
80 bpNichol Lane
Toronto ON M5S 3J4
Canada

416 979 2217
800 367 6360

mail@chbooks.com
www.chbooks.com